SECRET SISTER

September, 2011

To Niagara Falls Public Library

I hope you enjoy!

thany,

SECRET SISTER

Sharol

SHAROL LOUISE

FIVE STAR

An imprint of Thomson Gale, a part of The Thomson Corporation

THOMSON

GALE

Detroit • New York • San Francisco • New Haven, Conn. • Waterville, Maine • London

THOMSON
GALE

LIBRARY OF CONGRESS CATALOGING-IN-PUBLICATION DATA

Louise, Sharol.
 Secret sister / by Sharol Louise. — 1st ed.
  p. cm.
 ISBN 1-59414-532-6
  1. Young women—Fiction. 2. Orphans—Fiction. 3. Family secrets—Fiction.
4. Survival after airplane accidents, shipwrecks, etc.—Fiction. 5. Sisters—
Fiction. 6. Inheritance and succession—Fiction. 7. Impostors and imposture—
Fiction. 8. Scotland—Fiction. 9. London (England)—Fiction. I. Title.
PS3612.O82S43 2006
813'.6—dc22
                                        2006015847

U.S. Hardcover:
ISBN 13: 978-1-59414-532-2
ISBN 10: 1-59414-532-6

First Edition. First Printing: October 2006.

Published in 2006 in conjunction with Tekno Books and Ed Gorman.

Printed in the United States of America on permanent paper
10 9 8 7 6 5 4 3 2 1

To my sister, Pat Mack.
Because every writer needs a sister Pat
And to Tomás, life partner *extraordinaire*

ACKNOWLEDGMENTS

I gratefully acknowledge my "magnificent seven support group," who made the journey possible:

Lynette Alison Moore
Hildegard McKissen
Susi Cradduck
Jeff Schell
Jennifer Vlasman
Rachel Joseph
Linda Hoversland
And my patient editor, Alice Duncan

CHAPTER ONE

London, 1794

Mrs. Pickett screamed.

Fortunately, she was sitting in a stout, overstuffed chair, so Mr. Bartlestaff was not overly concerned she might faint.

Mr. Bartlestaff, of Redigen, Bartlestaff and Porter, was accustomed to female clients swooning, crying, and throwing tantrums. Thus he insisted there always be a fresh supply of laundered handkerchiefs and smelling salts on hand. The gentleman was married, with five grown daughters. This stood him well; emotional women no longer rattled him.

Composing a sympathetic, fatherly expression on his face, he waited for the ranting.

The weak ones screamed, then fainted. The reasonable ones sighed, then composed themselves. The annoying ones, such as Mrs. Pickett, screamed and then ranted—as if the law firm were to blame for their misfortune. As if she could bully them into changing the dried ink upon the old will.

"That is impossible! My Harold would never have agreed to such a clause in his will. Never!" The feather in her outrageous hat bounced in agreement, as did her multiple chins.

"The encumbrance was tied to the deaths of both Mr. Harold Pickett and his previous wife, Lady Jeannette Pickett. Since he never mentioned it to you, Harold Pickett was either unaware of it or unconcerned about the possibility of his own death."

The bright light from the side window glinted from Mr.

Bartlestaff's spectacles.

"How did we not hear of this before?" she asked with a sneer. "This law firm must be either mistaken or grossly negligent. Perhaps both."

Mr. Bartlestaff removed his glasses. Eyes closed, he pinched the bridge of his nose and sighed. "I assure you the clause has always been there, Mrs. Pickett." He opened his eyes and focused his direct gaze upon the glaring woman. "When your husband first married, due to his wife's sizeable fortune her family insisted upon the clause."

He could still recall the first wife's unhappy father, a long-standing client. His lordship had been concerned with his daughter's choice of husband, but it was a father's intuition. Not finding a suitable reason to forbid the marriage, he indulged his daughter's wishes to marry the handsome Harold Pickett, but tied a legal knot to protect her. The stipulation? Only a portion of the estate was touchable each year. This had been sizably generous, however, so the bridegroom readily agreed.

What the greedy young fellow had not realized was that the larger portion would remain in trust for any offspring of Lady Jeannette's. Her husband Harold would never touch the bulk of her inheritance.

"As I've already explained, madam, the greater part of the fortune that came from Mr. Pickett's marriage to his first wife will not be in your control." He wiped his glasses with his handkerchief. "The will is very specific: your two stepdaughters inherit equally."

"*Two* stepdaughters? You are again mistaken!" She almost crowed with smugness. Shifting in the chair, she tugged impatiently at the purple skirt bunching tightly at her hips. Her impatience just as quickly transferred to him. "There is no second daughter, Mr. Bartlestaff. Only my dear, sweet Eleanor. Surely your recordkeeping is not so incompetent that you did not know Harold's second daughter died?"

"I realize it was presumed the baby died with its mother when the first Mrs. Pickett met her tragic death. However, we now have evidence the young girl survived to adulthood." It had, in fact, been the most startling of surprises, he reflected— the confidential letter received upon Miss Madeline's eighteenth birthday. "It was this firm's unfortunate duty to contact her and inform her of her father's death. The father she apparently never had a chance to know."

Mrs. Pickett made a rude noise. "Let me tell you something, sir—I've raised my Eleanor since she was two years old. I am the only mother she remembers, and she is the most biddable of daughters. I am confident she will look after her dear mama with the money she inherits from her father. That is what she calls me," she sniffed, " 'Mama.' For we are very close, and her own mother deserted her."

She pointed her pudgy finger at the lawyer, punching the air as she spoke, "But . . . she will not share one farthing with this imposter. Eleanor's sister is dead. And even if she were not, she deserves nothing. As you admitted, she's never even known her father. So why should this stranger profit from Harold's death? You know she's only interested because of the inheritance."

Mr. Bartlestaff stopped wiping his glasses. "Miss Madeline has not been informed of the specifics of her father's will, so she knows nothing about the size of the legacy." He replaced his spectacles upon his nose. "Furthermore, whether you feel Miss Madeline is 'deserving' does not signify, Mrs. Pickett. The terms of the will shall be carried out in accordance with the law by this firm."

"It's not fair!" Mrs. Pickett was red in the face. "I demand to speak to the owner of this establishment," she ordered, as if she were at the local haberdashery.

Mr. Bartlestaff did not take offense.

The fact that Mrs. Pickett was not a member of the nobility, however, made it a bit more enjoyable to take his time, sit back in the leather chair, let it squeak a couple of times in the silence, and then to steeple his fingers before replying, "I am one of the two senior partners of this firm, madam."

Her brows lowered in a frown. He knew exactly when she realized there was no other way to push, for her face turned ugly and she rose to leave.

"This is intolerable! That is all I have to say. Good day, sir."

He let her get almost to the door. "Mrs. Pickett?" he called clearly.

She stopped, and he saw the tension in her shoulders; knew she did not want to turn around or acknowledge him.

"Your stepdaughter, Miss Madeline, will arrive within a fortnight for the reading of the will. I assume you will be bringing Miss Eleanor?"

She did turn now, and he saw she was white. Whether from rage, shock, or a combination of the two, he could not discern, though he was normally quite a discerning gentleman.

She turned her back on him and marched out.

CHAPTER TWO

"Hell, Emerson . . . I have more important things to do than spy on a child." Mr. Jace Remington picked disdainfully at an imaginary piece of lint on the elbow of his olive riding coat.

"She's hardly a child, cousin." Emerson leaned forward, speaking earnestly. His waistcoat buttons strained across his paunchy stomach. "Why, she must be almost twenty by now, as her older sister Eleanor will soon be twenty-one. *If* she really is Eleanor's sister—which we seriously doubt. So keep that in mind—she's not an innocent young thing, but a greedy, scheming liar trying to steal my fortune . . . Of course, I mean, my beloved Eleanor's fortune. Or, rather, *our* fortune, since we are engaged."

"What are you going on about? Give this to me again. Slowly." Jace sat back, eyed his cousin impatiently. With one ankle crossed over the other knee, and an arm stretched along the back of the settee, Jace's large frame took up most of the sofa. "I'll admit I still owe you a favor since Whitson's card party, but all you did was introduce that Pembrooke chit to me. Yet it appears you are asking me to go sleuthing across the country, whereas *I* merely asked you to walk across a ballroom. So . . . I'll listen, but I must understand what you're asking of me before I agree."

"But I've already given you the pertinent facts."

"Then summarize, and no rambling this time," ordered Jace.

"When Eleanor was about two years old, her mother, Lady

Jeannette—that's the *first* Mrs. Pickett—gave birth to a second daughter. No one understands what happened those many years ago, but it appears Jeannette Pickett ran away, taking the baby, Madeline, with her. Later, the family learned Jeannette Pickett and her daughter Madeline died . . . it appears of a carriage accident, but that was never made clear either."

Jace pushed up from his chair, and strode over to pour another brandy. "Yes? Go on. More brandy?"

"Don't mind if I do." Emerson continued talking to his cousin's back. "As I said, this Jeannette Pickett was confirmed dead, and the family was told her dead infant was found with her."

Emerson's snifter was refilled. "Where was I? Oh, yes—this left Mr. Pickett free to remarry, which he did fairly swiftly. You know the current Mrs. Pickett. She was formerly Mary Marple. Actually, I don't know if I ever told you, but that's how I met my Eleanor. Mary Marple Pickett is a distant cousin on the other side of my family. My mother's side and—"

"Emerson—does this have anything to do with the story about this imposter?"

"I suppose not." He sniffed prissily. "I just thought you might like to know the family connections, but obviously you don't."

At Jace's impatient sigh, he hurried on, "I'm simply pointing out that I have other connections to Mary Pickett besides through my dear Eleanor, and I truly begrudge seeing either of these deserving ladies deprived of their rightful inheritance—"

"Emerson—the imposter, please?" Jace closed his eyes and massaged his forehead. "And no whining?"

"Yes, yes. All right. About a year ago, when the dead child *would* have reached her eighteenth birthday, a letter was mysteriously received by Harold Pickett's solicitors . . . or so they say. They evidently never told Mr. Pickett about it—well, he's dead now, isn't he, but Mrs. Pickett is sure he didn't know about it, as nothing was ever said to her, and she tells me he didn't keep any secre—"

"Emerson," Jace threatened softly.

"Right, right. These solicitors received a letter that claimed Miss Madeline Pickett had never died with her mother. It claimed she was alive and well and living in the country all these years. Can you believe that? But did those solicitors tell anyone about it? No, the sneaks simply stuck it in their files with the other legal papers and wills of the family."

"So. She is alive. Then she stands to inherit? Get to the point, man."

"That *is* the point, yes." Emerson leaned so far forward, he was about to fall off his chair. He puffed out his ruddy cheeks. "This woman—whom no one has ever met, who has been assumed dead these many years—conveniently comes to life in time to inherit half of the Pickett fortune—*half.* Have you ever heard of anything so unfair?"

"Whether or not—"

"I tell you, cousin, it just galls me that this imposter is trying to take food out of dear Mrs. Pickett's mouth."

Jace's eyes twinkled. "Emerson, have you looked at your future mother-in-law lately? I hardly think she'd waste away if a few crumbs fell by the wayside."

Emerson opened his mouth to protest, but Jace held up a hand. "Sorry. Sorry. Your image struck me as funny, is all. So . . ." Jace drained his snifter. "You are asking me to . . . what? Locate this imposter?"

"Oh, no. Not that. We've already been given her direction. In fact, she may already be on her way to London for the reading of the will. No, I want you to go to where she hails from. Learn enough so that we may prove she's a counterfeit."

Jace looked suspicious. "I interview local folks in the area. About her. That's it?"

"Anything you can dig up in a timely fashion. Shouldn't take long, as we're already convinced she's a phony."

Jace didn't answer immediately. He stood and paced once, twice across the room, pondering. "Don't you think that's quite a request, Cousin Emerson? This hardly seems a fair exchange for the favor I owe."

Emerson played his trump card. "Look at it this way, Jace. By returning this small favor, *you* are protecting Eleanor's dowry. *I* shall share Eleanor's dowry. That means *I* won't be borrowing money from *you* in the future."

Jace spun, a finger in the air. "Now—that clarifies matters, Emerson. Very succinct. Why didn't you say so in the first place?" He strode to the side table to retrieve his hat and gloves. "Give me the directions, and I'm off to uncover an imposter."

"The reading of the will takes place in fifteen days."

"I'll be back in three."

CHAPTER THREE

Redfern Manor

The crumpled paper twitched in the middle of the carpet, struggling to untwist.

Madeline spied it as she slipped through the library doors in response to her grandfather's summons. Squinting against the bright afternoon light, she saw his outline at the far window. Out of habit she picked up the wadded ball and placed it, unopened, upon his desk. She was used to Grandfather's tempestuous outbursts as he handled his affairs.

"You asked to see me, sir?"

"Madeline," he began with a tired sigh, as he turned from the window, hands clasped behind his back.

Oh, dear, what had she done now? Her mind raced through the last few days, but she could recollect no transgressions. "When I was little, you know, you could always get me to blurt out my misdeeds with that very sigh. However, I can't accommodate you this time." She smiled her affection. "I do believe I've finally become the perfect granddaughter."

"Ah, but perhaps I've been less than a perfect grandfather."

She noted his slow shuffle toward the desk—he seemed older than he had yesterday; was that possible? She met him in the center of the room and took his hand in both of hers. "Grandfather? Is everything all right?" She searched his face.

"I've received rather disturbing news today."

"What's wrong?" her voice caught. "You're not ill, are you?"

"No—no, child." He opened his arms, pulling her against him.

She leaned, relieved, into his woolen jacket, aware of its usual scratchiness. Disconnectedly, she wondered—did all older gentlemen have scratchy clothes?

"I've received a letter from my solicitor in London." He continued toward the desk, Madeline enclosed at his side. "But sit." He handed her into one of the burnished leather chairs facing his desk, then took the seat next to hers, their knees touching, his hand still holding hers. "First, I have a story to tell you. One I should have told you long ago."

Madeline studied his face. What could be in the letter? It couldn't be good; she'd never seen him so pale. She swallowed without noticing the dryness of her throat, and pressed her lips in the tightest of smiles to control their slight quivering.

Sir Arthur waited as the clock's carillon bells cheerfully announced the hour in the silence, then shook his head softly, and spoke even more so. "I remember thinking, that night, that the hounds of hell had been released.

"I was riding home against freezing winds. I can still hear them howling and chasing through the trees, and then they'd hit like an ocean wave. All I could think of was a warm fire awaiting me. I could practically hear the welcome crackling of the logs . . . then I realized it was the sound of splintering tree limbs. It became a tattoo of popping, followed by leaves—thousands of leaves—as a heavy mast came down to barricade the road. I'm lucky it didn't crash my skull."

He raised haunted eyes to Madeline. "If the sycamores hadn't cut off the moonlight, I might have seen her in time." He took an audible breath. "I still see her huddled over, clutching her dark cloak around her. I couldn't stop. I heard her scream as my horse reared up and came down sideways, striking her."

He contemplated Madeline's hand in his, but Madeline

suspected he stared at a time and place that did not exist in this room.

He'd sat next to her bed, his broad shoulders slumped. He should have sent a groom into the valley to fetch the doctor, but he'd given this woman his sworn word he would not. She'd been feverish and hysterical, insisting her baby would be taken away and murdered if he told anyone she was here.

Was this the reason he hadn't summoned the doctor—because she'd begged so pitifully? Or, was it because he did not want the rumor spread that he was a murderer? He had ridden down and killed an innocent young woman. A mother carrying a child.

The child would soon be motherless; of that he was sure. He'd seen enough men die during his lifetime to recognize the lamp holding her tenuously on this earth becoming dimmer. He studied her sleeping face, and was again lost in turmoil. Why did she believe her baby was in danger? And . . . why should he care? He'd lost his son—his only son. He was no longer capable of feeling compassion for others.

His manservant tiptoed in, bearing a tray with brandy.

"May I send Mrs. Whiting up with some dinner, Sir Arthur?"

"No." He turned and lifted the snifter. "Leave us."

He heard soft steps retracing; the closing of the bedroom door. He breathed in the apricot vapors of the brandy, its thin glass shell warmed by his large hands. She was as fragile as the glass, and most likely would not last the night.

She knew it as well. He'd seen the resignation in her eyes. But she was not at peace. Probably because she worried about the child. It was his fault the child would be morning's orphan. He looked over, willing her to wake, needing to release the guilt that overflowed within him.

As if she heard his thoughts, the woman's eyelids slowly

blinked open. She looked at him through clear, though pained, eyes. "Where am I?" It was almost a whisper.

"Madam, this is my home—Redfern Manor. And I am Sir Arthur Halvering."

Her eyes widened as if in shock, then fluttered closed, as though the effort of keeping them open was too much.

"We spoke a little earlier. Do you remember? You asked about your child. The baby is fine, madam. I brought you here after my horse struck you down on the road." His voice broke. "I didn't see you until it was too late. I'm so sorry," he raggedly breathed out, reaching for the white hand lying atop the counterpane.

She tried to shake her head back and forth, but looked ill from the effort, as if the tiny motion made her nauseated. "Do not . . ." she began.

He leaned forward, struggling to catch her words. "No, don't talk . . . don't talk. Please, save your strength, madam."

"But I must tell you." She could hardly turn her head, but was able to open her eyes and slide her gaze to his. "Do not apologize. I . . . I believe I was already dying. Fever. And terrible pain when I cough. I was foolish to travel so far. To sleep on cold ground. But . . . but it is better I should die than my baby." She tried to grasp his hand lying on hers, but her fingers had not the strength to grip. "He will kill her if he finds her. Please . . . please don't let my husband find her."

He wrapped both weathered hands around hers and clenched his jaw with resolution, biting back tears—she would not die alone. The least he could do was keep his vigil.

No—that wasn't true. There was more he could do, and he must tell her now, before it was too late. "Madam." He held her haunted gaze. "I make a promise to you." He raised his voice slightly so both she and his god should witness. "I will care for your baby. I take full responsibility—I shall raise your child as my own."

She said nothing; just closed her eyes against the tears that escaped anyway. They ran in a narrow rivulet, etching the hollow of her cheek, and then toward her ear.

He took his handkerchief and wiped the tears, first one side of her face, then, carefully, the other.

She swallowed. "I am Lady Jeannette Pickett. But I have not told you who Madeline's father is."

"I don't give a damn who the father is." He glanced at her still-closed eyes, hoping he had not offended her with his honest response. "Though," he corrected himself, "if he plans harm to the child, perhaps I must know?" He despised himself for making her talk, but she might not live to see daybreak, and he must be able to recognize the enemy.

She did not answer, but lay breathing raggedly. A jolt of panic coursed through him that she might no longer be conscious. He despaired of her answering, when her eyelids fluttered open.

"My husband—the evil oaf whose name I bear—is Harold Pickett. He can no longer hurt *me,* but if he discovers this child, he shall indeed kill her, as he threatened to do before she was born." Her fever-glazed eyes were intense. "When I said Madeline's father, I meant her true father."

She coughed, a wracking cough that left her face slick with perspiration. Sir Arthur reached for a dampened cloth and sponged her forehead and cheeks, as he'd been doing the past several hours.

"I fell in love with another man. My husband suspected as much. He killed him. I know he did it, though none could ever prove it. He returned to the house, and with those same hands that had just destroyed the man I loved, he beat me and kicked me—hoping I would lose the baby I carried. I protested it was his child. But it wasn't.

"He grabbed my hair and pulled back my head. I don't know if there really was a knife. I could smell his foul breath next to my ear. He said . . ." Her soft voice dropped to a lower whisper. "He said if the baby did not look like its sister—if the baby did not look like him—he would take it to the river and drown it like a rat."

She winced in pain, but continued. "After she was born, I watched her. Every day I watched her for any sign. Immediately I saw the birthmark. It was the same birthmark as the man I loved. I'd seen it so often. But, my husband would not recognize it. It was not a birthmark that showed . . ."

She might have blushed, but her face was already flushed with fever, so he could not tell.

"Then I discovered—her true hair was growing in. The same color as *his*. Spun white gold. I knew it as her death toll, and I took her away. I had to hide her in a safe place. I could not raise her as my own." She moaned. "God forgive me, I left her sister, knowing she would be unharmed until I returned. And now I shall never see her again." She shook, but the fever had dried up any tears; her eyes were glazed but dry.

"Shall I know who the real father is, then?" he asked. "Should we know her relatives?" He was revolted at himself. Did he think to foist this child off upon others once she passed away?

Lady Jeannette turned her face to his. She sucked in breath, suffering visible in her face.

"Your son sired this child."

At daybreak, when night's sky turned softly lighter, he snuffed the candle. She tried to turn her head toward the window, but could not, so she merely made the effort to turn her eyes. He leaned forward, grasping her hand to let her know she was not alone. She smiled faintly, then let her lids drop closed.

He recognized that final rattled breath, but waited a minute before gently putting his fingers to her throat. He could not detect a pulse, and already she seemed cool to the touch; but that was not possible, was it?

He rose and poured himself another drink, pondering what she'd told him. He was hesitant to believe her story. Yet she'd insisted his son Adrian had told her about his childhood home; insisted she'd been on a pilgrimage to this very manor. Why didn't he believe it? It was obvious she was a lady of quality. Would she tell such a lie in order to provide a home for her deserted child? He swirled the liquid in his glass. She knew Adrian's name.

He noticed the print on the walls gaining more color with the steady rose light from outside. He thought about Adrian. He'd lost his only son almost a year ago. They said he'd been robbed and brutally murdered by footpads. If she'd been pregnant by his son, before Adrian's death, how old would the baby be? Did he want to believe it?

He pulled the bell and instructed his manservant that she be buried in the estate's cemetery. He needed to retire to his bed for a few hours of rest. If thoughts of Adrian had returned to haunt him, it would be a restless sleep.

He stood, setting down the untouched drink. A knock at the door was followed by his housekeeper's tentative entry.

"Sir? The wet nurse has arrived. I hope it was not presumptuous on my part. She's already with the baby."

"Thank you for your quick thinking, Mrs. Cork."

She nodded, hesitating, but did not leave.

"Yes?" he said.

"Sir Arthur—I am sorry, but there was another reason I interrupted you."

"Don't apologize. Yes?" His clear gray eyes inquired with barely a lift of his bushy brows.

"It's the baby, sir. When the wet nurse unwrapped the baby to change her, this fell out of her bunting." She held out a fist, without approaching any closer.

He came to where she stood, and she finally opened her hand, palm upward. He saw the glint of light as her fingers slowly unfolded. He stared, but did not immediately reach to take it. The bright gold shimmered in her hand.

He knew what it was before he gently picked it up. It was his son's ring. And Mrs. Cork had obviously recognized it. She had tears in her eyes. Of course. She'd been nurse to Adrian as a child.

"There's something else," her voice trembled, ending on a choke. "I think you should see for yourself."

He followed her out the library door and up the wide staircase toward the nursery, though it was unnecessary. He already knew what she would show him.

He knew before they entered the small room, and before she pulled back the soft blanket to expose the tiny girl's thigh.

It was there—his son's Maltese cross birthmark, on her left thigh.

He simply nodded, and left the room.

Madeline wiped her eyes as her grandfather finished his story, but new tears threatened. "I wish I'd known her. And I wish she hadn't died because of me."

Their deep leather chairs almost touched. She reached across and touched the old man's arm. "And I'm so very sorry about your son, Grandfather."

"He was your father, as well."

"Yes. My father," said Madeline, testing the foreign phrase on her tongue. "I was afraid, when you started telling me this story, that I must not be your real granddaughter. Especially since our names are different." She squeezed his arm.

He placed his hand on hers and patted gently. "It would not have mattered one wit. You know that."

Madeline ducked her head in pleasure. "Still, it gives this sad story a happy ending. Like a fairy tale."

"Well, this tale hasn't ended. There have been some very recent events." Sir Arthur leaned slightly to pull a handkerchief from his side vest pocket. He wiped his forehead, then methodically refolded it and placed it back before continuing. "The man who was your father by name, Harold Pickett, has recently passed away."

"But wasn't he the evil man in the story?" Madeline grasped her throat. "He's the man who wanted to kill me."

"Yes. But he's dead now. He can no longer hurt you. I kept your existence secret from him all these years. I promised that to your mother, but I'd have done it regardless, after the story she told that night."

"Then—they never knew I lived here?"

He shook his head. "No. They didn't. I made sure the news reached London that the baby died with its mother. Excuse me, dear." He once again took out his handkerchief. "I hadn't noticed how warm it is in here. I should have worn a lighter vest. Now, where was I? Oh, yes. When you turned eighteen, my solicitor advised we contact the Pickett family lawyers—we understand they originally had loyal ties to your mother's family."

Madeline shuddered. "But was it safe? If Harold Pickett was still alive?"

"My man in London confirmed that Harold Pickett was drinking himself to an early death, and should no longer be a threat to you. Besides, I was assured they would be discreet."

"Did Harold Pickett ever remarry? After my mother died?"

"Yes." Sir Arthur raised a disdainful eyebrow. "It seems he married the first woman to come along—a widow by the name of Marple. Mary Marple. She's now Widow Pickett."

"I have a stepmother?" Hidden dreams pooled just below the surface of Madeline's eyes. "Will I get a chance to meet her?" Could she dare to dream?

"There's more. Your mother, Lady Jeannette, had a daughter prior to you, by Harold Pickett. Which would make that daughter your half sister." At Madeline's shocked expression, he muttered, "Not a real sister, though they may suppose so. I doubt they knew with certainty that Harold Pickett was not your true father."

"I have a sister!" Madeline jumped up and wrapped her arms about herself. "A sister, like in the stories we read when I was little." She spun to face him. "Please, when shall I meet her?"

Sir Arthur looked down at his gnarled knuckles. "You make me feel ashamed, Madeline, that I've kept this from you for so long." He looked up at his granddaughter, a soft plea in his eyes. "You realize it was for your own protection, don't you?"

Nothing could dampen her enthusiasm now that she had such wonderful news.

She reached down and hugged him, protesting, "No, no, please don't feel that way. It's just that this is a dream for me. I'm so very excited! Please, *will* I meet her?" She plopped down into the chair and placed a hand on her grandfather's knee.

"I'm considering it. These solicitors happen to be asking for your appearance in London at the end of the month. It appears your mother's family has left an inheritance, and they'd like you to attend the reading of the will—"

She gasped. "This is wonderful!"

"Well, I haven't fully made up my mind. You know, dear, as my only survivor, you are an heiress in your own right. You don't need anything they should deign to bestow upon you."

"But I wasn't talking about the inheritance. I don't care about the money—I don't, Grandfather. I want to meet my stepmother, and my sister. And, who knows? Perhaps I have aunts and cousins . . . a whole family."

She saw the hurt in his eyes, and regretted her words immediately. "I meant a large family. And female relatives. You *know* I'll never be as close to anyone as I am to you. But this is so new to me. The idea of a sister . . . and a stepmother. Please forgive my rudeness." She blushed. "I must seem so selfish."

"No, it's a fair reaction. I realize you've never had female company other than your faithful Mrs. Cork."

"And I love Mrs. Cork. You know that."

"Yes, yes, but I imagine 'sister' is a magical word to a young woman. I do understand, Madeline." He slapped a hand on his leg, having reached a decision. "Well, it seems a trip to London is what is called for."

Madeline pulled in a breath of joyous disbelief. Her stunned smile was uncontainable. "When do we leave? How soon? I cannot wait to meet my sister."

"I have the letter from the solicitor right here, dear. Let's peruse it together, shall we?"

He craned to look at the Aubusson carpet behind them, but Madeline cleared her throat. He glanced at his granddaughter, who nodded her chin toward his desk. The crumpled wad of paper perched in the middle. He smiled and stood to retrieve the letter.

He reached out but faltered, his hand frozen mid-air. He gasped and began to collapse.

He would have fallen to the floor except that Madeline jumped up to support him, bending helplessly under the weight.

"Jerome!" she cried. "Jerome, please! Come quickly! Jerome!"

CHAPTER FOUR

Doctor Crombley escorted Madeline from the gentleman's bedroom, closing the door behind them.

"Your grandfather will be fine, Madeline."

"Is it his heart?"

"No, no. He has a very strong heart. It appears he's had a relapse of that intestinal disorder that put him in bed last year. His fever has made him weak as well."

"We were going to leave for London . . ." Madeline's shoulders drooped. "But how thoughtless of me to mention it. Poor Grandfather. I'll decline the summons from the lawyers, of course. I can't leave him alone. Not now."

The doctor set his bag on the console table and snapped it shut, then started toward the stairs. "Well, don't make a hasty decision. Let your grandfather rest today, and perhaps you two will discuss it tomorrow."

Madeline nodded in silence, following the doctor.

As he descended, he said, "I'll be back tomorrow to check on him. I'm confident he'll continue to get stronger, Madeline, but he must have absolute quiet and bed rest for several weeks." He turned to her with a thought, one foot a step above the other. "You know, I do think you should talk to your grandfather about keeping your plans to go to London. You could take Mrs. Cork with you as companion. After all, there's nothing you can do by staying here. In fact—don't mistake my concerns, but this may be ideal for your grandfather—to have complete bed rest while you are gone."

"But he'll be so bored. In bed, with no company."

"Now, you know I'm not about to allow his chess game to get rusty. I'll be here, checking on him every day." He turned to continue down the stairs.

"I don't know. I did want to go, and that makes me feel self-ish."

They reached the ground floor, and Doctor Crombley donned his hat. "Discuss it with him—but, not today. He needs to rest now."

"All right. Thank you, Doctor. I'll see you to the door."

The next afternoon, Madeline sat on the counterpane of her grandfather's bed as she massaged his hand in hers. "So, if you don't want me to go, I would completely understand."

"I wish I could accompany you. But you know . . ." He glanced at Doctor Crombley, whose back was to them as he tidied his bag, "I have this curmudgeon of a doctor who doesn't believe in my having any fun."

A loud harrumph from the corner had Madeline and her grandfather smiling.

"I don't know, Grandfather. How can I leave you alone?"

"Pish-posh. Doctor Crombley says my condition will not change. Other than getting better, that is. And I can understand how excited you are to finally meet your sister. It would be a shame to miss the reading of your father's will due to my unfortunate timing. So I took the liberty this morning of send-ing a message to Duncan, and he will—"

"Duncan?"

"Yes, yes, you must remember Duncan. From Scotland. And he will—"

"Duncan? Your servant at the hunting lodge?"

"Well, I'd hardly call him a servant, Madeline. He's more of a hunting partner and friend. Anyway, let me finish, child. I expect, unless he has other commitments, he'll be arriving within the week to accompany you."

Madeline froze.

"Speechless? This isn't like you," he teased.

"But—but, I don't even know him, Grandfather. He's a stranger to me."

"I would trust Duncan with my life, Madeline."

She ignored the reproof in his tone. "But I wouldn't feel comfortable traveling with a stranger. Can't I please take Mrs. Cork and one of the footmen here instead?"

"No. I'm going to stand very firm on this. If I cannot accompany you myself, then I shall only feel secure if I know Duncan is with you. And, of course, Mrs. Cork will accompany you as well."

Doctor Crombley cleared his throat. "Arthur, you need to rest," he reminded gently.

"Yes, yes, I know. Madeline?"

"I . . ." How could she be accompanied by a complete stranger? But she knew she must let her grandfather sleep. "Of course, Grandfather. I will await Mr. Duncan. I . . . I wonder. When do you expect he might arrive?"

"You have a comfortable number of days before you must be in London for the reading of the will. I would expect Duncan could be here in three or four." He fell into a coughing fit.

"Come, Madeline. Your grandfather must rest."

"Of course." She touched the old man's shoulder and dropped a quick kiss upon his temple before exiting.

"Mrs. Cork, I have an idea."

"Uh-oh. And what is it this time, miss?"

"I'm serious."

"So was I, miss."

Madeline sifted through her jewelry box while Mrs. Cork carefully tissued dresses. Turning her head to throw a smile at her maid over her shoulder, Madeline returned to sorting necklaces and pins.

"I've been thinking about our coming trip these last couple of days, and I have the most ingenious idea: This Mr. Duncan, the Scotsman who is going to accompany us to London—he is the man Grandfather shares all his adventures with. His outdoor adventures, right?"

Mrs. Cork paused, quieting the rustle of wrapping paper. "I'm not sure I'm following, miss."

"I'm saying that this Scotsman—this Mr. Duncan—he's the expert woodsman who accompanies Grandfather on every hunting trip at Grandfather's lodge in Scotland. And fishing—*all* of Grandfather's fishing tales include his exploits with Mr. Duncan, whether it's fly-fishing or angling. I'm sure I can recite most of the stories by heart."

"Is that the idea? To recite stories to Mr. Duncan?"

"No . . ." Madeline held an open hand toward Mrs. Cork. A blood-red spot glittered on her palm. "Do you remember this garnet pin, Mrs. Cork? Grandfather said it was called a witch's heart. He brought it back from Scotland." She gingerly dropped the pin back into its case. "Ever since I was a tiny girl, I was entranced by Grandfather's stories of Scotland and his sporting trips with Mr. Duncan. I've always dreamed of having an experience like that. You know how I've begged Grandfather to take me to his hunting lodge, but he refuses."

"I know you always scandalize Sir Arthur by asking."

Madeline chose to ignore her maid's astute observation. "It's just that this will be the first time I've been away from the house and on a trip of my own. And—it may be the last, if I know my grandfather."

"I must admit I was as surprised as you to learn we were off to London. Imagine!"

Madeline carried the carved jewelry box to the bed and sat down next to the rainbow mountain of dresses. "I've given this matter a lot of thought, Mrs. Cork, and I'm determined. I do believe this is the perfect opportunity to have *two* journeys. I'm sure I'll never get another chance like this."

"Two journeys?"

"Yes! One . . ." She counted on her fingers. "We are going to London to meet my new family—my sister. I'm so excited." Madeline hugged herself. "And two . . ." She ticked off the second finger. "Well, why not?"

"Why not?"

"Yes. Why not have an outdoor adventure on the way to London as well? Grandfather already said we have a leisurely number of days before we must arrive in London. Isn't that ingenious?"

Mrs. Cork's brow wrinkled in concentration as she continued folding. "Well, now, I'm not sure. What exactly is an outdoor adventure?"

"You know—it's what Grandfather is always telling us about. How on his trips to Scotland he and Mr. Duncan go fishing, how they go hunting. And sometimes, when Mr. Duncan is trapping further afield, they take along an old wedge tent and spend the night far from the lodge. Grandfather talks about building fires at night and cooking the fish they catch over the crackling wood, and how it smells so wonderful, and how they see the night constellations so clearly." Madeline's eyes sparkled like those stars, repeating the childhood tales she'd learned on Grandfather's lap.

"Just think of it, Mrs. Cork! I've always begged Grandfather to take me with him, but he never does. Now, we shall have Mr.

Duncan with us, and you and I will finally have our own outdoor trip."

"And what if this Mr. Duncan refuses?"

Madeline frowned. She hadn't considered that possibility. "But he can't. He won't. We'll command him to do it. I'll insist that Grandfather has given his approval."

"Oh! That's fine then. Has he?"

"Of course not." Madeline studied her cuticles.

"You mean you're *planning* to ask Sir Arthur for his approval, but you've just not had an opportunity?"

"Not quite. Anyway, I'm sure he would say 'no.' "

"But—but, what if *I'm* asked if it's true? What am I to say? I'm not good at fancying tales, miss. And you said yourself this Mr. Duncan is a giant of a man, according to your grandfather." Mrs. Cork's eyes were round with apprehension.

"Don't be such a worrier, Mrs. Cork. Here, I'll make this easy for you. If I were to give you a direct order about how you should answer, would that make it all right to fi—to agree?"

"Oh, yes, I'd feel ever so much better about it then."

"All right." Madeline jumped and paced to the dresser, then spun around. "Mrs. Cork—" Madeline cleared her throat with a theatrical gesture. "You are hereby *ordered*, should anyone formally ask whether this was my grandfather's wishes, to say, 'That was my understanding as well.' "

"Very good, miss. Thank you."

Madeline picked up a small statue from her dresser, with careful idleness. "Mrs. Cork, did Grandfather by any chance already tell you we could do this?"

Mrs. Cork looked incredulous. "Of course not, miss! No, he's said nothing to me at all. I thought you just now dreamed this up."

"Mrs. Cork," Madeline said, with an exaggerated toe-tapping,

"I am *formally* asking you. Did Grandfather tell you we could do this?"

"Oh! Oh. I see. Yes, he did. Rather—" She straightened her shoulders and recited, " 'That was my understanding as well.' " She bobbed her head convincingly.

"Very good, Mrs. Cork. That was well done."

CHAPTER FIVE

Jace swung a booted leg over the saddle and dropped to the ground.

He still hadn't decided how to present himself, or what reason to give for his presence here at Redfern Manor. He'd tried so many phrases on the way.

He'd originally planned on stopping in the village first, to interview shopkeepers and neighbors. But he'd had second thoughts. What if one of the townspersons took offense and headed up to the manor to inform the family? No, it made more sense to Jace to begin at her home, and then work his way down to the village.

He planned on chatting with the staff; perhaps he'd begin in the stables. Young stablemen usually knew the manor's gossip, and weren't averse to sharing with strangers. If she were a vile schemer—and perhaps more—well, he had no doubt these young roosters would be eager to crow.

She probably didn't go by the name "Pickett" either; he'd have to keep that in mind.

According to his cousin Emerson, there was no danger of crossing paths with her. Miss Madeline Pickett would already be on her way to London, if not already ensconced there. Of course, his cousin Emerson was not all that worldly—Emerson probably hadn't learned that most ladies were incapable of packing in less than two days.

What should be his story, should he meet her? Perhaps he

should try the truth: *Good day. I've been sent by your stepmother to ferret you out.* That made him smile. Or, *Greetings. Your so-called stepfamily thinks you're an imposter.* Better yet, how about, *Hello. What makes you think anyone wants to see you after all these years?*

"Hello."

He jumped at the voice, and turned. "Madam." He bowed, not taking his eyes from her. Holding the reins at his side, he planned to drink in this vision as long as possible. Tying up a horse could wait.

"You're late, you know."

"Late?"

"We expected you here yesterday. Actually, it was hoped you'd be here two days ago." Her voice softened the chastisement.

Jace reacted cautiously; he'd not give anything away. "I see . . ." But he did not.

"Oh! Forgive my poor manners. I should be appreciative of the fact that you've come at all, shouldn't I?"

"Should you?" *What the devil?*

"This was very generous of you, doing something like this for him."

Jace gave up trying to understand. If she were referring to his cousin, and that weasel Emerson had made this public already, Jace would kill him. "That's what friends are for, I suppose."

She simply nodded, then looked at the sky. "Weather looks good. And it's still early. What do you think?"

"About . . . daylight? I like it in its place. During the day . . ."

She narrowed her eyes, as if she suspected he was making fun of her. "Mr. Duncan, I'm anxious to get on the road to London. Are you, or are you not, prepared to leave immediately?"

He chose not to answer her question. He'd learned long ago to stay silent in an unknown situation; simply listen and absorb. Or, sometimes, repeat.

"Immediately?"

Her eyes flashed with impatience. "Mr. Duncan, I'm due in London. One never knows what delays we may encounter. Can you think of a reason we should not leave now? Today?"

"No, I cannot . . . Miss . . ."

"Madeline. But I suppose you ought to call me Miss Pickett. I don't know how you address women in Scotland, but we English are quite formal, you must know."

He smiled.

"You find that funny, Mr. Duncan?"

"No. Oh, no. I'm sure I thought English women who lived in cottages wouldn't have such fine city manners." It was worth saying just to watch her eyes flash again.

"This is not a cottage. And I am beginning to think that Scottish men, regardless of where they live, have no manners at all."

She pulled on her gloves with an unnecessary yank. "Shall we say goodbye to Grandfather? If you'll please place my trunks in the carriage, I shall fetch my maid and say my good-byes. I'll let him know you'll be in as well."

She spun around imperiously, spoiling the effect by running up the few steps to the kitchen entrance.

Jace chewed their conversation in his mind like a West Indies sailor with a cheek full of tobacco. What facts did he know?

First, this was Madeline Pickett—though she did say she *supposed* he should refer to her as Miss Madeline Pickett. Was she admitting that would be her alias? If so, was this Duncan person an accomplice in her impersonation plot?

Second, she didn't know what Duncan looked like. That was obvious.

Third, if he hesitated to go now, this Duncan person would be arriving shortly. Apparently Mr. Duncan was already overdue.

Fourth, she was impatient to leave for London. Well, he was also impatient to return to the city.

Finally, what better way to uncover the Imposter than to travel with her as a confidante?

Chewing done, he bent down and hoisted one of the trunks that stood in the drive as impatiently as their mistress, and looked around for the traveling coach to load.

"Mrs. Cork, Mr. Duncan is here. Are you ready to leave?" Madeline stood in the doorway, one hand on the knob.

Mrs. Cork surveyed the empty wardrobe and bare dressing table. "Yes. I am, miss. What's he like? Is he wearing a kilt?"

"No," Madeline answered slowly. She shook her head.

"Is something wrong?"

"I don't know." Madeline moved further into the room. "I can't put my finger on it, Mrs. Cork, but . . . but, to tell you the truth, I don't think I like the man."

"But you just met him, child." Mrs. Cork delivered the admonition with a snap of the smallest travel bag.

"I know. But he doesn't appear to be very bright. He has this confused look about him. And I had the distinct feeling he was making fun of me."

Madeline walked to the window to see if Mr. Duncan was in view, but he was not.

She let the curtain drop back into place. "I guess it's true what they say about brains and brawn being distant cousins. He can't help it if he's not too intelligent, though I'll admit he does look strong enough." *Be honest,* she told herself. *You found his broad shoulders very appealing. Yes, but not his personality!* "Well, even the dumbest of dogs are loyal, and he certainly has Grandfather's trust."

"Miss Madeline! Shame, child." A chuckle belied the gentle scold.

"I know, I know. After all, he is doing us a wonderful favor. And I promise not to compare him with a dog again, Mrs. Cork.

If Grandfather says he can take care of us, I'll have to believe he can do so." Madeline backed out of the room, one hand on the door. "Speaking of Grandfather, I'm going to say my good-byes, and let him know Mr. Duncan will be up to see him as well. I'll join you at the coach."

Doctor Crombley was coming down the hall as Madeline closed her door and hurried toward him. He put out a hand to detain her.

"If you are on your way to visit your grandfather, Madeline, he's just fallen asleep."

She stopped and looked wistfully toward Grandfather's room. "Oh, dear. I was coming to say good-bye. Mr. Duncan has finally arrived, and I thought we could leave immediately. However . . ."

"Would you like me to let your grandfather know? I told him I'd pop back in after I check on the Misses Willow at their cottage." He joined her at the landing and they descended the stairs together.

"I'm not sure I should leave. I don't want him to think I left without saying good-bye . . . and I'm sure he'd like to have Mr. Duncan pop in to say hello as well."

Dr. Crombley looked over the top of his spectacles. "If you don't mind my opinion, Madeline, the less guests these first few days the better. I promise to tell your grandfather you're safe in Duncan's company, and I'm sure he'd prefer you were on the road while it's early."

"You're sure, Doctor?" She stopped, her hand frozen on the banister.

"Absolutely," he replied in his sternest, doctor-advice tone, at which he was expert.

"Well . . . I suppose if I slipped in and kissed him good-bye, that would not disturb his sleep?"

"I know you'll be very quiet. And I'll report that you stepped in and gave him a kiss good-bye."

"Thank you, Doctor Crombley. And . . . you have my direction in London, if . . ."

"He'll be *just fine,* Madeline. By the time you return, I promise he'll be up and about."

One last look around, Madeline thought, climbing the final flight of stairs to the top floor. Eighteen stairs—she knew without counting—only little girls counted steps. *Sixteen, seventeen, eighteen;* she smiled at herself.

Seeing Grandfather looking so fragile in his sleep had upset her. As she'd left his bedroom and passed through the dressing room on her way out, her imagination painted a familiar scene: her healthy grandfather standing in front of his mirror, a younger Madeline just entering the room. He would spin around and smile at her, his hands busy tying the cravat at his throat. He'd ask for her help—to the dismay of his butler, of course. Very importantly, the young girl would take hold of the cloth, fold it round itself, and give a good tug. By the time she became a young lady, Madeline wouldn't even wait for him to ask.

Gently she'd closed his hallway door, and just as gently she now opened the door on the highest floor. This had been her schoolroom. The tiny desk still squatted next to the globe upon worn planks. She walked softly, not knowing why. Putting a slender hand upon the globe, she spun it, hypnotized as she'd always been.

Her fingers brushed across the desk, then lifted the hinged top. Her initials were black against the burnished wood, as fresh as the day she'd carved them while pouting. Afterwards she'd been wracked with guilt and fear of discovery. Grandfather had, of course, discovered. She could still hear him exclaiming, "Why, look, Madeline! The carpenter who made your school desk put his initials of workmanship right here. And, see, his initials are the same as yours. Isn't that a coincidence."

She'd frowned, her lips still in a tiny red pout, wanting to confess.

When he'd risen to leave the room, she blurted out, "Grandfather, I did that. I carved those initials on my desk. I'm so very sorry."

He turned slowly, and smiled even more broadly than before. He held out an arm, and she ran right up against him, burying her face in his wool coat.

"I knew you did, pox. And I'm proud that you admitted it. Very proud of you indeed."

She never understood how he could magically take her misbehavior and turn it around so she was the best child imaginable. A tear dropped onto the wood, and sat in a bead on the glossy, waxed surface. She rubbed it away with her thumb, and closed the lid.

No, nothing she'd forgotten to take with her in this room. Nothing except memories here, and they would be with her during her travels. She left the room, closing the creaking schoolroom door.

She could not delay any longer. It was time to go.

CHAPTER SIX

"Stop! Please, stop the coach," Madeline shrieked out the carriage window, shouting at their driver over the clattering wheels and horses' hooves.

Jace pulled back on the reins, bringing the coach to a creaky, swaying halt.

Sticking her upper body precariously out the coach's window, Madeline could see him leaning down from his perch.

"What's wrong?" He coughed, waving away the cloud of dust stirred by the horses.

"We're not going to the inn," she hollered, each word separate and loud.

"You don't have to yell, Miss Pickett . . . What did you say?"

"If you can't hear me clearly, it's obvious I need to yell. I said—" she jerked back, as he was now in her face at the small door of the carriage.

"I said," she continued, as he opened the door and peered in at the two ladies, "we're not going to continue on this road."

"We're not?"

"No. According to my map, we're going to take this next crossroad." She raised a grease-spotted, wrinkled paper.

"And why would we do that?" He sounded doubtful.

It was now or never. She sucked in air, so that she wouldn't sound out of breath, or wavery. She hated it when her voice wavered.

"Grandfather agreed we might have an outdoor adventure.

Oh, my, didn't he tell you in his letter, Mr. Duncan?" She scrunched her face in feigned disbelief.

He just stared at her. *All right, there's a good start,* she thought. *At least he's not refusing.* She would continue her speech as planned.

"He and I fully discussed this. In fact, we had many discussions. He helped me plan this. It's practically his plan, really."

The staring continued. But she saw no skepticism there; only a blank look, as usual. Perhaps this was going to be easier than she'd anticipated. This gave her the courage to rush on.

"Since this is my first trip outside our home—I mean, of course, I go to the village practically every day, but I mean farther afield—Grandfather agreed it might be my only opportunity for an outdoor experience."

"An outdoor experience," he repeated.

Why must he repeat everything? Perhaps if she spoke more slowly. "Yes . . . you know, the kind you two are always having."

He grunted; he seemed to be understanding at last, she was pleased to see. Well, perhaps he was not as ignorant as she assumed outdoorsmen to be.

"So," she continued, with a bit more confidence and authority in her voice, "rather than spend a night at the inn, we will take this road." She punched her finger at a spot on the map. Following a hidden trajectory, her finger lifted off the map and pointed toward the hills on their right. "And go about three miles. There, we'll find a nice forested area, near a river." Satisfied, she folded her map.

"And?"

"And?" she repeated, raising her eyebrows imperiously, sitting up straight against the squabs, hands folded in readiness on her lap. Her tone demanded, "Why aren't we on our way?"

"And what in Hades do you think we'll do when we get to the forest and the glens?"

Wrinkling her brow, no longer quite so self-assured, she waved a hand in dismissal and said, "Why, we'll do whatever you two do on your trips, of course. Fishing. You know . . ." She held her breath for his reaction.

"Fishing? Just . . . fishing?" He looked terribly skeptical, as if he couldn't believe he'd heard her correctly.

"Well, what else do you and Grandfather do on your excursions in Scotland?"

He hesitated, opening his mouth to answer, and then appearing to think about it some more.

"What did you *think* we did?"

"I know he says you go hunting, but . . ." She scrunched her face in distaste. "We're certainly not going to run about spearing little defenseless animals. Nor shooting them," she hastened to add. "Besides, I did not bring my rifle."

"You have a rifle?" This, in a tone of incredulity.

"Well, Grandfather's rifle."

"That's a relief," he smiled. "And your spear?"

"I don't have a spear, and you know it. That was just a figure of speech—hunters' talk."

"I see; and, no bows and arrows? No knife?"

"I wish you would stop this. I'm sure you think you're very clever. I did bring fishing poles. Grandfather says you both love to fish."

"So, we're to go fishing. Like we men do . . . your grandfather and I, that is . . . when we're outdoors."

"Yes." Oh, Zeus. She didn't mean to sound so hopeful. She meant to sound authoritative.

"And that's it," he said. "We fish, then we continue on to the inn."

"Not quite. We have other things to do as well as fishing. We . . . we must spend the night in the woods."

"What?" He hollered into the small space of the coach.

"You don't have to shout, Mr. Duncan. I said we must sleep in the woods, beneath the stars. I even brought along the small wedge tents that Grandfather told me you use. Besides, we'll need more time for our other activities."

"What other activities?" He lowered just one brow, speaking slowly.

"Well, I have this list. . . . somewhere."

"What list? Of what?"

Madeline was having a difficult time hiding her impatience. "I have a list of what other things we'll be doing on our excursion." She dug furiously through her handbag. "Oh"—she looked up as she realized—"I must have tucked it into one of my other bags." She grabbed the side of the door, preparing to alight. "If you'll just excuse me, I'm sure I can climb up and locate the correct bag very quickly."

He held up a hand, still standing in the doorway, effectively barring her exit with his body. "There's no need to find that list right now," he said. He looked up the highway, scanned the clouds in the sky, then contemplated the hills in the distance. He appeared to be considering something. "You say your grandfather agreed to this?"

"Are you questioning my honesty?" she asked, imitating the very words Grandfather would have used, and attempting to imitate her grandfather's tone as well. However, she couldn't bring herself to make eye contact, instead choosing to turn to her maid with an exasperated expression that clearly said, "Can you believe he is questioning my honesty?"

Mrs. Cork's head bobbed. "That was my understanding as well." She reddened. "I mean, that her grandfather agreed . . . not as to whether you're questioning her honesty, though it certainly sounds—"

"No one's calling you a liar, Miss Pickett. It's just—I have to be honest. I'm a bit surprised your grandfather would be foolish enough to allow his only granddaughter to spend the night in the woods." Jace shook his head in disbelief. "In fact, it's the stupidest, most ridiculous idea I've ever heard."

Madeline's mouth froze in the shape of an embroidery hoop.

He ignored her shock and continued preaching. "Ladies belong in inns. That's why they built them."

She felt her face flush hotly. "What fustian! And don't you dare criticize my grandfather. I thought you were his friend, Mr. Duncan. He's a wonderful guardian, and he's not foolish, and I think you are pompous, sir. Why shouldn't a woman be able to spend a night in the woods, if a man can do it?"

They stared one another down.

Madeline's mouth was dry. She licked her lips, ready to play her final card. "My grandfather not only agreed, he insisted it would be an educational experience. Mr. Duncan, please. It might be the last chance I ever have. Ever. For the rest of my life." Drat! She hadn't planned on pleading.

It was her last gamble. It was now or never. They went straight, or they took the crossroad.

Jace ran his hand through his hair. Fists on hips, he turned once more toward the hills, then back. "Hell. All right, we'll take the detour. This is ridiculous!"

He slammed the coach door and stomped off to take his seat atop the coach.

She held her breath until they were rolling forward, then, covered by the noise of the horses and the squeaking wheels, she squealed and hugged her maid.

"We're going on an outdoor adventure, Mrs. Cork!"

CHAPTER SEVEN

"That doesn't look very stable, Mr. Duncan."

Jace got up from where he'd been kneeling and threw down a peg in disgust. "Miss Pickett, you've done nothing but follow me around, criticizing. Are you now telling me how to set up a tent?"

"No," she backed away. "I was simply making an observation. Grandfather says you snap those tents up like flags. I just thought you'd be done by now, is all." She walked around to the back and eyed the sagging canvas wall. "And, I thought . . . I thought it should look a little safer."

"What was that?" he called from the other side. "I can't hear you."

"Nothing, Mr. Duncan." She reappeared at his side.

He bent to retrieve the peg. Kneeling again, he twisted to see if she still supervised. She did. "Are you in a hurry, Miss Pickett?"

"Yes. I mean, we have this whole list of things to do, and—it's almost noon."

"And? What else do we have to do, madam?"

She didn't appear to hear his reply. "That reminds me: I must find my list. I'm sure it's in one of my trunks."

"The trunks are under that elm tree," he said as he pointed with the wooden stake. "Why don't you go busy yourself finding it?"

This she heard. "I don't think you should be bossing me

around, Mr. Duncan. After all, *you* are the servant here."

"Then do whatever you like. Just get out of my hair."

"That doesn't sound very respectful, either."

A disgusted sound accompanied the pound of the tent peg. "Miss Pickett, let's begin again. What would you like to do at this moment?"

"I believe I will go find my camping list." She strode away, calling back over her shoulder, "Grumbling is also rude, Mr. Duncan."

"Here we are." She unrolled a long parchment as she walked toward him, her nose buried in her list. "Oh, my"—she looked up—"aren't you done setting up that tent yet? You still have to set up your own shelter, you know."

"I don't need one." He was down on one knee, lacing leather strips through grommets.

"Are you just saying that because it's taken so long to—"

"I don't need a tent!" he roared.

"Well, all right. There's no need to shout."

His back to her was his only reply.

"Mr. Duncan, would you care to hear my list?"

"Could I stop you, woman?" He didn't look up from where he knelt on the ground.

Madeline scowled. "I don't understand how Grandfather can claim you are the best of companions. I am not enjoying your company one whit."

He stood abruptly, and in two strides he was in front of Madeline. Placing his hands on her upper arms, he moved her back exactly one pace. She squeaked, afraid she'd pushed him too far. But he didn't look angry. In fact, he looked as surprised as she, dropping his hands as if her fabric burned him.

"I'm sorry," he said. "I just wanted us to stand back and get a good look. I didn't mean to be so abrupt. But—just look at that." He turned to view his work. "Isn't it something?" Looking at the lopsided tent brought a proud fatherly grin to his face.

Madeline wrinkled her nose. The tent looked awful. And he was so pleased, you'd think it was the first time he'd ever put one up. The man was an enigma.

"Yes," she stuttered, "it's . . . beautiful, Mr. Duncan."

He turned and looked at her; really looked at her. "Thank you, Miss Pickett." He brushed his hands together. "What's next on our list?"

She hid her smile by looking down at the long sheet of paper. She could practically recite it from memory:

"Going fishing. Grilling the fish we catch over a fire. Brewing tea in an iron kettle. Doing our laundry in the river. Cooking potatoes in the coals. Sharing ghost stories . . . when it's dark." She smiled up at him. "Cooking breakfast at sunrise. Hanging our clothes to dry on a line between the trees. Looking at the stars. Taking a hike—"

"Good God, Miss Pickett—exactly how many days are you planning on staying in this forest?"

She drooped. "Just today." Quietly, she asked, "We won't be able to do all of these activities today?"

He visibly softened, sighing loudly. "Give me your list. We'll see how much we can do."

He scanned it quickly with furrowed brows, then handed it back. "All right. Where are the blasted fishing poles?"

Mrs. Cork yawned. "My goodness, I'm tired. I could take a nap. And I don't usually care for naps." She sat on a fallen log near the tent and patted her mouth on another yawn. "It must have been the fishing . . . not that it wasn't exciting—just standing there and all . . ."

Madeline sat across from her, bursting with enthusiasm.

"Grandfather claims that's what being outdoors does to you, Mrs. Cork. He says it gives you a fierce appetite, and it helps you sleep soundly."

"Is there anything," drawled Jace, "that 'Grandfather' does *not* say about being outdoors? Any little minor detail without an anecdote? Without an opinion?"

"That's rather rude, Mr. Duncan," said Madeline in surprise. "I thought you and Grandfather were close friends."

"Aye. Forgive me. It must be my Scottish humor."

Did he just insult her grandfather? Or himself? What an odd man. She turned to her maid and asked, "Would you like to take a quick nap?"

Mrs. Cork set down her knitting needles quickly enough, but spoke with hesitation. "It certainly is an appealing thought . . . but I just couldn't. It would hardly be proper, now, would it?" She looked round-eyed at Madeline, hopefully. "Would you think?"

"Oh, for Hades' sake, what is it with women and propriety?" Jace's face mirrored the incredulity in his voice. "Who is around to report it? Do you think we'll read about it in the *London Gazette,* or the *Bath Journal*—'Miss Madeline Pickett unchaperoned for half an hour in the forest?' "

"Ignore him, Mrs. Cork." Madeline shook her head. "Of course it would be proper and acceptable. I've got my book, and I'll be happy to sit here and read while you nap. I'll not be more than ten feet from the tent, should I need to call you."

"Should you need to call her?" repeated Jace. "And why, may I ask, would you need to call her? Do you think I'd be wanting to make improper advances to you, Miss Pickett? Are all men suspect in your diary, I'd like to know?"

As if Mrs. Cork's face was on a string, she turned from Madeline to Jace and back during their conversation volley.

"You're being crass, Mr. Duncan." Madeline's spine stiffened, and she sat up even straighter on the log. "Perhaps this bad temper is due to the fact that, evidently, for the first time in your life, you were unable to catch any fish—unable to get even one small nibble on your line, in fact? I don't know how it is on the moors, with no humans for company, but in polite English society there are certain conventions we follow. Leaving a woman unchaperoned is not one of them. However, as I pointed out, I will be sitting right here outside Mrs. Cork's tent, and we've agreed that would be acceptable."

"Well, let me assure you again that you'd be the last woman I'd be making advances to, Miss Pickett."

"That's welcome news, as you'd be the last gentleman I'd acknowledge advances from, Mr. Duncan."

Each turned and angled pointedly away from the other.

Mrs. Cork looked one last time from Mr. Duncan's scowling face to Madeline's prim indifferent expression, then shrugged her shoulders and popped into the ladies' tent for a quick nap.

Madeline read, and Jace relaxed. Now and then a soft snoring came from the tent.

He was deliberating how best to involve her in a discussion. Unlike women of his acquaintance in London, Miss Pickett appeared quite artless. She was as easy to read as his first schoolroom primer. He had to admit, though, it was refreshing not to be constantly sparring with coy innuendoes and *bon mots*. Not that this young lady didn't spar—her verbal spears hit their mark.

She was more straightforward than he'd experienced with women in town—she'd probably tell him everything he needed to know if he'd ask it casually. Then he could return to London to reveal what his cousin Emerson waited to hear.

Jace wouldn't leave immediately; no, he would not leave the two women alone on the highway. He'd taken on the guise of their bodyguard, and his honor bound him to escort them safely to London.

Honor? There was no honor in what he did. She'd never know he was a spy, would never even suspect. Now that he'd met Miss Pickett, he wished this dirty business were done. Even more, he hoped she was genuine; all his instincts told him she was.

He should take advantage of this private time to learn the truth from her. Unfortunately, it was his own fault she wasn't speaking to him at the moment. He hadn't meant to let his temper escape—he'd been angry and annoyed with himself, not her. He'd failed at every task they'd given him, and she'd finally stopped criticizing. Now all that remained in her eyes was pity. And pity annoyed him most of all. He ground his teeth and determined to get this over with.

"Let us call a truce, Miss Pickett."

Madeline looked up with disinterest from her book. "And why would we, sir?"

"Because I'd like to apologize for my bull-headedness. And, I'd think, for your grandfather's sake. I'm sure, knowing him as well as I do, that he would be pleased if we'd get to know one another."

"Very well." She put her marker in the open pages, and closed her book. "What do you wish to discuss?"

Jace sat on the ground, one arm draped along the fallen log he leaned upon. "Tell me about yourself."

"What would you like to know? I'm sure Grandfather must have bored you with stories of his only granddaughter."

Of course—he must remember there were certain things he should already know. He'd have to be more guarded. "But there's so much he never mentioned." He hazarded a safe guess. "Such as—whether you were tutored at home?"

"I was, as a matter of fact. I suppose most females are. I

think I would have enjoyed going away to school, though."

"Never say that! I hated it."

Madeline set aside her book and leaned forward, her hands locked between her knees. "Tell me why. I desperately want to know what it was like."

Jace sat up straighter, bending one leg. He paused to give her question fair thought before answering.

"Mostly," he said, "I spent time feeling sorry for myself because I missed my family. I was the eldest son, but I suppose I *was* a little coddled by my two older sisters. I remember standing at the school window that first day, and watching my father climb into his coach, leaving me to some horrid fate." He chuckled. "Well, it wasn't really horrid, but the headmaster did declare I reminded him in looks of his obnoxious nephew, so you can imagine what a great start that was."

Jace recalled himself—*he* was supposed to be grilling *her*. "Tell me why you desired to go away to school, Miss Pickett."

Madeline picked up a nearby twig and doodled in the powdery dirt. "I suppose it's because I never had any siblings."

Well, well, the little schemer. *Looks like I'll be lucky enough to uncover the ruse here and now*—wasn't she admitting that Eleanor was not her sister? This was going to be much too easy.

"Any other relatives?" he asked with careful nonchalance.

"No. I wanted so badly to have playmates, but Grandfather's home is quite isolated, and I was never allowed to go to the village to play. Grandfather was always reading stories to me— stories about children who had friends." She looked up with an impish grin. "Do you know, I was even jealous of Hansel and Gretel! I would have gladly faced a witch if I had a loving brother next to me on my adventures." She laughed at herself.

She has a beautiful laugh, thought Jace.

Madeline continued scratching figures in the dirt. "I even made up an imaginary friend: Teeter Thomas—" She peeked up at him through her lashes. "—and don't you dare laugh, sir."

He pressed his lips together, emphasizing the crevice in his cheek, but he didn't laugh. He studied her, encouraging her with a nod to go on.

"I was never allowed to go anywhere. I was certain I would be eighty years old before Grandfather would allow me to see London . . . that is why this is so exciting for me. I have to pinch myself to be sure it's real. I don't know what I've anticipated more: London, or this outdoor adventure." She tilted her head and eyed him to the side. "Do you want to know a secret, Mr. Duncan?"

Oh, do I. "Yes?" he asked in measured tone.

"Every year, after Grandfather returned from his hunting trips with you in Scotland, I would force him to spend the next several nights in front of the fire, telling me stories. I loved sitting cross-legged at his feet, watching his face as he recounted your journeys, with the hearth warming my back. And I relished every tale. Every detail."

She stared at some unseen space that did not include Jace.

"I loved you, you know," she said, still staring into her memories. "Oh!" she blushed. "I mean, I *used* to love you . . . I mean—forgive me, Mr. Duncan—I loved the memories of you in the stories. They were so real to me. Grandfather made you sound such a grand companion and hero." She held her hands palms up. "You were the hero of my stories, so I couldn't have loved the real you, because I'd never met you. Not, of course, that I love you now we've met—oh, dear me, perhaps I'll stop talking," she said, shaking her head in embarrassment.

Jace experienced a twinge of jealousy for this Mr. Duncan. He wished he really were the man, if only to bask in the glow of that admiration.

"Enough about me, Mr. Duncan. You mentioned two sisters. Any brothers?"

"One younger brother. A real rascal. I love him dearly, though I'd be tortured before I would admit that to him. And, lots of cousins. Too many cousins. Most of them very annoying. You?"

She raised her brows in question.

"Cousins?" he repeated.

Madeline shook her head. "No. No one. Just Grandfather. Grandfather and me. I arrived at his doorstep as a baby, and he took me in and raised me. And," she added with a smile toward the tent, where soft snoring sounds escaped through the flaps, "of course, Mrs. Cork. She's the closest to a mother I've had, and she's been wonderful to me. Although her title is lady's maid, over the years she's been my nursemaid, my companion, my confidante . . . my best friend, really."

Madeline abruptly changed the subject. "Tell me about Scotland. I want to hear all about it—I've only ever read about it. Tell me about growing up on the moors."

Jace cleared his throat, stalling for time. Good God, now what? He'd never seen a moor in his life. Wasn't even sure he could spell the word.

"But I'm still curious. What of your mother and father? You mentioned your grandfather and Mrs. Cork raised you—" He apologized with his eyes. "I'm sorry. Perhaps it's painful to speak of?"

"No. At least, it shouldn't be . . . I never knew either of my parents. When I was very young, I assumed every child was raised by her grandfather. As I got older, I learned that my grandfather would not tolerate any questions about mothers or fathers. I could have badgered Mrs. Cork, but not knowing made it more mysterious. I thought maybe they'd been spirited away by trolls."

"Do you still?"

Her answering smile started out right side up, but the corners of her mouth turned it upside down. "Grandfather only told me the whole story a matter of days ago. Yet, that made it seem more real. So recent . . . so very sad."

He hated himself. Why was it important to uncover the truth? He'd only just met Miss Pickett, yet already felt more loyalty to her than to his unlikable cousin Emerson.

"My mother died when I was an infant. I guess I always knew that, but I didn't know the circumstances—" Madeline swallowed, so that she wouldn't cry. A hard lump burned her throat, and she chose not to continue.

"Don't. Please don't think about it. That was rude of me to pry, Miss Pickett." Jace stood up, uncomfortable with her pain and helpless to ease it.

He held out his hand, and Madeline took it and rose. She shook out her dress, looking down. Jace noticed she was avoiding looking at him.

"Are you all right?"

She nodded, mute. He put a hand under her chin and raised her face. As he suspected, her eyelashes were heavy with wet tears.

"I'm sorry," he mouthed silently. He reached for her, to pull her into his embrace, but saw the movement at the tent opening.

Mrs. Cork was stepping out to join them, so instead he squeezed Madeline's upper arms, a silent support, then stepped a proper distance away.

He'd wanted to embrace her.

CHAPTER EIGHT

A quiet threesome huddled around the pile of cold sticks. Madeline and Mrs. Cork pulled blankets round their shoulders, while Jace knelt at the pyramid of wood, rapidly rubbing two sticks together.

"Will it take much longer for a flame to start, Mr. Duncan?" asked Madeline.

"How the devil would I know?"

"Grandfather says you always insist on starting your fires by friction. Shouldn't you know by now approximately how long it takes?"

He looked up at her as he continued to rub one stick against the other. "It takes as long as it takes, Miss Pickett."

The minutes elapsed as the women sat patiently, hands clasped on their laps.

"Well, look on the bright side," chirped Mrs. Cork into the silence. "We may not have a fire for cooking our dinner, but even if we did, we have no fish to fry."

Jace pivoted on his knee to face Mrs. Cork, and then swung back to Madeline. "Do you mean to tell me we have no other provisions? You were depending on catching fish in order to eat a meal?"

Madeline reddened. "But Grandfather told me you *always* catch more fish than the two of you can consume." She brightened suddenly. "Oh, now I see! That's what's referred to as a fisherman's tale. Well, and how was I to know?"

He grunted without elaborating. "And, what were we going to cook over the fire for breakfast? More fish?"

"Of course not. I brought along a special surprise for breakfast. Oh! And I did bring some small potatoes to roast. Shall we cook those now? I mean, assuming you can remember how to start a fire?" She rolled her eyes comically at Mrs. Cork, but was mortified to find him watching her when she turned back.

"Do you think you could do any better, Miss Pickett?"

"I'm not the hired outdoorsman," she said primly.

They continued to huddle quietly.

"Let's sing a song," suggested Mrs. Cork.

Jace and Madeline looked incredulously at her.

"I just thought it might lighten the mood," Mrs. Cork said with a slightly defensive tone. "It was on your list, wasn't it, miss?"

But no one started a song.

"What else is on your list?" Jace asked, swiping a sleeve across his sweating forehead.

"That doesn't involve a fire? Not much, I'm afraid," said Madeline, sitting desolately on a log, chin in hand.

"Go take a walk, then."

Madeline sat straighter. "I beg your pardon, Mr. Duncan? How dare you order us about like that?"

He paused, staring at the cold stick in each hand. "I'm just suggesting you let me work at this, and you ladies take a walk down to the river. Wasn't that on your blasted list?"

Perhaps, Madeline pondered, moving about *would* keep them warmer than sitting here with no fire. She'd take the wool blanket about her shoulders as a shawl.

"And gather some smaller kindling while you're at it," he added. "Do you think you can do that without getting into trouble?"

That was it. Madeline jumped up, her hands fisted. The blanket fell in the dirt. "Mr. Duncan—we are not your servants. I must insist you stop ordering us about. If you want kindling, gather it yourself. Let's go, Mrs. Cork."

He called without turning from his task, "When you're outdoors, everybody pitches in—if they want to eat."

"You surely wouldn't dare say that to Grandfather."

"Aye, I would if he were here."

She stared at his back in disbelief. "Are you telling me my grandfather gathered kindling?"

"Aye."

"And you *let* him gather kindling?"

"Aye."

"I have to tell you, Mr. Duncan, your Scottish is getting on my nerves. Would you please stop saying 'Aye'?"

Now he turned to face her. "You bring back kindling, Miss Pickett, and I'll try not to speak my native Scottish tongue for the remainder of our trip. I promise."

"You, sir, have a deal."

Madeline and Mrs. Cork returned shortly with small bundles of twigs. No cheerily burning fire greeted them. Madeline noted Mr. Duncan's hair fell in sweaty locks over his forehead, which was beaded with perspiration.

She was no longer angry and felt herself softening with sympathy. "Mr. Duncan, perhaps you should try a different pair of sticks. When I asked Grandfather to explain its workings, he said the hard wood is rubbed against a softer wood, and the smoldering flakes jump right off and onto the dry moss and twigs."

"Hmmm . . ." Jace muttered to himself. "Maybe that's it. Makes sense. Perhaps I've two pieces of hard wood here." He dug a fingernail into each stick as if to judge its hardness. "Or maybe they're both soft. Excuse me, ladies. I'll be back shortly. I think I'll find some different sticks."

Jace strode into the forest. Madeline looked at Mrs. Cork, who returned the look, raising both brows and rolling her eyes.

"If you ask me, miss, our Mr. Duncan is not quite the woodsman."

"I know what you mean, Mrs. Cork. But I can't imagine . . ."

"You can't imagine yer grandfather making up all those hunting stories?"

Madeline sighed. "No. It's just not like Grandfather." She picked up a nearby twig, and broke it into smaller pieces as she contemplated.

"Either that, or Mr. Duncan is just having a very unlucky day," said Mrs. Cork as she turned to pick up her knitting bag.

"Now that I think of it, I was always pestering Grandfather for stories and for detailed explanations. Perhaps it was *my* fault if Grandfather made it all up."

Madeline brushed dirt and twigs from the rough blanket she'd retrieved. She folded it methodically. "But then, why didn't Mr. Duncan simply admit to us that he does not start fires by hand?"

"Perhaps he's seen how important this outdoor adventure is to you, and he doesn't want to disappoint you?" asked Mrs. Cork. She shook her head, answering herself. "Though I doubt it. That man doesn't strike me as the type who would go out of his way to do something nice for anyone. He'd just as soon spit vinegar at ye."

"Why, that's it, Mrs. Cork! Of course—he doesn't want to disappoint us."

"Where are you going?" asked Mrs. Cork.

Madeline was already at the edge of the clearing. "I'll be right back, Mrs. Cork. This is all my fault. I just want to tell Mr. Duncan it's all right—we understand. I don't want him wandering around trying to find sticks. It will be dark soon."

Mrs. Cork couldn't make out Madeline's last words, as she walked away: "That poor, thoughtful man. He—"

Madeline disappeared around the curved path.

"Mr. Duncan! Halloo, Mr. Duncan," called Madeline loudly, crashing through gorse bushes crowding the narrow trail. Several deer paths had crisscrossed the edge of their tent clearing, but she was sure this was the direction Mr. Duncan had taken.

She stopped to look around. It was silent once she'd stopped snapping dry pine needles underfoot. Birds called long distances across the forest floor, and a woodpecker drummed among the tall tree poles. Looking up, she had to shade her eyes against the amber light refracted through needled branches. This was heaven. It was more than she'd imagined.

Madeline inhaled and closed her eyes; she wanted to remember everything: the smell of berries warmed by the sun, and the resins lingering as pine trees gave up their afternoon heat.

A scratching startled her eyes open. Not twelve feet away, a squirrel skittered sideways through the cleft of an ash tree. She stood very still, watching with a contented smile until the squirrel scampered out of view in the canopy above.

Now—where was Mr. Duncan? Grandfather said the man was an excellent scout and could find his way back, no matter how deeply they ventured into dark forest. Though Madeline began to suspect this piece of lore as well. The man could not be lost, could he?

A cloud's shadow swept the sunlight from the trail and the chill air suggested the forest might not be so welcoming in the night. She quickened her steps. The path ahead became a bit darker as overgrown vines crowded its edges, attempting to touch hands and form a tall tunnel. Bramble thorns caught at her heavy traveling skirt. Madeline looked down to tug the bombazine free, and walked into a fine web. She batted furiously at the sticky threads, shuddering. Imagining a spider in her hair, she shook her locks, running her fingers frantically through her hair.

A twig snapped. But Madeline had been standing still.

She swung around, looking back along the trail. Nothing could be seen through the thick bushes. It was eerily quiet now. Even the birds held their songs, hiding from the intruder.

Maybe it was just a gentle doe returning home to her fawn. But as Madeline tried to conjure up the pastoral scene, she envisioned instead a wild boar with sharp curved tusks.

Or it could be a bear. Grandfather said they scavenged the bushes for ripe berries. She'd eaten a few temptingly juicy berries along the trail; maybe the beast smelled it on her breath. She wanted to cry.

Up ahead, the trail thinned out, allowing greater visibility. It appeared to enter a grove of old fir trees. She'd have more room to escape in an open space, she thought, hurrying away from the claustrophobic curve of the trail.

And then she heard it.

A low growl, and a slow snapping of twigs. Something was advancing slowly . . . one large foot at a time. She closed her eyes, her breath coming in short, shallow intakes of fear.

A hand grabbed her shoulder from behind, and she screamed.

"Miss Pickett! Are you all right?" It was Mr. Duncan.

"Mr. Duncan!" She spun into his arms, and grabbed onto the front of his shirt. "There is a beast nearby. I'm so glad you arrived." A tiny sob escaped as she hid her face against his chest.

Jace's eyes opened wide as she grabbed onto his shirt. He sucked in his breath as her fists buried themselves in a twist of fabric, and he could feel the warmth of her hands against his chest. A protectiveness welled within him . . . and more.

"Shh. You're safe." He smoothed her hair with one hand, his other holding her close.

"Do you see anything?" she asked.

He realized Madeline couldn't see, as her face was buried in the cloth of his shirt. The sweet scent of her hair was distracting.

"Is there anything there?" she repeated, then turned her face, and opened just one eye, venturing a peek. Seeing nothing, she opened both eyes.

He stared at her as she lifted her face to his. Her eyes were beautiful—open and innocent, with a soft touch of fear. He leaned slightly toward her, knowing he was going to kiss her.

"Well?" she demanded, breaking the spell.

Jace leaned back. "Well, what?"

"Do you see a beast or not? Why are you just standing there? There's a wild animal nearby! Aren't you going to do something, sir? Shoot it or something?"

He didn't bother pointing out there was no rifle about. "What kind of wild animal?"

"How would I know!" Her voice was rising to a near-hysterical pitch. "It's most likely a bear or a wild boar!" She buried her hands deeper into the fabric of his shirt.

"Ow!" he said, as she pinched chest hairs along with the wool.

"Don't jump like that! You scared me," she scolded.

He chuckled. "You made me jump, madam. In case you haven't noticed, you've got more of my shirt in your hands than I have on my back."

She recoiled in embarrassed horror. "I'm . . . I'm sorry . . ." Then her look hardened. "What are you laughing about? We're in danger! Are you crazy, Mr. Duncan?"

"There are no animals about, Miss Pickett . . . At least, none that I can see."

"But I heard it. Do you doubt my word?"

"No. Not at all. But perhaps you could tell me exactly what it sounded like?" He looked at her expectantly.

"It was very low. Low in tone, I mean, not in volume. Well, yes, it was quiet as well. I barely heard it." She looked defiant. "But I did hear it. I'm positive."

"A low sound. That's all?"

"A growl. It was definitely a growl."

"A very low, quiet growl . . . hmmm. Did it sound like this?" Jace made a soft growling sound, pitch-perfect to the one Madeline had heard.

Her expression went from fear to disbelief to fury in a matter of exactly four seconds.

"You scoundrel!" She pulled her hands from his shirt, but then changed her mind and pushed her fists against his chest.

Jace caught her balled hands, and smiled his wicked smile, one corner of his mouth higher than the other. He laughed aloud, and she pulled away forcefully.

"You are a despicable cad!" she cried, spinning on her heel and stomping back along the trail.

"Wait! Wait," called Jace, laughing as he hurried in her wake.

He caught up to Madeline and put a restraining hand on her arm. She halted, and he almost ran into her.

"Don't . . . you . . . touch . . . me," she said.

He raised his hands in the air, palms toward her.

"All right. All right. I promise not to touch you. But, please. Let me apologize. It was just a small joke, Miss Pickett."

"That was your idea of a joke? I did not find it to be one bit funny."

"Not even one bit?" he couldn't resist asking, holding his fingers in a pinch near her. "Don't you think your grandfather would have thought that was funny?"

He could see her struggling not to grin.

"Just a wee bit, lass?" he added in his best Scottish burr.

Madeline looked down at the path, but couldn't hide the smile.

"Ah, does that smile mean I am forgiven, Miss Pickett?"

Her chin jerked up at him, and she narrowed her eyes.

"It won't happen again. I promise, Miss Pickett."

Now she did smile, and trying to hold it back only deepened her dimple. "All right, Mr. Duncan. You are forgiven . . . just this once."

"And how can I make it up to you?" His eyes twinkled with mischief.

Madeline leaned toward him to whisper intimately. He held his breath.

"How about a warm fire?" she asked with a hint of sarcasm, then turned and continued picking her steps along the path.

"You certainly know how to break a mood, Miss Pickett."

He smiled ruefully as he brushed by her to lead the way. His back to her, he sighed loudly in mock resignation. He was pleased to hear a small chuckle behind.

The two approached the campsite, where a tiny glimmer of light floated.

"What the devil?" said Jace.

"Where is that light coming from?" asked Madeline at the same moment.

In the center of the clearing, Mrs. Cork sat contentedly knitting in the twilight, by the light of a fat beeswax candle.

On top of the neat cairn of twigs, she had wedged the stub of wax, like the topping on a one-year-old's birthday cake. Within another half of an hour, it certainly would not provide enough light to see by.

"Mrs. Cork! How did you . . ." Madeline came right up to

the pyramid of wood, and peered down, as if she could not believe her eyes. "How did you light this candle, Mrs. Cork?"

"With a tinderbox, of course," said Mrs. Cork. "How else would a person light a candle?"

"What tinderbox?" asked Jace, looking around.

"This one. In my pocket." Mrs. Cork pulled out her round tin canister.

"Mrs. Cork—why didn't you mention you had striking flint with you?" asked Madeline with amusement.

"Why, I thought you wanted to have Mr. Duncan show us how he prefers to do it." She turned a guilty look toward Jace. "It's nothing; I was just waiting for you to return and light the fire properly, Mr. Duncan."

With that said, she leaned forward to pick out her candle from the stack of wood, and she blew it out.

Jace and Madeline looked at one another, then burst out laughing. Mrs. Cork looked confused.

An hour later, a different threesome sat outlined in orange. A fire lit their circle, and Mrs. Cork and Madeline sat cozily on a log, facing Jace.

"This is so much fun. Thank you, Mr. Duncan." Madeline held out her tin plate. "May I have another small potato?"

Jace dug in the coals, and pulled a steaming bud from the hot ashes.

"More tea, Mrs. Cork?" he grabbed the kettle with a cloth wrapped around the hot handle, and refilled her mug. He held the steaming teakettle toward Madeline, but she didn't notice. Her head was tilted straight back, her mouth open as she perused the constellations.

"Just look at the stars! It's true they're brighter when one is in the hills. That's what Grandfather says."

"And don't you think a fire is brighter outdoors as well?"

Mrs. Cork asked no one in particular.

In answer, the three sat mesmerized by the red and cobalt layers floating above the wood. The snapping of bark and the popping of moss played a sleepy symphony. Or perhaps it was the occasional wisp of smoke that stung the eyes closed before it pirouetted away.

"Could we tell stories?" Madeline asked. "Ghost stories, or perhaps fairy tales?"

"Are you sure it's on our list? It may be too dark to read and confirm."

"Oh, but it is!" Madeline looked up at Jace, but stopped when she saw his grin.

"Of course it's on our list." He smiled, stretching out his long legs. "I doubt there is anything that is not on that list."

"I'll begin," Madeline said, ignoring him. "I've always been partial to the story where a princess waits in the tower for the prince to rescue her. He is so brave—coming to her rescue, knowing the witch could return at any moment. And all for true love."

"Wait," interjected Jace. "He doesn't even know her at that part of the story. How can you imagine he loves her?"

"Why else would he risk such danger? Of course he loves her. He does it because he's seen a glimpse of her at the tower's ledge and he's fallen hopelessly in love with her."

"In love with her? He has one glimpse of her while riding through the forest, and now he loves her? You think that's why he's helping her?" He snorted. "Humph—there's a word for that, but it's not 'love.' "

"How can you be such a cynic?" She stood abruptly. "I don't think I want to tell any more fairy tales in front of you, Mr. Duncan. You would shrivel all the love right out of them. Good night." She turned toward the lopsided tent.

"I have a story," Mrs. Cork said in the still darkness.

Madeline stopped in surprise. "Why, that's wonderful, Mrs. Cork. I'd love to hear it." She settled onto the log again, fanning out her skirt, and directed a challenging glare at Mr. Duncan.

"I'm all ears, Mrs. Cork," he said, looking directly at Madeline instead.

Mrs. Cork began, "This is a tale told me by my granny when I was a young girl. It's a true story, as it happened to herself." She looked at the others, but all that could be seen in the light of the fire were their floating faces.

She closed her eyes and reached into her memory. "Granny was a young maid at the time. Her mistress received an invitation to visit a cousin's castle, a remote spot in the northern highlands of Scotland. It was a huge castle overlooking the sea, with pointed turrets, and over a hundred bedrooms. Do you know it, Mr. Duncan?"

Jace gave a quick shake of denial, and she went on. "My granny remembers climbing circular stairs to the rooms in the corner tower they were to occupy. The other servants warned her that those rooms were haunted, but she laughed, figuring they thought she was a country mouse, easily frightened. They whispered that it happened about two hundred years ago—the earl discovered his only daughter was planning to elope with a young lad. The earl became furious, especially as he found the young man to be unsuitable. Well, he foiled their plans by locking his daughter in one of the attic rooms of the tower. That night, she thought she could escape out the window, and she tied her bed curtains together. Rich silk fabrics from the east, they were, flimsy, and the next morning the servants saw them fluttering like doves at the window. But she'd fallen to her death in the dark, and her young broken body was found on the rocks below. That's the story they told my granny. That the young maid had fallen from that very tower she'd now be staying in.

And that's why it was haunted. Granny laughed to their faces, but she told me she had a feeling inside, a suspicion about that place. Folks always said my granny had the second sight. When they first arrived, she said she'd seen a hand—a very pale hand—at one of the windows, parting a lace curtain to the side, and a shiver went up from her spine to her scalp.

"When they reached the room in the tower, she said there were cobwebs in the neglected corners of the ceiling, and a large carved bed of the darkest wood imaginable. One of the slitted windows overlooked the church and graveyard. The cemetery gate was closed when they entered the room. But by the time the sun went down, it was open . . . and they'd never seen anyone in the churchyard who could have done it.

"Her young mistress was unsettled, and ordered her maid—my granny—to sleep with her in that huge four-poster bed. Well, during the night my grandmother woke up. She said she heard an extra set of heartbeats through her pillow. Like it was comin' from the mattress, or the bed itself. She knew it weren't her mistress's, because she could hear it in her ears and head as clearly as she heard her own. A thump-thump, thump-thump. Two sets of heartbeats, and only one was Granny's."

Mrs. Cork opened her eyes and looked at Madeline and Jace. Madeline was staring at her.

"That's it?" breathed Madeline softly in the dark.

"That's it," Mrs. Cork said. "It still gives me shivers, it does."

An owl assented. The fire had become a mound of embers; Madeline smelled only the pungency of charred wood. The sky was now as dark as a mourning shroud. She lifted her teacup to her dry mouth, but only tasted cold, bitter tea leaves at the bottom of the cup.

She jumped when Jace spoke softly near her ear.

"Mine is also a true story, also one of doom. Would you prefer something lighter, another romantic fairy tale perhaps?" His teeth gleamed a ghostly white.

"No. I am not afraid. Are we, Mrs. Cork?"

Mrs. Cork's eyes were wide, but her head shook obediently.

"Well, unfortunately, mine does not take place in Scotland."

"Why is that unfortunate?" asked Mrs. Cork.

"Because it takes place near here. Perhaps in these very woods beneath our feet."

Madeline swallowed when he wasn't looking in her direction.

"It happened at the time of the Norman invasion," Jace began in a low, somber voice. "Harold, the Earl of Wessex, was rushing to battle with William, the Duke of Normandy. He was accompanied by his fearless fighters—Anglo-Saxon housecarls—the toughest fighters in Europe. The legend holds that one of the housecarls discovered that his wife had slept with a comrade-in-arms. The warrior went berserk. He slew his fellow soldier with a battle-axe, then began to slay the others around him. They were able to subdue him with their swords, but only by cutting through his sinews and his neck. He was covered in ribbons of blood. As his life ended, the forest floor a red sponge, he cursed his wife. And he cursed any woman who should enter the forest where he died."

Mrs. Cork gasped. Madeline opened her mouth to speak, but Jace held up his hand. "None believed him, of course."

Madeline and Mrs. Cork looked over their shoulders. In the dark, they could no longer discern where the clearing ended.

"However . . . well, perhaps I've said too much. Shall we retire?"

"However, what?" Madeline asked. "There's more?"

"There have been rumors over the years, of women losing their rings in these woods."

"Oh. Is that all?" Madeline looked down at the golden band she wore on her middle finger. "Women lose rings every day. I have no fear of that. Mine is quite tight. Unless they were magicked off their fingers." She laughed nervously.

"No. They are removed with fingers still attached. Cut off. By an axe. But no one has ever been seen. It happens as they sleep."

"I can't remove my ring." Madeline twisted the gold band.

Jace shrugged. "It's just an old wives' tale."

"Old wives' tales usually have truth in them." Mrs. Cork popped her ring off and rolled it into her pocket, then sat looking around the pitch-black woods.

Madeline stood. She was still working the slender band of gold against her knuckle. "Perhaps it's time to retire, Mrs. Cork? Mr. Duncan, will you be sleeping outside our tent? Are you a light sleeper? Will you make sure the fire does not go out?"

"Aye. Good night, and sleep well, lasses."

Jace rolled a blanket into a tight sausage, placed it under his head, and turned on his side. He was surprised to discover a smile lurking at the corners of his mouth. It had been an enjoyable evening. Perhaps this would not be such a bad trip back to the city after all. Perhaps his debt to his cousin would not be such a difficult chore.

He chuckled once more, then was soon asleep.

The night was interrupted with a whoosh and muffled screams. Jace jumped up, still half asleep. It was pitch dark, except for red embers glowing in the fire pit. He ran to the tent. Only— there was no tent. All he could see was a writhing mound on the ground, with flailing limbs poking about.

Chapter Nine

Madeline groaned as she stretched the next morning, rubbing her lower back. The hard ground last night had been bone chilling. Once the tent fell down, they hadn't slept well at all. She was in a snappish mood, and was convincing herself it must be the Scotsman's fault.

She stared resentfully at his broad back as he tended to the pan hanging above the crackling fire. "You know, Mr. Duncan, Grandfather always made you sound bigger than life. He said you were a giant, very strong, all muscle. But you're not. Not really."

He added another log to the roaring blaze. "Well, I've found that most muscle-bound men still have a good share of fat. It just happens most of it got pushed up into their brains."

She considered this. "And you're not very tall. Grandfather said you stood heads above other men."

"Any other complaints, Miss Pickett?"

"I'm certainly not complaining! But, since you ask . . . where is your kilt?"

"Kilt?" he repeated with disdain.

"Yes. I understood you always wore your kilt. I've never seen a man in a kilt. Why would you wear it with Grandfather, and not with us?" For some reason, this revelation annoyed her further. "Are you implying this isn't a real outdoor trip?"

He stirred a spoon around the edges of the iron pan before answering. "I may wear a kilt when your granddad expects it,

Miss Pickett, but I'm not about to don one to satisfy your curiosity. Anyway, in my opinion, kilts look like they're for . . . let's just say effeminate men, and leave it at that." He turned to her and held out a hand. "Now, pass me those plates, and we'll have some breakfast."

Madeline watched as Mr. Duncan ladled the sticky mess onto the dishes. He handed her a full plate. Glancing at Mrs. Cork, she saw her maid found it unappealing as well. When his back was turned, each hastily scraped half the slop into the bushes next to where they sat.

All three pushed forks around their plates with a distinct lack of interest.

Madeline almost brought a bite to her mouth, in an effort to be polite, but manners failed her. "Did you like the breakfast surprise, Mr. Duncan? I heard haggis is a favorite breakfast in Scotland."

"Haggis. It is quite a surprise, I must admit."

"You're not eating much," Madeline observed.

"I'd say it's appetizing, but I'd be lying. What's this made of?"

"Oats, and a few other things. You're from Scotland. Don't *you* know what's in haggis?"

"What do you mean, a few other things?"

She pushed the gray mass around on her plate. "I can't tell you."

"Why not?" Jace was beginning to look ill.

"I asked our cook to provide it, and when I asked what was in it, she said, 'Oats, miss. And you don't want to know what else.' " Madeline lifted a rubbery edge and peeked beneath. "She wouldn't elaborate. The only other thing she said was, if this was your favorite dish, you deserved to be a Scotsman."

"My apologies to your cook, Miss Pickett, but I say let's feed this to the plants, and get to an inn where they serve real food."

He stood, eyeing his breakfast with suspicion. "Give me your plates, ladies. We can be ready to leave shortly."

"But we haven't done everything on my list!"

"And what could possibly be left on that blasted list?" Jace reached for her plate.

"Let me see . . ." She handed him her dish, then pulled a piece of paper out of her pocket and unfolded it. "Grandfather says you wash clothes in the river in the morning, and he also said—"

"Wash clothes? Wash whose clothes? No—don't answer that. I'm not about to wash clothes. Not mine. Not yours. You're lucky I set up your tent and lucky I made a fire. I took you fishing, I cooked breakfast. And, now we're leaving, and that is my last word. You have precisely fifteen minutes to prepare to leave, ladies."

Madeline jumped up and stamped her foot in the dirt. "I don't understand why Grandfather raves about you! You can't cook a decent meal, you're a horrible companion, you cannot build a fire, you can't set up a decent tent. I suppose you don't even know the first thing about washing clothes, either!"

She knew she sounded like a shrew. She hated when she sounded like a shrew. But, what on earth did Grandfather see in this arrogant man? And why did he have to saddle her with the Scotsman as bodyguard and servant? Being in the woods alone and helpless with this man was no better than being in the woods alone and helpless with the elderly Misses Willow from the village. At least those near-sighted sweethearts wouldn't hesitate to beat away a bear with their canes.

She stared down his scowling countenance. She squinted right back at his squinting eyes. She frowned when he frowned more deeply.

And then he jumped up and started toward her. Once more she mirrored him, but this time in reverse.

"Aye, lass, I may not cook a meal to your satisfaction."

He continued stalking her. She continued backing away, and caught her balance as she stumbled on a thin branch.

"And I don't feel a bit abashed that I'm not a chatty companion for two overly chatty females. *And* I don't apologize for taking longer than you'd like to build a fire. But—"

To her shock he grabbed her by the waist and threw her over his shoulder. He was so quick and strong, she was certain he was going to fling her right over his back, and she'd continue flying through the air right into the brambles nearby. But he did not. He held her firmly as he strode across the small clearing to the other edge of their campsite.

"—don't question me about my ability to launder, as it happens I've got that well mastered."

With that, he lifted her away, raised her over the deep pool, and dropped her into the freezing water.

Madeline came up gasping, sputtering. She began to screech, but had to gasp again as the icy water continued to suck her breath from her chest.

"Now, could I get some soap for ye, lass?"

"I can't—" she gasped, then coughed.

"What's that? Can't talk? Well, well, we'll have to wash clothes more often."

"I can't—" she gasped again, but didn't complete her sentence as her head bobbed below the water.

"Can't wait to apologize? Is that what you were about to say?"

Her head bobbed up again, and she sputtered, then her long hair was left floating above the water as she dipped below once more.

"You great oaf!" yelled Mrs. Cork, running down the path to the water. "She's trying to tell you she can't swim!"

★ ★ ★ ★ ★

Madeline tried not to cry. She was frightened, humiliated, perhaps still in shock. And, worst of all, she was wrapped like a baby in a cloak, trapped by Mr. Duncan.

They sat close to the roaring fire.

He'd plucked her from the water, and wrapped her in his voluminous cloak. He insisted on rubbing her arms vigorously through the wool.

"This is most improper . . ." Her teeth chattered, and she couldn't finish her sentence. "I've got to learn to swim."

"Why? So some lout like me can throw you in the water on a regular basis?"

If she hadn't been so upset, she would have laughed. Actually, she let out a tiny laugh, but instead of merriment her eyes overflowed with tears. Her nose began to run, and she sniffed.

Jace got up. "Let me put on more wood. We've got to keep you warm."

Madeline didn't point out that they already had a bonfire going. She felt the sudden chill where his warm body had leaned against the damp wrapper. She shivered again.

"Are you all right, miss?" Mrs. Cork's hand was gentle on Madeline's shoulder.

Madeline kept her voice low. "What am I to do, Mrs. Cork? This is so very shameful. If Grandfather knew . . ."

"Stop that!" Mrs. Cork whispered fiercely. "Now, you stop blaming yourself. It was that oaf who threw you in the water. It weren't *your* fault."

"But I baited him. I've been nothing but rude to poor Mr. Duncan all this trip. And he's Grandfather's friend . . . or at least he was."

"Humph. You know what they say about having friends like that, miss."

Jace carefully added three split logs atop the fire, and returned to her side, a small flannel cloth draped over his shoulder. He bent over Madeline, massaging her wet hair with the toweling.

She closed her eyes, enjoying the warmth from the blaze and the warmth from his large hands. The deep scalp rubbing gave her a different chill—a delicious chill. She hardly noticed when he sat back down beside her, but jumped at his touch as he pulled her back against his chest.

"What are you doing, Mr. Duncan?"

"I'm merely keeping you warm. You're still shivering." He wrapped both arms around her.

"I am sure this is not proper."

"And I don't give a damn whether it's proper. I'm not about to let you die of a cold because of what society dictates." He pondered. "Are there etiquette rules governing conduct in the middle of the forest? For that matter, should a lady be on an outdoor adventure at all?"

She stiffened. "If there are any outdoor rules for men, I'm sure tossing young ladies in the creek is not considered a proper outdoor sport."

"I deserve that, Miss Pickett. I know it's not a good excuse to say I have a temper—but I admit I do, and I work hard to control it." She felt the sigh released deep in his chest. "I can't believe I did that. An apology seems much too hollow for such a detestable act."

She pulled back and looked up at him. "It must be your Scottish blood."

He smiled crookedly. "Aye. That would explain it."

Madeline knew she should also apologize, but had trouble looking him in the eyes. She leaned back again. "Mr. Duncan, I have an apology of my own to make . . ." The colors licking at the logs were hypnotic. "I also have a temper. Quite a temper, according to my grandfather."

"Shhh. No, Miss Pickett. There is absolutely no fault of your own that this happened. This was totally my brutishness. I won't hear of an apology."

"No. No, please hear me out," she rushed on. "I realize you're in a strange land, Mr. Duncan, and that it's not easy being this far from home. I'm sure you're lonely and homesick. And then, to have to look after me . . . I'm sure you weren't prepared for that. And then, to be treated like a servant . . . well, even though you are . . . a servant . . ." She peeked up at him. "Somehow, that wasn't as pretty an apology as I'd planned."

His lips quirked. "It's forgiven."

Jace was much too aware of the young lady in his arms, even though she faced away from him.

He cleared his throat, wishing he could clear his physical thoughts away as well. "So, what is the first thing you plan to do in London?"

"See my sister." He could hear the smile in her voice. It was as soft and sweet as claret.

Jace was confused. "I thought you said you had no siblings."

"I didn't when I was growing up. But . . . I do now." She laughed. "I know that makes no sense—but, I also have two fathers now."

Jace's suspicions were at full alert. "How unusual. Tell me about it."

"My real father's name was Adrian. Adrian Halvering. And then, there's Mr. Harold Pickett . . . rather, there *was* a Harold Pickett. He recently died, but I never knew him."

Aha. Finally, the truth is coming. The little actress. "Tell me more about Harold Pickett. I don't believe your grandfather ever mentioned him."

"There's nothing more to tell, as Grandfather never mentioned him before this month. At least not to me. I'm going to London for the reading of Mr. Pickett's will, but he's not my real father. Though, Grandfather says perhaps I shouldn't tell anyone. But I know I can trust you, Mr. Duncan."

"And why shouldn't we tell anyone?" He was oddly disappointed. He should have been elated, but the fact that Emerson and his crude fiancée's family should be right about Madeline saddened him.

"According to Grandfather, Harold Pickett threatened to murder me when I was young. It's why my mother took me away. It's a long story."

She proceeded to explain.

Jace heard the whole story; heard the honesty in Madeline's words. He believed she told the truth—but what did that mean? Even if Harold Pickett was not her real father by birth, he was her father by name. She would still inherit as long as she could prove she was his daughter by name—his and Lady Jeannette's daughter.

Still, the less doubt she cast upon her background, the better. According to Emerson, his fiancée's mother was a greedy battle-axe. Wasn't it possible she cried "imposter" in order to keep more money for herself and her daughter?

The fire crackled, and Madeline lay peacefully cocooned within his arms, having finished her tale. She no longer shivered, but Jace was hesitant to release her.

"I've been thinking, Miss Pickett. About your father . . . your real father, that is."

"Mm-hm?" Madeline half turned to look at him with sleepy green eyes.

"I don't think you should tell anyone in London what you just told me."

"Why?" She said the word on a soft breath. He could see she struggled to keep her eyelids raised.

"I'll explain later," Jace said.

"Mmm, this is so cozy . . ." Madeline squirmed, burrowing

deeper, like a kitten, and he became uncomfortably aware of her every curve.

"Miss Pickett?" He looked down and swept her damp hair away from her face. She was asleep.

He leaned his chin on the top of her head and thought about everything she'd told him. She truly did deserve her portion of the inheritance. After all, the fortune came from the first wife, who'd died saving Madeline's life.

Madeline cuddled even closer. His first instinct was to cuddle her and kiss her perfect ear, but a second instinct made him glance to the side.

Mrs. Cork sat with her arms folded, her sharp knitting needles held like swords, staring at him. He met those dour daggers in her eyes. With an inward sigh, he simply patted Madeline's shoulder with great exaggeration, in as fatherly a manner as he could imagine, offering a weak smile to the guardian.

Madeline yawned, and began to stretch, coming out of a deep sleep. She found herself wrapped in wool, and a solid body beneath. She inhaled sharply, sitting up.

"Excuse me," she stood abruptly and looked at Jace. "I'm . . . I'm warm now. I'll just go change my clothes . . . and pack." She stepped on the edge of the cloak, stumbling a half step.

Jace caught her elbow, helping her catch her balance, but she pulled away, red-faced. Scooping up the edges of the large garment, she hurried to the tent. Mrs. Cork followed to assist.

CHAPTER TEN

The housekeeper at Redfern Manor opened the kitchen door to shake crumbs from the breakfast linens. She made clicking noises with her tongue, calling to the sparrows and chickadees to come for their share.

A giant shadow fell across the doorstep, blocking out the bright morning sun. She dropped the napkins with a tiny squeal, then squinted against the dark outline edged with glaring light.

"Sorry to be startlin' ye, madam."

She didn't acknowledge his greeting, but crossed herself instead.

"I'm looking for Sir Arthur Halvering. My name is Albus Duncan."

He still didn't receive a return greeting, as she fainted in the doorway.

"Hallo! Hallo! Is there anybody home? I have a woman here needin' some help."

Doctor Crombley happened down the stairs, not a moment too soon. Hearing the commotion, he rushed to the kitchen.

"Here, my man. I'm a doctor. Please, bring her in here. Lay her on that couch," he pointed to the closest settee.

The giant carried the housekeeper in, then bent carefully over before he let her roll from his arms onto the satin couch.

"What happened?" asked the doctor.

"I couldna tell ye," replied the gentleman in his heavy burr. "One moment she was standin' in the doorway, and the next she fainted. I myself had just walked up. I dinna think I startled her that badly."

"What was she doing in the doorway?"

"Makin' wee little birdie sounds . . . oh, and she crossed herself."

The doctor shook his head, then raised a skeptical eyebrow. "Might I inquire your name, sir?"

"Aye. Lost me manners. It's Duncan. Albus Duncan, at yer service. I was summoned by Sir Arthur."

Doctor Crombley went as white as his shirtsleeves.

"Duncan? Did you say you are Mr. Duncan? Of Scotland?"

"Aye, that's me. He should be expectin' me. Though I'd of been here sooner if I'd been home to receive his message."

Doctor Crombley looked around hastily. "Perhaps we should lower our voices, sir. It might be best if no one else hears of this."

"Hears of what?"

"Hears of the fact that you have arrived."

"But I already told ye. Sir Arthur is expectin' me. Is he not well?" the giant brow furrowed in concern.

"He is resting at the moment. However, I'm not sure his heart could stand the strain. I . . . I must think of what to do."

"What strain? What's wrong with his heart? I dinna understand anything that's comin' from yer mouth. And who are *you?*" the bushy brows rose in suspicion.

Doctor Crombley saw the tension in those broad shoulders, the large hands curling in readiness to defend Sir Arthur, and hastened to explain. "Mr. Duncan—I don't know that I understand either."

The giant took a threatening step forward, and the doctor rushed on. "I am Doctor Crombley. I am Sir Arthur's physician. He had a setback recently, and I've been tending to him every day. He will, however, be fine in a matter of weeks. He just needs more rest." He remembered whom he was talking to. "Unless, that is, he should suffer a shock. He is still quite weak. Seeing you would not do his heart good, I am afraid. We must disguise who you are until we decide what to do."

"Yer not makin' any sense, man!" the huge visitor said in a frustrated explosion.

"Mr. Duncan, please bear with me. Why exactly did Sir Arthur send for you?"

"He wrote and asked if I would escort his granddaughter to London."

Doctor Crombley closed his eyes in anguish. "That's what I was afraid you would say."

"Ye've got to talk faster, Doctor."

Looking at the huge fists, the doctor blurted, "Another man appeared here. Yesterday. He claimed to be you. He took her."

The teeth ground like huge boulders. "Slow down, man. Start at the beginning. I'm trying to catch up to ye."

"Sir Arthur did say that you—I assume he meant you, Mr. Duncan—would be arriving to escort Miss Madeline to London. Miss Madeline Pickett is his granddaughter."

At that moment, the doctor remembered the housekeeper, who was lying like a dishrag between them. He loosened the apron ties at her waist, and began to fan her. Looking back up at Mr. Duncan, he continued. "When you arrived—I mean, when this man who claimed to be Mr. Duncan arrived—the young miss was already anxious to be on her way. I assured her . . ." The realization hit him that he was at fault. "My God, it is all my fault! I assured her that her grandfather—Sir Arthur, that is—needed his sleep, and that she should get an early start on the road, and I would inform her grandfather she was now in safe hands."

The doctor's face was strained, as if he'd seen something horrible. "Except she isn't. She's in the hands of some stranger, and they left yesterday. She's been gone overnight with a stranger. Of course, her maid is with her. But he might have disposed of the maid by now! Good God, we don't even know if she's on her way to London."

"Doctor, Doctor! Calm yerself. Can I get ye some smellin' salts er somethin'?"

Doctor Crombley recalled himself. "Oh, my, I don't know what to do. I should go wake her grandfather, and let him know. Only . . . I'm afraid the shock may harm his recovery!"

"Ye say they left yesterday? In the mornin'?"

"Aye," the doctor unconsciously imitated the visitor.

"Then don't say anythin', Doctor. Let me go after the cur. If I overtake them, then no harm's been done, and I'll send word to ye."

"I can't *not* tell him!"

"If ye don't hear from me in two days, then let him know. But also let him know this—I will be on the man's trail. He knows I *always* catch my quarry, Doctor. He'll know I can find her, and I will." He rose, and put a ham-steak hand upon the doctor's shoulder. "But, ye've got to tell this woman here to keep quiet."

The doctor looked down at the housekeeper. "I can manage that. She's a very discreet member of his loyal staff. Aren't they all?"

Albus rolled his eyes. "Not the ones in Scotland, Doctor. Bless ye, I hope yer right about Sir Arthur's servants."

He started in bounds toward the door, then the mountain spun around. "Is there anythin' else ye can tell me, Doctor? About the lass? About the lad who's impersonatin' me?"

"She has silver-blond hair. Folks couldn't miss her. He looked to be mid-twenties, thirty at the most. He's tall, but not as tall as you. Not as heavy either—I mean no offense, of course!" He broke off nervously, then continued. "He has dark hair, lots of it; somewhat curly . . . and . . . a dark look about him . . . sinister. I should have known. That was the word that came to my mind when I first saw him. I thought it was because he was a hunter . . . like you," he finished lamely.

"Aye. Sinister. That's not surprisin', since he fooled everyone here. Just what's his plan, I'd like to know."

"Miss Madeline is only nineteen years of age. So innocent. So innocent, and it's all my fault she's been abducted."

"Shhh. Remember, we're not to let anyone know. Until two more days at sunset, then. Give me until then, and I promise I'll have word back to ye."

"Bless you, Mr. Duncan. Godspeed, sir."

Madeline finished folding the last item to be packed. The vitry canvas of the tent filtered the sunlight into a tawny radiance that glazed everything within.

"Hasn't this been a wonderful outdoor trip, Mrs. Cork?"

"You almost drowned! We're both starving. And you must be freezing still . . . and you're having a wonderful time? Do you have a fever, child?"

"No!" she laughed. "Look around you, Mrs. Cork. Have you ever seen a light so grand? Look. Even where the moths have eaten through the canvas . . . these little pinpoint holes. Look how the sunlight tries to send a prism through. It's almost like starlight . . . in the middle of the day."

"I wouldn't know, miss. I just see little holes that need darning. Little holes that will let in rain and cold air. Here. Let me feel your forehead."

Madeline stood obediently while Mrs. Cork measured her temperature with a discerning palm.

"Hmmm . . . You don't feel hot. Perhaps you're faint from hunger?"

"I'm fine. Really I am. I'm just having such a wonderful time.

And now I'm off to London to see my sister. This is such a wonderful, wonderful—"

"Don't say 'wonderful' again," warned her maid, "or I just might be tempted to dunk you myself."

Madeline chuckled, but Mrs. Cork was already on her way out of the tent. Madeline stooped at the opening, and bumped into Mrs. Cork.

"Get back!" cried Mrs. Cork. "Hide, child!"

"What? What is it?"

Mrs. Cork turned and shoved her. "Hush! We've been ambushed. Hide yourself!"

Madeline fell on her bottom. She couldn't believe this was happening to them. Ambushers! What would Grandfather say? He'd tell her she should have known better than to go into the woods.

Mrs. Cork squatted behind the tent flap, peeking out.

Could Mr. Duncan save them? Guilt coursed through Madeline for thinking they'd have been safer with the Willow spinsters.

And what if Mr. Duncan needed her assistance? He hadn't proven himself terribly competent so far. In truth, his outdoor skills were woeful. Of course he would need aid, and it would be cowardly of her to stay hidden. Madeline scurried out of the tent on hands and knees, just in time to see Mr. Duncan fall to the ground. He'd been felled by a giant.

Mrs. Cork screamed. "He's killed Mr. Duncan. Run, miss, run for your life!"

Madeline did run, but not away from the campsite. She ran to the supplies and grabbed a fry pan, then she rushed the large ambusher with the pan held over her head. He grabbed the pan, and held it high, Madeline still clamping it tightly. Mrs. Cork screamed again.

"Stop!" roared the giant. "Stop yer bansheein' woman. I'm

lookin' for Miss Madeline." He eyed Madeline's bright head of hair.

"She isn't here," screeched Mrs. Cork.

"I'm right here," said Madeline, dropping her grip on the pan and stepping back warily.

"Yer Miss Madeline? Sir Arthur Halvering's granddaughter?"

"Yes," Madeline said, her defiant voice reflecting her stance. "And who are you, sir? And why have you hurt poor Mr. Duncan?"

"*I'm* Albus Duncan, lass. That man"—he nudged Jace with a booted toe—"is an imposter. I'm just glad I found ye two ladies before he did ye any harm. He dinna harm ye, did he?"

"Dinna?" repeated Madeline.

"Aye. He dinna harm ye none, did he?"

Grasping his meaning, Madeline shivered. "No, sir, he did not. Well," she frowned, "he did try to drown me."

The giant roared, and looked about to do more bodily harm to the first Mr. Duncan, so she hastened to explain. "But I think he didn't realize I couldn't swim. And, he did dry me and hold me very tenderly."

This seemed to make the man even angrier, judging by the redness of his face.

"I'm fine, Mr. . . . Mr. Duncan. Really." She wrapped her arms about herself, overwhelmed. She and Mrs. Cork had narrowly escaped disaster. But . . . how did she know this man was telling the truth? She'd blindly trusted the first Mr. Duncan. She pinned the intruder with a skeptical look. "And—how do we know you truly are Mr. Duncan? Can you prove it?"

The man scratched his grizzled jaw. "But I am."

Madeline thought for a moment. "Tell me something of your adventures with my grandfather." Goodness, she groaned inwardly, why hadn't she thought of this test for the other Scotsman?

The big man smiled; it split his log of a face. "Yer granddad and I have had some mighty adventures, lass."

"Then tell me . . ." She racked her brain for one of Grandfather's favorite stories. "Tell me of the grouse you tracked into the swamp."

His laugh shook the tent behind her, or so it felt. "Aye. I thought the old man—beggin' yer pardon, I mean yer granddad—I thought he was goin' to sink into the peat like a dinosaur to leave his bones for the scientists. I reached for him with a tree limb, and him holdin' the other end for dear life . . . turns out the grouse just walked out ahead of him. The bog, it were only a few inches thick. We scared each other."

Madeline laughed. "Yes, that's the same way Grandfather recollects it. Yes. You are definitely Mr. Duncan. And, I love your accent, Mr. Duncan. That man"—she looked with contempt at the heap of a man on the ground—"never really sounded Scottish. Now, why didn't that make me suspicious?" *Perhaps because I found him attractive,* she thought guiltily. "But, then who is this imposter? Do you know him?"

"Nay, miss. Never set eyes upon him before. And ye don't know why he kidnapped ye?"

She shuddered. She'd been kidnapped. He was right. "No. No, I don't. Perhaps for Grandfather's money? Do you suppose he was going to hold Mrs. Cork and me for ransom?"

He looked over at Mrs. Cork, perhaps weighing his next words. "Well . . . I daren't think of what he might have done with Mrs. Cork, since he didn't need *her* body to retrieve yer grandfather's fortune."

"Mr. Duncan! Please!" Madeline rushed over to put a protective arm around her maid, who looked about to faint.

"Beggin' yer pardon." Duncan looked sheepishly at Mrs. Cork.

Madeline looked down at Jace, and whispered, "What should

we do with his body?"

"Oh, he's not dead. I just gave him a tap. He'll be up and about soon enough. But, we won't be here when he wakes. Are ye ladies ready to leave?"

"Yes, we are," said Madeline. She looked around the clearing. "I suppose we can leave the tent here. I, for one, would rather not be here when he awakens." She gave a second thoughtful look to the tent. "Unless . . . that is . . . Mr. Duncan, we were supposed to have an outdoor adventure, but that imposter bungled everything. Well, not surprising, since he's not you."

"An outdoor adventure?"

"Why, yes. I explained to Mr. Dun—to that man—that Grandfather had agreed he—I mean you—would take us to the forest. Perhaps if we took the tent, and found a different spot, we could—"

"Absolutely not. No," said the giant.

"But, surely, just one extra night on the road—"

"Absolutely not. No," he repeated—never raised his voice. Simply stated it as an absolute fact.

"You don't understand, Mr. Duncan." She batted her eyelashes, and stopped. His bushy eyebrows were lowered, and he crossed his arms. "All right," sighed Madeline. "I suppose I'm lucky I did get to spend at least one night in the woods, under the stars . . ."

This made her think a bit more kindly about the stranger who'd abducted them. She smiled. He wasn't a woodsman, yet he had taken her for an adventure. He couldn't be a bad person, could he? "Are you sure he'll live, Mr. Duncan?"

"Oh, trust me, I'm not worried about that." Duncan looked around. "I'm thinking though, that I'll find a good hangin' tree before we leave. We ought to make an example of him for others who think to kidnap innocent women. Do ye have any spare rope in all this mess?"

Madeline gasped. "No! Mr. Duncan, I forbid you to hang Mr. Duncan—I mean—him. He didn't do us any harm. He was a perfect gentleman."

Mrs. Cork cleared her throat, and Madeline continued, "Oh, all right, Mrs. Cork, nobody is perfect. But . . ." She smiled. "I did enjoy our adventure. Couldn't we let him live, Mr. Duncan? Please?"

Albus Duncan shook his head, but said, "All right, lass. I'm not sure I follow ye, but . . . all right." He looked around the campground. Other than the tent, all was ready to pack onto the carriage. Mr. Duncan hefted up a few bags, and tossed them easily onto the carriage roof.

Madeline and Mrs. Cork watched as he climbed up, tied them down, and unceremoniously said, "Into the carriage, ladies."

Madeline hesitated before stepping up into the vehicle. "Shouldn't we take his horse with us, Mr. Duncan?"

"Good, God, woman, yer a bloodthirsty one! If yer not wantin' to hang him, ye'd be signin' his death sentence just as easily if ye did that. Even your granddad wouldn't leave a man out here in the middle of nowhere without a horse. No, we'll be long gone afore he awakes. No need to worry. I don't think he'll be foolish enough to be pursuin' us."

"As you wish, Mr. Duncan." She was embarrassed that he thought her "bloodthirsty." She turned the conversation to a lighter, safer topic, "I do like your kilt, Mr. Duncan."

"Why, I thank ye, miss."

"That man—" Madeline pointed her chin at the prostrate form lying in the dirt. "—he said kilts are for . . . well, he said they are effeminate," she confided primly as she stepped into the carriage after Mrs. Cork.

They both looked out the window, waiting for the coach to move forward. Instead, they saw Mr. Duncan descend from the carriage. He turned and walked back past the fire, to where Jace's horse was tethered. He untied it and gave it a good smack, which sent it galloping off.

"Effeminate, huh?" He spat in the dirt by Jace's feet, then climbed to his perch atop the coach.

Early that evening, Mr. Duncan maneuvered the team into the dirt courtyard of the narrow stone inn. He disappeared through the green door. Madeline and Mrs. Cork waited until he returned to the coach, filling the door with his huge frame.

"I think it would be wise to stop early this evenin'. That way, ye can get a good hot meal, and freshen yerselves up for our arrival in London tomorrow." The man blushed, looking at Mrs. Cork. "Not that I'm saying ye need freshenin', beggin' yer pardons."

"That's all right, Mr. Duncan," Madeline said. "A hot meal and a fire sound absolutely sinful."

"I agree heartily," added Mrs. Cork.

"Then, if ye'll go ahead inside, the landlady's wife will show ye to yer room. I bespoke a dining parlor as well. I'll join ye shortly, but I have to send—that is, I have an errand to attend to."

He handed Madeline down from the carriage, and held out his large hand for Mrs. Cork.

"Your errand, Mr. Duncan," she paused on the step and spoke softly so only he should hear. "Will you be letting Sir Arthur know his granddaughter is safe and well?"

"Yer a smart woman, Mrs. Cork." He nodded. "But it's the doctor I'll be sendin' a message to. We thought it best not to worry her granddad, ye see . . . I'm sorry to be soundin' so dishonest, but, on top of his other ailments . . . well, the truth is we didna tell him, so he doesn't yet know." He looked embarrassed.

"Oh, Mr. Duncan." He heard her relief.

"Albus, if ye please."

"Oh, Albus." She put a hand to her chest. "Here I was, sure the master thought me a terrible companion, letting her get kidnapped and all." She leaned toward him, and planted a quick kiss on his cheek. "Thank you, Mr. Duncan. I mean . . . Albus." She stepped down, and hurried after Madeline.

The Scotsman turned one shade more red than the threads of his kilt's tartan. He realized it had been the doctor's suggestion not to tell Sir Arthur. Well, he'd have come to the same conclusion himself, wouldn't he now? He climbed up to retrieve their luggage, rubbing his cheek as if afraid it had left a mark for all in the inn to see.

CHAPTER ELEVEN

Miss Eleanor Pickett stood at the window, frowning down upon the carriage that rattled up the long drive of Gresham Park. The coach was smart enough—its black lacquer reflected the sunlight, which also glinted on hardware and handles. By what Mama had told her, she'd pictured her sister as a country mouse arriving in a tattered excuse of a dogcart.

Yet . . . something looked not right. For one thing, the driver was oddly out of proportion—he dwarfed the coachbox. As if that didn't call enough attention, the man was dressed in garish colors. He chose that moment to look up, and Eleanor took a quick step back. When she ventured to peer again, the giant jumped from the top, and she gasped—he was wearing a skirt!

Well, perhaps this would be more entertaining than even she had hoped. She hurried to tell her mother their guest had finally arrived.

In Mrs. Mary Pickett's sitting room, the young maid bobbed her head to signal she understood, as her mistress ranted.

Careful to keep her features from showing the slightest emotion, the girl was close to tears. She'd heard the last three maids had each been turned away within a fortnight, and she was determined that would not happen to her.

She desperately needed this job. Her mother was trying to keep the youngest children together at home, and it was up to her and her brother to send money for food. If she could not help, which of the tiny ones would mother send away? And where did unwanted children go? She had no idea, and she shivered at the thought.

"Is that a problem?" Mrs. Pickett thrust her chin out at the girl.

The maid panicked. Had her mistress still been talking about the green chiffon? She hazarded a guess. "Oh, no, ma'am! I just had a shiver, I did, thinking how awful I'd feel if yer dress was not ready soon enough. It's the first thing I'll see to, ma'am, I promise I will."

Her mistress seemed appeased by this, but had to get in a final barb. "You would feel even more awful if you were out on your ear without a reference, so I'd see to it that it is ready, if I were you."

"Yes, ma'am." The maid bobbed her head vigorously as she confirmed the command.

Mrs. Pickett stared, and raised one eyebrow imperiously. The girl realized that was her signal to scoot. She turned and rushed out the door, almost knocking down Miss Eleanor in her haste.

"I'm so sorry, miss. Beggin' yer pardon, miss," the maid reverted to heavy brogue in her nervousness.

Eleanor didn't acknowledge the maid. She looked right through her as she sailed into the room. "Mother, *she's* here." She couldn't bring herself to say, "My sister."

"Is she, darling? I assume she's in the parlor?"

"No—I mean the coach is just arriving. And . . . there's a man driving the coach. In a skirt!" Eleanor blurted.

Mrs. Pickett wrinkled her small nose in distaste, like a rabbit eating rotten cabbage.

"What will the neighbors say? This is intolerable. If only dear Harold were alive, he would know exactly how to handle this disaster."

"But, mother, if father were alive, we wouldn't have these

visitors arriving for the reading of his will."

"Don't be impertinent, Eleanor. That's not at all becoming."

Madeline and Duncan paced the parlor. Each passed the other, weaving individual patterns in the carpet. Mrs. Cork had gone belowstairs to join the staff members.

Madeline could not slow her breathing, though she tried. She was about to meet her long-lost sister! And a stepmother. She clasped gloved hands in prayerful fashion, holding them against her mouth. She inhaled. She would not cry; she would not cry. Would her stepmother hug her? Would her sister cry in happiness? She wanted to freeze every motion, to remember each crystalline second forever.

Footsteps sounded. Madeline held her breath as the door opened. She wanted to close her eyes, as on Christmas morning, but was afraid she might miss even one tiny detail of this treasured moment.

In walked a maid.

"Good afternoon. May I bring refreshments?"

"Yes," said Duncan, before Madeline could decline.

The maid stared at Duncan's knees. With pink face, she bobbed a curtsy and exited.

Duncan and Madeline continued pacing in crossing paths that never quite collided.

The latch turned, and they spun toward the door as one. A woman in her mid-forties entered, a round plum in a billowy purple frock. She was immediately followed by a slouch-shouldered young woman about Madeline's age. Except for the hair color—this young lady's was a dark blond—she and Madeline could have been twins.

Madeline and Duncan stood on one side of the room, facing the two women who stopped just inside the door. Madeline had the oddest feeling; it felt like a duel, and each was waiting for the other to draw a pistol.

Especially looking at the sour mouth on Mrs. Pickett—the woman with those downturned lips wasn't about to rush across the carpet to plant a kiss on Madeline's cheek.

"Yes?" demanded Mrs. Pickett.

"I'm . . . I'm Madeline . . ." She hesitated; should she add "Mother?" Duncan cleared his throat, and she hurriedly added, " . . . ma'am. And this is Mr. Albus Duncan, a dear friend of my grandfather's. Mr. Duncan was kind enough to escort me here from my home."

Perhaps now was not the time to share a laugh over her adventures—the imposter, the kidnapping, the camping trip and the rescue. No. Looking at those two beady eyes squinting at her, she knew now was not the time. Maybe not ever.

"Madeline who? What is your last name, girl?"

"Pickett. Madeline Pickett, ma'am." This time she remembered to curtsy. "You were expecting me? I mean, you did receive my letter?"

"Humph," was all the response she received, as Mrs. Pickett looked her up and down.

The maid entered following two raps. Mrs. Pickett never even turned her head. "Set it down and leave us," she commanded.

Madeline heard the loud ticking of the clock, and the swish of the maid's starched apron against her bombazine skirt. After the maid exited, only the ticking of the clock remained.

"Eleanor, you will serve us. Sit."

Duncan and Madeline looked at each other. Was she telling Eleanor to sit while she served tea, or was she telling them to sit?

Mrs. Pickett glided regally to a small settee and spread her voluminous skirt before seating herself, pointing her steely eyes at Madeline like ammunition pellets. Madeline decided she was supposed to take a seat as well. Duncan followed her lead, sitting next to Madeline. Madeline wished she'd chosen a sturdier couch, when it groaned and swayed as the large man dropped onto the cushion.

The clock continued to tick. The china cups clinked in the saucers Eleanor handed round. Spoons stirring in symphony were a relief, almost a cacophony against the silence.

But the stirring stopped at once, and all sound was sucked out of the room, to be replaced by a swirling fog of uncomfortable silence. Madeline silently rehearsed all the lines she had practiced several times each day: *"May I call you Mother?" "I can't tell you what it means to me to have a sister." "I've always dreamed of women to share my life with."* They all dried on her tongue, like the old currants in the bun that rested quietly on her plate.

"According to our family lawyer . . ." Mrs. Pickett emphasized "our." "You claim to be Harold and Jeannette Pickett's daughter." She set down her cup, pulling her pudgy finger out of the delicate handle to reach for a bun. "Let me tell you that I, for one, find that hard to believe."

"Good God, woman!" thundered Duncan in exasperation. "Open yer eyes. Dinna tell me ye can't see the similarity between these two young lasses."

Madeline and Eleanor looked at one another. Madeline's eyes began tearing, but Eleanor only stared a few seconds and looked away.

"For all we know," sniffed Mrs. Pickett, "Miss Madeline could be a twice-removed cousin. Or . . . well, we don't need to mention the other possibilities, do we? Perhaps when she heard from others that there was an uncanny family resemblance, she chose to cash in on dear Harold's death." She sunk tiny sharp teeth into her pastry.

Madeline's world was turning upside down. She'd been

anticipating affection and camaraderie. These people thought she was a vulture.

"Else," continued her stepmother, speaking around a mouthful, "why haven't we heard from her in all these years?" She waved her half-eaten bun in the air. "Why show up now, at such a private family moment? Why not remain in your little home in the country?"

Madeline felt ill. This woman hated her. "I hadn't known. I only learned of this last week, from my grandfather."

"And who is this grandfather?"

"He is the gentleman who raised me. My mother arrived at his doorstep as she was dying, and he promised to raise me as his own. His name is Sir Arthur Halvering. He'd never told me about my mother—or my family in London—until just a few days ago."

Mrs. Pickett looked straight at her, and lifted one thin eyebrow in obvious skepticism.

"Please, believe me," Madeline said. "When Grandfather received the letter from London about Fath—about Mr. Pickett's death—and, I am so very sorry for you both. Truly, truly sorry for your loss—then he told me everything. I never knew. I've dreamed of a sister all my life!" This last on a choked sob, as Madeline turned to Eleanor.

Eleanor looked at her stonily, and then at her mother for direction, as if Madeline had not even spoken.

Perhaps they are too full of grief; perhaps that is why they act like this, thought Madeline. But no, she knew that was not true.

"Put yourself in our shoes, miss. Wouldn't this make you suspicious?" Mrs. Pickett carefully chose a biscuit with pink icing; she didn't bother to make eye contact.

Madeline bowed her head. Of course they would find it suspicious. She'd been thinking this herself; one of her cursed traits was that, in fairness, she tried to always think every problem from both sides.

She rose. "I . . . I'm so sorry. I'll leave, of course."

"Sit down," that cold voice commanded, and Madeline sat. "I will not have relatives gossiping that we turned you out. For I do not care what *you* think, but I do care what the rest of society says, and this would give them a day at the fair."

Mrs. Pickett made a face as if inspecting an unwelcome bug on the cushion where Madeline sat. "You shall stay with us until the reading of the will. Then, we shall decide what to do with you."

She picked up a silver bell from the tea tray and rang vigorously; the happy chimes were incongruous in the chilled vault of the parlor. The maid opened the door so suddenly, Madeline wondered if she'd been standing outside, listening. No wonder all of London society knew everyone else's business.

"Show Miss Madeline to her room. And?" Mrs. Pickett raised an eyebrow at Duncan.

"I'll be stayin' on me own," he said with a curtness Madeline hadn't heard from him before.

As Madeline stood, Duncan rose and turned toward her, his huge body blocking her from the sight of the others in the room.

"Don't stay here with them, miss," he said quietly. "They're poison, and they don't want ye. I'll take ye to the inn, and we'll send a post to yer granddad."

Madeline was tempted to take his advice. All her dreams were unraveling and tumbling, like the tent in the forest.

"I can't," she said as much to herself as to Duncan. "I'll be fine, Mr. Duncan. It's only for a handful of days. A dozen at most."

Perhaps . . . perhaps when they got to know her? Perhaps she and her sister only needed time to get to know one another. "I'll be fine," she repeated, but this was said to convince herself.

★   ★   ★   ★   ★

Meg stood outside the bedroom door and tugged at her apron, hoping to yank the wrinkles out, though by now it had become a nervous habit—one her mistress never failed to ridicule and bring to her attention. The maid had been instructed that she was to "see to any of their guest's needs."

She knocked ever so gently. Meg lived in fear of knocking too loudly, thus incurring her mistress's wrath. She usually waited outside a room thirty seconds, then knocked again with a firmer rap. Most times her mistress ignored the first knock, and became furious at the incessant interruptions of the second. Anticipating yet another demanding, whining overseer, Meg was taken by surprise at the soft voice calling "Come in, please" after her first tentative knock.

Meg opened the door softly, and briskly curtsied as soon as she was within the doorway, with an efficient "Good evening, miss." Perhaps she should have said "madam"? Sweat broke out on her palms, and she placed them against her apron, trying to wipe them surreptitiously.

"Good evening," returned the young woman seated at the desk, as she put down her pen and twisted toward the maid. "And what is your name?"

"Meg, if it please you, miss."

"And, what would be your name if 'Meg' did not please me?"

Meg was confused, not knowing what to answer. Then, seeing the smile on miss's face, she realized it was a jest. "I guess it would have to be Margaret, then." She smiled shyly.

"I am teasing you," said Madeline, "as you can guess, and it is a very bad habit of mine. I have driven all of my grandfather's servants to Bedlam, or so they tell me."

"I am sure, miss," bobbed the maid, but then realized how terrible her reply sounded. "I mean, I doubt that, miss," she stammered. But this young lady had not become red in the face, as her mistress would have. Meg moaned to herself. If she had a fault, it was babbling replies when none were solicited. "I was sent to ask if there is anything you need, miss."

"Besides new relatives?"

"I beg your pardon?"

Madeline forced a smile, but it was half-hearted. She'd finished drying her eyes just minutes earlier, and was penning a falsely cheerful letter to her grandfather. "No, there's nothing I need, thank you. My own maid has traveled with me."

"Very good, miss." Meg began to back out the door.

"Wait. Yes, there is one thing you can do."

"Yes, miss?"

Madeline stood and walked over to Meg, surprising her by taking one of the maid's hands in both of hers. "Would you seek out my maid—Mrs. Cork? Would you make her feel welcome? It is an unfriendly house upstairs."

Meg was touched by the young woman's kindness. Yes, the lady was right. They were a sour lot "abovestairs." "It's fine, miss. I can assure you it's a true family for those of us below-stairs, and I'll go and find your Mrs. Cork directly, and make sure she feels welcomed."

Tears again touched Madeline's eyes. "I wish I could join you and Mrs. Cork. Thank you for the kindness."

Meg bobbed her head, curtsied, and left.

Chapter Twelve

Clutching a pillow, Madeline stood in an apricot chintz dressing gown and looked down onto manicured lawns sparkling with early morning dew. A park faced the stately homes on this block, and an occasional delivery wagon rattled by with an echoing clip-clop of hooves.

So this was where her father by name had lived all those years; this was where her mother had slept. Madeline hugged her pillow closer. Perhaps Madeline had been born in this very house. Had her mother stood in this bedroom? Had she looked out this window?

It didn't feel like home. Grandfather was her home, and she missed him terribly. She hoped for news of his health soon, having sent a message of her safe ensconcing in London.

Duncan had originally planned to deliver Madeline into her stepmother's care and then to leave London temporarily, returning only after the reading of the will. But he changed those plans. He informed her he would be nearby at the Golden Hart Inn, awaiting word should she need him. He said he would stay there as long as Madeline stayed at her stepmother's. When she was ready to return, he'd escort her home to the country. She had to smile—Mr. Duncan, the intimidating giant, was really a protective mother bear.

Eleven more days until the reading of the will. Should she stay? Did she still care? Grandfather had explained she'd most likely inherit a part of her mother's fortune. He also told her she didn't need the money, as she was his sole beneficiary.

Madeline didn't care about the money. Her secret wish was to discover a keepsake hidden all these years in the lawyer's vault. She prayed her mother might have left a piece of jewelry for each of her daughters . . . a brooch, or a necklace with fine links to connect Madeline with the woman she'd never known. Or perhaps a miniature likeness in a cameo had been safely tucked away, to be presented to Lady Jeannette's younger daughter.

Madeline's shoulders drooped like the wisteria branches outside her window. Why did she suppose there might be a sentimental trinket? Her other dreams had already been doused with cold tea. She could not stop picturing the pinched face of her stepmother in the parlor, her sister's look of resentment. What had Madeline done to incur such emotion from her half sister?

Well, the imposter was right. His advice not to tell them Eleanor was only a half sister had been justified. That might have made the relationship even worse.

She froze. How had he known what their reaction would be? And why had her mysterious kidnapper felt compelled to warn her? A sign of compassion from a man who had brutally misled them?

She straightened her shoulders and prepared to go downstairs to breakfast. Pasting a faint smile upon her lips should not be too hard. These people were nothing to her, after all.

She should have gone straight to the breakfast room. Upon reaching the first floor, the butler had clearly instructed her to proceed to the third door on her right. But she'd found herself too curious to pass up the first two doors.

She glanced down the hallway in both directions as she stood in front of the first room. No one was in sight, so she stepped within and glanced about. It appeared to be a music room, with its highly polished mahogany floor and a bandbox at one end of the room, while a grand piano stood sentinel at the other. The drapes were of heavy golden damask. A tasseled silk cord held them aside and sheer under-curtains let in morning light.

She inhaled, aware of a light floral scent. Lemon in the wax, certainly, but something else she could not quite place—almost a honey. She entered a step further and saw the curtained doors open to the terrace. Of course; it must be a flowering vine or shrub offering its delicate perfume. Wandering to the French doors, she peeked outside.

There it was again—honeysuckle? No. More like vanilla. She peered back into the room, toward the doorway. Perhaps she could take the quickest of peeks. A gardener at heart, she couldn't resist. Stepping onto the paved patio, she followed her nose to the right, where trellises were burdened with clematis. While appreciating the pink display, she heard a throat clearing, and spun around in dismay.

"Have we had the pleasure of meeting?"

As she faced the tall stranger, she saw his eyes widen, almost as if she'd startled him.

He answered his own question. "No, of course we haven't met, for you are her sister, the one they've rattled on about. It's obvious. Do you realize how alike you look?"

"Yes," she said, still standing a few feet away. Should she curtsy? Hold out her hand? Was this simply another rude relative come to berate her and accuse her?

"Except"—he tilted his head and narrowed his eyelids—"now that I study you, you don't look alike at all. Yes, the features are the same, and the shape of the face, but you have an innocent appeal Eleanor could never achieve."

"I—Shall I know your name, sir?"

He continued as if she hadn't spoken. "And your lips are

fuller. Well, perhaps Eleanor's are simply trained like her mother's—into a tight-lipped cynicism."

As he pointed this out, he aimed the stem of his pipe at her. So, she realized, it was the tobacco she had smelled. She smiled at her own ignorant anticipation of discovering an unusual plant.

"Ah. You have a dimple when you smile. No, your sister will definitely not be pleased. Do you have any idea how much they shall despise you for that dimple?"

"You are too frank, sir. Is this how men speak in London? I am not sure this conversation is proper."

He changed the subject. "Why did you smile a moment ago?"

"I came out upon the patio because I smelled the most wonderful flower. And it turns out to be common nicotiana, so the jest is on me." She saw the confusion on his face. "Nicotiana . . . tobacco," she explained, with a grin.

"I see . . . the Latin name . . . you have an interest in botany. Well, now I am positive you are not related to Eleanor. Perhaps I will stay to breakfast after all. I am sure the friction that is about to descend shall be delicious."

"Then you are too late. It fell yesterday, and today could not possibly be any worse."

"How so?"

She could not believe she was confiding in this stranger. "I had dreamed of finding a loving family—a mother and a sister."

"Some dreams are preludes to nightmares."

"You will excuse me, Mister . . ."

"Remington. Bennett Remington." He bowed, but before he straightened, she ducked back inside.

Madeline heard voices in the breakfast room. Taking a deep breath, she entered. Eleanor sat at table with her stepmother and a portly young gentleman with frizzled side-whiskers.

"You are late," Mrs. Pickett announced, not bothering to

look at Madeline.

"I'm very sorry, ma'am." Madeline pinkened; she felt the man's gaze. She looked to Eleanor, who turned her focus to the food on her plate.

"We eat our meals punctually, miss. While you are a guest in this house, you will observe those hours."

"Yes, ma'am," Madeline said, taking the seat across from her sister.

The gentleman, who sat beside Eleanor, half stood as Madeline slid into her chair. Madeline looked down as she unfolded the napkin in her lap. When she looked up, the man had sat down, but still rudely stared. He cleared his throat and glanced at Eleanor.

Eleanor looked at him with open exasperation. "This is my . . . relative, Miss Madeline Pickett. Madeline, my fiancé, Mr. Emerson Edwards."

Madeline nodded to Mr. Edwards. As she waited to be served, she watched Mr. Edwards tilt his head to whisper to Eleanor. Rudely, both laughed. Madeline was amazed at their lack of manners. Mr. Edwards was ruddy-faced, and Madeline unfairly suspected a fondness for drink, perhaps only because she took an instant dislike to the man. Curly hair outlined both jaws, which unfortunately only emphasized the smallness of his face. The sparse hair did not fully cover the sagging jowls, so one had the impression his beard had been pinned but had slipped upwards, and needed to be tugged back down into place.

Madeline was served, and pushed the greasy sausages and eggs with her fork, hoping her lack of appetite would not be noticed.

"Mr. Edwards also happens to be my cousin twice-removed." Mrs. Pickett bestowed a simpering smile on Emerson. "No relation to Eleanor, of course. Such a fortuitous match."

Emerson cleared his throat. During the course of breakfast,

Madeline noted he cleared his throat before delivering what he considered to be astute observations. This meant he cleared his throat quite often.

"I must agree. I was most happy when my cousin introduced me to her lovely stepdaughter," he said, smiling with greased lips at Eleanor. "And, what happens to bring you to London, Miss Madeline?"

Mrs. Pickett answered for Madeline. "She is here for the reading of dear Harold's will."

Emerson's greasy smile slid off his face. He lowered his eyebrows. Of course, this shrank the size of his face another comical degree.

"I do not understand. Have you determined her connection?" he demanded of Mrs. Pickett, speaking of Madeline in the third person as if she were not even in the room.

"Why, we told you about her. She claims to be Harold's daughter. Surely you can see the implications there, cousin?"

"Yes. But . . . but, I thought we had established that woman was an imposter. What is she doing here in your house?" Now he turned his puffy face to Eleanor. "I thought we agreed Mr. Pickett would be leaving the bulk of his inheritance to my dear Eleanor. This is most distressing indeed."

Madeline wished she could shrink through the floor. Perhaps she could finish breakfast quickly, and escape from this room. Perhaps if she focused on counting the number of times he cleared his throat?

"Ah! Bennett. Welcome, welcome." Mr. Edwards perked up again as the gentleman she'd met in the garden sauntered into the room.

"Just coffee, please," Bennett instructed the serving man, then took a seat at the end of the table.

Madeline chewed on a bite of pettiness, noticing Mrs. Pickett did not berate him for being late at table.

Emerson cleared his throat. "Miss Madeline, may I present—"

"Don't bother, Emerson. Miss Madeline and I are old friends; in fact, we've just come from the garden together."

Madeline blushed, and opened her mouth to protest.

"I don't understand," Mrs. Pickett said frostily, eyeing the two of them.

"Please don't be flippant, Mr. Remington," Madeline hastened to add. "Ma'am, I was late for breakfast because I took a turn in your beautiful gardens. I ran into Mr. Remington. For the first time. He . . . he was a perfect gentleman."

"Please!" protested Bennett. "You'll ruin my reputation, Miss Madeline." He put a hand to his chest in mock injury.

Eleanor tittered, and Mrs. Pickett relaxed. It was obvious Mary Pickett could be nice when she chose, and both Emerson and Mr. Remington seemed to please her.

Unlike me, thought Madeline testily. She speared a fat sausage a bit too aggressively, and the hot juice splattered onto Mr. Remington's wrist as he stirred his coffee.

Madeline caught her breath. "Oh, I'm so sorry!"

"No, it is nothing. Please, don't apologize."

The others looked with curiosity, not knowing what had occurred.

Emerson's spoon clinked like a bell clapper as he stirred his tea. "So, Bennett, any news? From your *brother*, perhaps?" he added pointedly.

Bennett looked askance at Madeline, and then sternly at Emerson. "I hardly think this is the time to discuss my brother, Emerson." He took a sip from his cup, glaring at Emerson across the rim.

"Oh." Emerson looked over at Madeline. "No, I suppose not." That conversation died.

Madeline was confused. She felt like Ulysses blown off course, so lost in this house with its innuendoes and undercurrents. She chose a safe topic.

"Mr. Remington, I don't believe you mentioned *your* connection to the Pickett family?"

"I am actually related to Mr. Edwards, Miss Madeline. We are cousins, on his father's side. Whereas I believe Mrs. Mary Pickett is a somewhat-removed relative on his mother's side. It is a tangle of a family tree, is it not?"

"It appears everyone in this house is a cousin," Madeline said. "Are there other cousins I've yet to meet?"

Bennett choked on his coffee, and coughing, set it down onto the china saucer. "Ah, and that is the question of the day, Miss Madeline. Relatives . . . and . . . non-relatives, now isn't it?"

Madeline noticed Emerson watching her with an intensity that almost frightened her. Looking away, she caught Mrs. Pickett eying her as well with a speculative look. She turned to face Eleanor, who simply stared back with a dull look.

"Please, may I be excused?" asked Madeline of the napkin in her lap, and rose without waiting for an answer. She feared for her sanity if she remained in this claustrophobic room any longer.

"Well? And what do you think?" Emerson looked at Mrs. Pickett.

"There's been no reason to change my mind, cousin. I still believe her to be a scheming little—"

"Where is Jace?" interrupted Bennett. "Wasn't he to have cleared this up?"

"He has not returned," Emerson said. "At least, we have not yet heard of his return. I had hoped you—"

"What? I thought he was only going for a short jaunt to the country seat where this Miss Madeline hails from. Wasn't that the plan? Just a day or two to ask questions—and return shortly? Shouldn't he have returned by now?"

"Well, yes," said Emerson. "I expected him by yesterday at the very latest. That was our initial agreement. Though I'm most unhappy at the way he chose to repay me. Our bargain was that he should return immediately. And he has not."

"What if something's happened to him, you self-centered fool?" Bennett spoke loudly. "You're concurring that he should have been back already? I've been expecting him these past two days." Bennett ran a hand through his hair.

No one answered. Each looked guiltily at his or her silverware.

"I suppose I had better go off in search of him. Tell me again, Emerson, *exactly* where it was you sent him off to."

Emerson gave the same directions he'd provided to Jace, but then a thought struck him. "You don't suppose . . ."

"Yes?" asked the others in the room, in one voice.

"You don't suppose there's even more to this fraud than we supposed?"

"What the blazes are you talking about?" Bennett set his cup down. "Get to the point, cousin."

"What if . . ." Emerson looked at each expectant face. "What if this Madeline Pickett is not only a scheming woman intent on stealing a fortune . . . what if she is even more nefarious?"

"I don't understand." Mrs. Pickett shook her head.

"What if this . . . this determined criminal . . . learned that Jace was on to her scheme, and . . ." Emerson chose to leave the thought unfinished.

The clock struck the hour, echoing loudly in the silent room. Mr. Bennett Remington took his leave immediately.

CHAPTER THIRTEEN

Lady Glynnis Chesterton pulled off her gloves and hat, handed them to the butler, and shed an exasperated sigh. She dreaded this visit.

The last time she'd set foot in this house, she'd sworn never to do so again. Her sister-in-law Mary Pickett was a windbag who exhaled her worthless opinions without pause. And Harold and Mary's dull child appeared she would possess all her mother's charm one day. That's all the *ton* needs, she thought—another Mary Pickett entering society. That thought turned up one corner of her mouth.

The butler prissily handed her accessories to a footman—ah, yes, Glynnis remembered this butler—then he minced down the hall ahead of her.

What was the name of that drawing room? She hazarded a guess to the butler's back. "Is your mistress receiving callers in the Topaz Room?"

"Yes, mum," he said, angling his chin to the side in a nod, without breaking stride or turning to face her.

"And does it still contain those ridiculous safari pieces?" she asked, not really expecting a response. Nor did one come.

He entered the Topaz Room, announcing, "Lady Glynnis Chesterton."

When he stepped aside, Glynnis sighed again, noiselessly. Two tight frowns looked straight at her. They reminded her of an arrangement of prunes at the market stand.

"Mary, such a pleasure to see you again," Glynnis lied smoothly to Mrs. Pickett. "And . . ." She looked at her niece Eleanor expectantly, waiting for a curtsy. No curtsy was forthcoming.

"Eleanor," droned Mrs. Pickett. Her daughter bobbed clumsily. "And our . . . relative . . . Miss Madeline." Mrs. Pickett didn't even bother to turn her body, but merely flung a hand dismissively to the side.

Glynnis turned and saw a young woman in a yellow day frock, book in hand, who hastened forward and executed a perfect curtsy.

"Lady Chesterton, I am so pleased to meet you." Madeline looked directly at Glynnis before dropping her gaze.

What a surprise, Glynnis thought—a canary in a den of dodos. "Please, dear, no need to be so formal. Aunt Glynnis seems appropriate. I assume you are the niece I heard about?"

"I . . . I believe so, Lady—I mean, Aunt Glynnis. Eleanor is my sister, and Mrs. Pickett is my step—"

"Oh, come now, we haven't proven that yet, have we?" said Mrs. Pickett in a disgusted tone. "Granted, she bears a resemblance to my dear Eleanor, but that's as much as we can conjecture at this point." Mrs. Pickett lowered her voice in mock confidence to Glynnis, yet spoke loudly enough for everyone in the room to hear. "Claims to be Harold's daughter, but we all know his second-born died soon after birth. Tragic, simply tragic. Died with her mother. We haven't quite straightened out this young lady's relationship to the family . . . Though, she claims there is one."

Madeline blushed in shame.

"Well, I don't know," said Glynnis. "And neither do I care. I think this young woman is charming, and I insist she call me Aunt Glynnis." She patted Madeline's forearm, and smiled her warmest smile to put the child at ease.

Madeline looked into her aunt's eyes and believed she might finally have found a friend in London. The woman's smile was warm, with no guile. *Please, please,* wished Madeline, *let me have a relative who does not despise me.*

All her expectations of meeting a family—a real family—had completely shattered yesterday. She held tears at bay, yet the warm touch of her aunt Glynnis brought them to her eyes in spite of her effort.

Tea was an awkward affair. Madeline was constantly spoken of as if she were not in the room. Every time Madeline found herself turning pink with embarrassment, she noticed a pitying look in Glynnis's eyes. Madeline didn't want to be pitied. She didn't need to stay in London and bear pity. Once again, Madeline considered sending word to Mr. Duncan and leaving this vile townhouse and this vile town forever.

And once again she reminded herself that if she could wait a handful more of days, she'd discover if her mother had left a token behind in the lawyers' dusty vault. If. If she could last another week and a half in London. And if she left sooner, did she trust Mary Pickett to send along a sentimental heirloom?

Aunt Glynnis rose to leave and Madeline rose with her, though Mrs. Pickett and Eleanor did not budge from their cozy cushions. "I will see you to the door, Aunt Glynnis."

"Thank you, Madeline. Don't bother, Mary. Eleanor. Good day," added Glynnis politely, though it was quite obvious even a fire would not entice either woman to move.

Glynnis linked her arm in Madeline's until they reached the entry. While slipping on her hat and gloves, Glynnis eyed her new niece intently.

"And how long will you be staying in town, Madeline?"

"Until the end of the month," Madeline said, without a glimmer of enthusiasm.

"Then, you must come to visit me as often as you like. Your father Harold was my older brother. My husband would love to meet you, though it never pleased him that he was Harold's brother-in-law . . . dear me, should I say he *is* Harold's brother-in-law, since my husband is still alive, though Harold is not? Never mind. We would both be honored if you would visit us. For you *are* my niece. I can see the resemblance. And even if I did not, I believe you, dear."

Glynnis took Madeline's hands, and gave them a squeeze. "Promise to come and see me, child."

"Thank you, Aunt Glynnis. I should like nothing more," promised Madeline.

Madeline peeked into the music room. Eleanor sat at the piano, practicing.

Madeline tiptoed to the closest chair in the room, one placed beneath a palm in the corner. She sat, but had to brush the fronds out of her face and hair, and scooted the chair quietly away from the pot.

Eleanor played beautifully, and Madeline studied her sister. Was it like seeing a mirror image of herself? She didn't think so. Eleanor dressed in frilly dresses; pastel colors, with ribbons dangling everywhere of the same hue. Eleanor's hair was thick, a shiny dark-gold twist.

Perhaps this was the same hair their mother had. Madeline fought the tears that hazed her vision. Had Eleanor known their mother? She was older than Madeline, but Madeline didn't know how much older.

Perhaps Eleanor could tell her stories about their mother. Madeline ached with the need for a sister. Or a female companion.

"What are you doing—spying on me?"

Madeline jumped, as if she'd been spat upon from across the room. Eleanor stood next to the piano, hands on hips, demanding an answer.

"I was daydreaming—I stopped in to listen to you play, Eleanor. You play beautifully, you know."

"I don't want you listening to me. I don't want you in this room." Eleanor wrinkled her nose, in perfect imitation of her stepmother. "And I don't want you in this house. Period."

"I . . . please, Eleanor." Madeline stood, and had to bat away a frond from her face. Moving from the corner, she held out her hands in helplessness. "Please. I didn't mean to intrude."

"Then why were you spying on me?"

"I meant, I didn't mean to intrude in this house . . . or in this family. I'd just like the chance to talk to you."

Eleanor looked to the side in disinterest.

"Please," Madeline addressed her profile. "Just a short talk, Eleanor."

"And stop saying my name. That annoys me."

"As you wish." Madeline's shoulders slumped. Should she turn and leave? Hopelessness engulfed her.

What would Grandfather do in this situation? He wouldn't run away. No. He'd fight for this chance. She felt her resolve straightening her back, lifting her chin in the air. "Just a few minutes of your time. In a matter of days, I'll be gone."

"What do you want?" Eleanor picked up her music sheets, pretending to be deeply engrossed in the notes.

"I never knew our mother. Did you know her? Do you have memories of her?"

Eleanor's eyes ignited. "She's not my mother! Don't you dare refer to her as my mother. Mary Pickett is my mother, not that . . . that . . ." Eleanor threw down the sheets of music on the carpet, and marched out of the room without another word of explanation.

The papers rustled as they fell slowly. Madeline shuffled across the room and picked up each piece, stacking them carefully, slowly, lining up the edges. She placed them on the piano and cleared her throat. It burned. If she allowed the tears to fall, they would burn her face. She wouldn't cry here, in this house, in front of anyone. She followed her sister's steps and left to find solace in her own room.

Nothing made sense in this house. Why did everyone hate her so?

Bennett entered his townhouse, and jumped at movement in the parlor across the hall.

"My God! You're here—you gave me a start, Jace. I was about to tear off to the countryside looking for you." His brother, having poured a brandy, turned around, and Bennett sucked in his breath. "What happened to your face? Are you all right?"

Jace limped gingerly to the plump armchair. He leaned slowly to set down his drink, but Bennett raced over and took it.

"Wait. Let me help you. Sit. No, just sit, dammit." He handed Jace his drink; reached out as if to touch Jace's face, but winced, and held back, knowing it would cause pain to touch the swollen purple mass around Jace's eye. "What the devil, Jace? Are you in need of a doctor?"

"No. It's just my face that took the beating. Well—and I guess when I fell unconscious I somehow twisted my ankle and knee. And, it appears I must have hit my head pretty hard, because there's this egg of a lump on it . . ."

"But you're fine. And not in need of a doctor." The sarcasm in Bennett's voice warred with his concern.

"I'm fine, mother Bennett . . . truly."

"Devil take you, Jace." Bennett crossed over to the sidebar, and twisted toward Jace before grabbing a glass. "Talk. Start talking. I want to hear everything."

Jace spent the better half of an hour regaling his brother about his trip to Miss Madeline Pickett's village, and the timely coincidence of arriving at the same time Miss Madeline was expecting her escort from Scotland. Bennett's mouth dropped open more than once as he sat, drink forgotten, on the sofa across from his brother.

Jace wove hilarious tales around their stay outdoors. Bennett's laugh was contagious, but it died mid-laugh when he heard about the blow Jace took from the giant.

"I was left without a horse . . . plus, the little shrew left me to freeze. If the temperature had dropped any lower that night, Bennett, I don't know that I'd be here to talk about it. When I woke in the foggy dark, I was shivering. I'd been lying on the ground, bone-cold." Jace stared into his snifter, swirling the liquid.

It was Bennett's turn to shiver. His voice was low as he said, "I was afraid something had happened to you, Jace."

"Well, I can't believe our Miss Pickett hasn't already told the tale to everyone in London. Surely she said *something* to our idiot cousin?"

"If she did, Emerson hasn't repeated it to me. The little weasel. If I find out that he knew you'd been ditched and injured, and he didn't tell me, I'll set his face to match yours. God, Jace, I was so worried . . ." Bennett shook his head, eyes downcast on the sculptured patterns of the carpet between them. He looked up at Jace. "How were we to know where you were? You were days overdue. And then that idiot Emerson convinced us Miss Madeline was a murderess."

Jace's head jerked up. "Did you say 'murderess'?"

Bennett looked sheepish. "He was sure she had not only murdered you, but he convinced himself your body was secretly buried somewhere between London and her village."

"Well, he had the part right about buried secrets—she's not

117

Harold's daughter."

Bennett stopped mid-drink. "The devil you say."

"Oh, legally she is. But he's not her father by birth. And, do you know what else, little brother? She admitted it to me the first day. No guise: just blurted it out as she chirped on about her grandfather."

"Then you'll be telling Emerson and Mrs. Pickett?"

"No. Don't intend to." Jace took a gulp. "It wouldn't matter anyway. She still stands to inherit. But no need for them to know of Lady Jeannette's private affairs."

"I met her, you know—Miss Madeline—at the Picketts' this morning," Bennett said.

"And she said nothing about me?"

"Would she know we're related?"

"Oh . . . I suppose not. And? What did you think?"

"You're right. No guise. Quite appealing in her openness." Bennett smiled to himself. "But how can she not be related to Eleanor? It's obvious they're sisters. By God, they could be twins. That's what's so comical about Mary Pickett making a cake of herself over this."

"They couldn't be twins." Jace looked at his brother in disbelief. "They're not at all alike, Bennett. How could you think so? Eleanor's face resembles her mother's. I find it ugly. The cynicism, the lack of friendliness, the pinched mouth. But Miss Madeline's face is clear, like a fresh pool. Innocent."

Bennett looked at his older brother speculatively.

Jace continued, "I made a mistake, agreeing with our cousin to get involved in this affair. Miss Madeline will be devastated when she learns they sent me to spy."

"Never tell me she doesn't yet know."

Jace had the grace to blush. "I'd planned to tell her the truth. Before we reached London. But, unfortunately, I let her believe I was the Scotsman until the moment I was knocked cold. I haven't seen her since."

The two brothers sat in companionable silence, each with his own thoughts.

Bennett broke the reverie with a chuckle. "You threw her in the river? Oh, big brother, now *that* was the heart of gallantry. No wonder you're avoiding her."

Jace yawned, stretching slowly and satisfyingly, but with caution for sore muscles. He lazily came to his feet. "I'm going to head home for some sleep, and for a soft bed, little brother. I'll see you tomorrow, I'm sure."

Bennett was still chuckling about the outdoor exploits. "If I might give *you* a bit of advice for a change, Jace . . . throwing her in the river just *might* have been a little overstepped. You aren't supposed to treat gentle ladies like you would your kid brother."

Jace slapped a hand hard over his own chest. "I know that! And I didn't treat her like a kid brother." As he passed behind the sofa where his brother lounged, he ruffled Bennett's hair. "I would have let my brother drown."

Bennett called to his brother's departing back. "Jace—out of curiosity—are you attracted to this Miss Madeline?"

"Don't be ridiculous. She's a child."

"I see. Mmm . . . then, you wouldn't mind if I were to pursue her?"

"Yes. I would mind." And Jace limped out of the room.

CHAPTER FOURTEEN

"I won't, I won't, I *won't!*"

The flounces on Eleanor's dress jumped as she stamped her foot. She scowled as she stared at her mother in defiance.

Mrs. Pickett pursed her lips. "I understand, darling. It is quite an inconvenience to take a guest to the recital, but you must realize there is no way we can avoid inviting her along."

Both Mary Pickett and Eleanor Pickett still refused to refer to Madeline as Eleanor's sister.

"Why can't we simply not tell her where we are going?"

Mrs. Pickett seemed to consider the idea for a moment, as her daughter threw herself onto the couch, lying back and crossing her arms. Harrumphing, Eleanor crossed her ankles as well, appearing a knot of discontent.

"I cannot think how we could slip out without her knowing, Eleanor. And, even if we could, our friends would think it odd of us not to include her. You know I do not care for gossip."

"I refuse to go, Mama, if we must pull that goose along everywhere. You told me she'll embarrass us all with her country manners," Eleanor whined.

Outside the door, Madeline stood frozen. Having heard the entire discourse, she thought furiously of what her options could be. She would not go where she was not welcome. She had no desire to parade before the *ton*, anyway. Yet her stepmother would most likely not allow her to be left alone. Inspiration struck, and she knew in that instant what she would say. She knocked.

"Good day." She greeted her stepmother clearly, crossing the threshold, pasting her expression into one of pleasant innocence. She continued to avoid any honorifics. Should she say, "Stepmother," or "Mrs. Pickett," or "madam"?

"Hello, Eleanor," she said with a smile, as if she could not have been more surprised to see her sister lounging around like a dumpling.

"We were just discussing this evening's plans," Mrs. Pickett said.

Madeline supposed her stepmother was anxiously fishing—wondering whether Madeline had heard any of the conversation. "Oh, how very selfish of me to have made plans of my own without consulting your schedule," Madeline said. "Of course, I shall cancel them."

Eleanor perked up from her reclining position at this announcement.

Mrs. Pickett's eyebrows arched to the top of her forehead. She appeared miffed at the audacity of her ungrateful guest making plans on her own. "That is most inappropriate, Madeline."

"Mama!" snapped Eleanor.

Mrs. Pickett looked at her daughter, whose pointed look prompted her to ask, "Ah, and what kind of plans were you speaking of?"

Madeline looked down at the carpet. She was not good at making up tales. How harebrained to not have thought this through. "My aunt Glynnis has asked if I might stop in to visit this evening. Perhaps if I send a note with the footman, I can ask her forgiveness and postpone until another day?"

"No, no, no, don't be silly. A visit with your aunt is most appropriate. Especially since you have only recently arrived in town. Most appropriate, indeed. We wouldn't dream of keeping you two apart, would we, Eleanor?"

"No, Mama," said Eleanor in an angelic chant, the picture of perfect filial obedience.

"Well, that's settled," said their stepmother. If Mrs. Pickett had been a cat, she would have purred and licked the cream from her fur. "Let us have our tea."

Eleanor and Mrs. Pickett were attacking their second plates of scones and clotted cream when a guest was announced.

"Mr. Jace Remington," intoned the butler.

"Oh, do show him in," said Mrs. Pickett, with an enthusiasm rare for the reticent woman.

Eleanor sat straighter, brushing crumbs from her lap onto the carpet. She flicked her napkin quickly, and additional bits flew.

Wiping her lips, she asked her mother, "Do I have food on my mouth, Mama?" She directed her next comment to Madeline. "Mr. Jace Remington is extremely handsome."

Mrs. Pickett looked at Eleanor speculatively. "He is your fiancé's cousin, dear. I don't believe it comely that you should always show such interest in him." She turned to Madeline. "He is Emerson's cousin," repeated Mrs. Pickett for Madeline's benefit. "Though I'll admit he does cut quite a figure. And Eleanor has so many gentleman callers. It quite reminds me of my own youth."

"Yes, ma'am," said Madeline, not trusting herself to say another word, keeping her grin tightly trapped.

She heard a masculine voice outside the room and froze. She knew that voice! As she turned, her abductor walked into the parlor.

"*You!*" cried Madeline, jumping to her feet.

Jace returned her look, and more.

"My dearest Mr. Remington! Whatever has happened to your face?" Mrs. Pickett cooed like a mother pigeon, bobbing her head this way and that as she looked him over.

The left side of Jace's face was swollen, amid a swirl of purplish colors. The bruised jaw showed red splotches, and the cheek looked like it had been clumsily stitched.

"I ran into a bit of Scottish masonry," he said, while still directing his gaze at Madeline.

Mrs. Pickett remained seated. "Madeline—have you met Mr. Jace Remington?"

"What is this man doing in your house? This man is a criminal!" cried Madeline.

Jace didn't say anything. His gaze flickered to Mrs. Pickett expectantly.

Mrs. Pickett stammered, "I don't know what you're talking about, Madeline. Of course Mr. Remington is not a criminal. Why ever would you say something so absurd?"

"This man kidnapped me from my grandfather's house! He abducted Mrs. Cork and me. He pretended to be someone he was not."

Mrs. Pickett looked confused. "Mr. Remington? What is Madeline referring to? That was not part of our bargain."

Madeline reeled as if she'd been slapped. "What bargain?"

"Madeline, do be quiet. I am asking Mr. Remington a question," said her stepmother.

"I will not be quiet! This man abducted me. What is he doing in this house?"

"Why haven't you told her, Mrs. Pickett?" asked Jace. He turned to Eleanor. "And where is that cowardly fiancé of yours, Miss Pickett? This was all my cousin's idea. Get him in here to explain."

"Cousin!" exploded Madeline. "Another cousin? Whom are you talking about?"

"Emerson Edwards," said Jace. "I was sent by Mr. Edwards to spy upon you, Miss Madeline. Didn't they tell you? Didn't you know?" he asked, his voice cold.

"Spy on me?" asked Madeline. She turned to Mrs. Pickett. "I don't understand."

"You will stop this drama at once. Emerson was only doing it for our protection. Can you blame him? We'd never heard of you—and after years of being assumed dead, you appear out of nowhere to claim part of dear Eleanor's inheritance." Mrs. Pickett sat straighter. "Don't look so indignant. You'd have done the same."

Madeline was crushed. "I can't believe you would do such a thing. You sent this man to spy on me. But . . . but why did you have him kidnap me?"

"We did not. You are wrong, miss."

She did not think she was wrong, but she blinked, looking directly at her stepmother, debating if there would be any value in a confrontation. She decided not, and blinked again, slowly regaining her composure.

"And do stop blinking, child. You have the most awful habits. You will embarrass us all, if not by your unschooled manners, then by your awful facial tics."

Eleanor sniggered, snorting on the inhale like a horse.

As if that braying won't embarrass them, thought Madeline. "Please excuse me," she said, and walked to the door.

"Miss Madeline. Please. I'd like to talk to you," said Jace.

She turned regally. "Yet I, sir, have no desire to talk to you."

"Hear me out. It's true I was sent to spy on you. I owed my cousin a favor, and he convinced me his future family needed to know your background. They asked me to go to your grandfather's cabin to inquire. That's all that was to have happened."

All her hatred of this man was balled in her fists. "It's not a cabin. It's a country manor."

Jace ignored her irrelevant comment. "Your grandfather would have done the same, if someone held a threat over his family. Be fair, Miss Madeline; you know I speak the truth. I admit it was wrong to let you think I was Mr. Duncan. It just happened so quickly. You're the one who called me 'Mr. Duncan,' and ordered the carriage to leave immediately. I simply took advantage of an opportunity. I didn't expect things to turn out as they did."

She stared right through him, saying nothing.

"I almost froze to death when you left me out there."

That sparked a reaction. "Well, Mr. Remington—or so you call yourself today—perhaps you wouldn't have frozen to death if you knew how to make a fire." She turned back to the door.

"One last thing—please. And then I'll leave this house."

Madeline paused out of curiosity, sure she should have kept walking out the door.

"Mrs. Pickett. Miss Pickett," Jace turned to Eleanor and her mother. "Please tell Emerson I came here today to say this young lady is telling the truth. I did check, as you asked, and she truly is Harold and Lady Jeannette Pickett's daughter. She is not an imposter."

Mrs. Pickett sniffed, a disagreeable sound. "Well, I hope she doesn't expect us to play the loving family. She is still an unwelcome intrusion to this household."

Madeline had meant to freeze Jace with her icy glare, but when she saw the pity in his eyes, her own filled with tears, and she exited the room.

Madeline sat alone in the library, engrossed in her book. It was a suspenseful tale of an orphaned gentlewoman and the cad who pursued her, intent on seduction.

She jumped in her chair when the butler cleared his throat.

"Mr. Emerson Edwards is here, miss."

"Oh . . . Umm . . . Please show him in, of course."

She closed her book and awaited boot steps outside the door.

Emerson appeared to list slightly to starboard, placing one foot carefully before the other. She narrowed her eyes; what was wrong with the man?

"Evening, Miss Madeline . . . Pickett." He bowed and almost lost his balance.

"Are you all right, Mr. Edwards?"

He nodded his head.

"I regret to tell you my sister Eleanor has stepped out for the evening."

"Ah." He looked around the empty room. "Is she with her mother?"

Madeline nodded.

"And . . . when do you expect them to return?" He took another unbalanced step farther into the room.

"I don't know. I believe it was a recital," Madeline offered.

"I see." Emerson eyed Madeline with an intensity that frightened her.

She wished Mr. Bennett Remington were here, but she wasn't sure why; except whenever she was around Eleanor's fiancé, she caught him watching her—and it made her uncomfortable. At breakfast, she'd had the strangest feeling Cousin Emerson was singling her out for attention.

That did not make sense, as the man was already engaged. Engaged to a young lady who was about to inherit a fortune. Several times during the meal, she'd looked down at her clasped hands to avoid his gaze as they were conversing. Whenever she'd glanced back up, he was peering at her bosom. Any other man would have been mortified at being caught out. However, Cousin Emerson simply raised his eyes to hers, and continued stentoriously droning on. She'd resolved to avoid Cousin Emerson.

Yet, here he was.

By telling the white fib to her stepmother, she'd allowed

Eleanor and Mrs. Pickett to go to their recital without her. And now she was alone with him.

"So, I'm sure you have no wish to stay, Mr. Edwards, now that you know Eleanor is not in. And, I must catch up on my correspondence," she added lamely when he hadn't made a move.

"May I confide something to you, Miss Madeline?"

Without moving her head, she eyed the bell rope in the corner of the room. Perhaps she should ring for a chaperone. Or for the butler to escort Mr. Emerson on his way.

"You are so different from Eleanor. You have a sparkle."

Madeline stiffened. "This is hardly an appropriate conversation, Mr. Edwards. May I remind you, you are engaged to my sister?"

"Ah, yes. And spunk as well. I like that. I enjoy a little fight in a woman. And you have the spunk of a fighter, I believe."

Madeline decided it was time to ring the bell. She stood and began slow steps around Mr. Emerson.

He followed her eyes, and realized where she was headed. He intercepted her, putting a hand on her arm. "Hold. Why are you summoning the servants?"

"I . . . I beg your pardon? Please unhand me, sir." She almost shivered. His touch raised the hairs on the nape of her neck.

He did not remove his hand. She tried to pull her arm away, but he tightened his hold.

"What's your game, Madeline?"

"Mr. Edwards! Let go of me. How presumptuous of you, sir, to address me by my first name. I . . . I expect you to address me as 'Miss Madeline.' "

"Perhaps I would if you were a lady. But we both know you're not."

Madeline was frightened. His hand was still clamped on her arm; he was crowding her. She could smell onions on his breath, and something else—a sour smell, as of old wine. Her eyes went to the bell pull again. If she could reach it before he stopped her . . .

"Don't be thinking about calling a servant, Madeline," he said as if reading her mind.

She tried reasoning. "I don't understand what you are about. You are engaged to my sister. Why would you jeopardize that?"

"You fool. I'm not jeopardizing anything. I'll still be engaged to your sister. I just expect to have a little sport with you tonight."

Madeline gasped, and put a hand to her throat. Emerson took a step closer, pressing against her skirts, and she stepped back. She was now farther from the bell pull, and farther from the door. She kept one hand behind her, so she would not inadvertently stumble over the furniture. Her mind was racing. How to hold him off? Perhaps if she kept talking, someone would arrive.

"I'll . . . I'll tell Eleanor. And I'll inform my stepmother as well. You are putting yourself at risk, sir. Perhaps you've had too much to drink, and you are not yourself."

His response was a derisive laugh, and a lunge, which she parried. His reactions were slow. So—he was drunk, as she'd suspected.

"They won't believe you, Madeline."

"What?" Her mind raced for a solution, an escape plan.

"If you tell them I made advances, do you think they'll believe you? They've already told me you are a scheming liar. What makes you think they'll take your word against mine?"

Oh, my God, thought Madeline. *He is correct.* They already hated her; of course they would assume she'd been flirting with Emerson.

Emerson's next move was not slow, as she'd hoped. He reached out and grabbed her hair. Madeline screamed.

Emerson began wrapping her loose hair around his fist, bringing her closer against her will; her scalp hurt as she struggled. Madeline was trembling, and put her hands out to shove him away.

"Madeline," called a woman's voice.

Emerson stepped away as if her hair were on fire. Both Madeline and Emerson turned to the door, where Lady Chesterton stood rooted. No one said anything for a full five seconds.

"Madam!" greeted Emerson, with a bow. "Do come in. Do join us. I came to deliver a message to Miss Madeline from her sister Miss Eleanor Pickett. Do you know my fiancée Eleanor?"

"Eleanor is my niece," said Glynnis with frost surrounding each word. "I am Lady Glynnis Chesterton. And you are . . . ?"

"Emerson Edwards, my Lady." He smiled and bowed again, then turned to Madeline. "I so enjoyed our brief visit, Miss Madeline. Do remember what we discussed—about family members and truth. That is so very important, don't you agree?" His teeth bared with the last word; it was not a smile.

Madeline nodded slowly.

"Good evening then, ladies." Emerson excused himself from the room.

Madeline's throat was dry. She smoothed her mussed hair behind her ear. What had her aunt seen? Would she condemn Madeline, as Emerson had predicted? Madeline thought she could trust Aunt Glynnis—but, what if the woman did not believe her? What if her aunt shunned her? Madeline didn't think she could bear that.

"Madeline, you are so pale, dear. Are you feeling well?"

Madeline fought the tears; she would not allow them to show. "Yes, Aunt Glynnis. I am fine," was her only reply. A whisper, actually, that came from the rip in her heart.

CHAPTER FIFTEEN

Madeline read the opening sentence of the novel yet another time. She next tried reading it aloud, but the words would not behave; they kept scrambling in her head and trying to swim away from her concentration.

Sighing, she stared at the myriad of knickknacks on all four walls of the Topaz Room, and the dust motes floating in the early sunlight; her plan was to hide away here until Mr. Bennett Remington arrived. Hopefully he'd received her note by now. She'd instructed the footman to show Mr. Remington to this parlor.

Her thoughts were interrupted by horse hoofs cantering up the sweep, and Madeline rose to peek. Bennett sat upon a handsome gray, waiting for the footman before descending, tossing the reins. As he swung down from the saddle his dark, close-fitting riding coat stretched across his broad shoulders. Madeline had noticed his height the first time they'd met. Today, he looked even taller with his flat-topped beaver hat and tasseled, knee-high riding boots.

He's a handsome young man, thought Madeline. How had her sister chosen Mr. Edwards when someone as kind and masculine as Bennett was available? Madeline speculated on the impropriety of matchmaking if the woman was already engaged to another man.

She turned away and carried the novel back to the shelf where she'd found it. She was careful to place it in exactly the right slot, thereby avoiding yet another transgression in this house. She carefully lined up the maroon leather spine with the books on either side, though her own worry brought a smile to her lips. Mary Pickett had made it clear to Madeline that there was no worse houseguest residing in London in the present century.

She never heard the well-oiled parlor door open. Bennett cleared his throat.

Madeline spun to face him. "Mr. Remington!" She wanted to rush across the room and hug the only person in the city other than Aunt Glynnis whom she considered as friend. Instead she stood frozen as Bennett crossed to her. "I'm so pleased to see you, Mr. Remington."

"But not too surprised, I assume, since you did request my presence? Though never say I am not truly flattered," he smiled, dipping briefly over her hand.

Madeline blushed, then leaned around him to check that no one stood at the door. She crossed the room quickly and closed it. Turning, she saw the surprise on Bennett's face.

"I have something private to ask of you, Mr. Remington. I'd prefer we weren't disturbed or overheard."

"I'm intrigued, madam." He followed her to the seating arrangement, and chose a deep-cushioned chair of bright gold velvet only after Madeline had taken a seat.

"I need your advice. Or rather, your opinion. You're familiar with this household—and my sister Eleanor?"

Bennett didn't answer right away. He raised one eyebrow and said, "Well, as to that, I don't know. I feel I know you better, Miss Pickett, in just these few days, than one might ever come to know this household. Particularly your sister Eleanor."

"But she acts so pleased with you."

"Ah. Now, that is only because Eleanor sees I am not prettier than she."

Madeline laughed. This man was easier on the eyes than

most. Could he be unaware of it? His bride would have cause for jealousy if the groom outshone her on their wedding day.

"You find that funny, Miss Pickett? Perhaps you should take it as a friendly caution."

Madeline met his eyes with a smile, then looked to the side, gathering her thoughts. "Mr. Remington—I've always wished for a sister. When I was young, it was like wishing for a piece of the moon. Only children in books had sisters. Still, I pretended. Then, overnight it seems, I found my wish had come true. But now, even though it is within my grasp, I find it just as elusive as the moon." Madeline twisted her fingers together. "I think . . . I'm thinking that perhaps if Eleanor and I were to spend more time together—"

"Then you need to get her away from her mother's eye, Miss Pickett." Bennett leaned forward and dropped his voice conspiratorially. "The one observation I can share with you about Eleanor is that she is mousy. She imitates Mary Pickett so well one would think she's a dowdy spinster. She will always strive for her mother's approval—and her mother has made it clear you are not welcome."

Madeline nodded, seriously studying her guest. "That was my suspicion as well. It is good to have it confirmed. So—I would like to invite her on an outing, but—" Madeline shrugged prettily. "I don't know London. Have you any suggestions about where we shall go?"

He leaned back and placed a booted ankle atop the other knee. "Is this why you asked me to come today, Miss Pickett? To recommend places to visit in London?"

Madeline bit her lip, studying Bennett's face for any signs of annoyance. "That does sound silly of me, and an imposition on your time, doesn't it?"

"Not if you replied, 'Why no, Mr. Remington. I asked for

your advice because I was hoping you would escort us on our outing.' "

Her eyes twinkled. "You are too good, sir."

"What's that? I didn't hear your answer, Miss Pickett."

"Mr. Remington, would you be so kind as to escort us on our outing?"

"It would be my pleasure. Now, where shall we go?"

"I don't know where her interests lie—" Madeline brightened. "But I did see a circular that a famous conchologist of the Linnaean Society will be lecturing tomorrow night!"

Bennett coughed. "This may be just a guess, but I should think she'll hate you even more if you make her listen to a scholarly dissertation on seashells in a hall full of naturalists."

Madeline's face fell. "Oh." She rolled her eyes to scan the parlor's ceiling, then snapped them back to Bennett. "I know. What about the summer art exhibition at the Royal Academy of Art!"

"Hmmm . . . Might I make a suggestion?"

Noting his grimace, she tried not to sound peevish. "But of course, Mr. Remington. It's what I was hoping for."

"Have you considered something more like Drury Lane?"

"The new theatre! That's brilliant. Have they already finished the remodeling, then? Do you know what is playing there?"

Bennett cleared his throat. "I wasn't thinking about a play . . . I meant Drury Lane itself. The market. And the shops. Or, perhaps Vauxhall?"

"Mr. Remington. You surprise me. Aren't those a bit . . . low?" asked Madeline with a frown.

Bennett laughed, then spread his hands. "May I be blunt, Miss Pickett? At the risk of having you call me out in defense of your cherished sister Eleanor, she strikes me as the type who might be happiest at a cockpit."

Madeline's mouth formed an "O."

"I'm sure she'd enjoy Vauxhall. We could take along a picnic meal."

"Vauxhall. I've only heard of it. You do think she would enjoy that?"

"I'm sure of it." He considered. "Are you inviting Mr. Edwards along as well? Is it seemly she should go somewhere without her fiancé?"

Madeline shuddered at the idea of being in the company of Mr. Edwards. "I shall bribe her. I'll convince her that we'll pick out a gift to surprise her Mr. Edwards. I'll offer to pay for it myself."

"Excellent thought. That should work. And I shall do my part to give the two of you plenty of room to stroll together and to talk."

"Thank you, Mr. Remington. You are a true friend." Madeline stood and held out a hand.

"I shall leave before we are discovered alone, or they may insist on making us more than friends." Bennett's lips hovered a respectable distance above her knuckles, and he took his leave. Madeline watched from the window, shaking her head in wonder that this charming gentleman could be related to the devious Jace Remington and the obnoxious Emerson Edwards.

Biding her time, Madeline knew Eleanor would be practicing on the piano just after tea. She waited outside on the terrace until she heard footsteps crossing the polished floor.

"Hello," Madeline greeted, stepping through the twin doors.

Eleanor watched her with dark eyes, but chose not to answer. She moved to the piano and sat erectly. Before she could place fingers to keys, Madeline said, "I wanted to ask you . . . I was wondering if you might like to go on an outing, Eleanor."

Eleanor's hands paused on the ivory keyboard, but still she made no eye contact. "What type of an outing?"

"I was thinking of Vauxhall." Madeline held her breath.

"That is rather expensive. Has Mama approved?"

"I hadn't mentioned it to her yet. I thought I would ask you first. But I would pay for our entertainment. In fact, perhaps we could purchase new ribbons for our hair just for the occasion. My treat, of course."

"I . . ." Eleanor struggled. "I don't know if Mama would approve."

"Perhaps not. I suppose we should not go. I'd been so looking forward to this outing with Mr. Remington."

"Bennett Remington?"

"Yes. It was his idea. And he asked me in particular to be sure to invite you. He thought we might also bring a picnic lunch. However, I'll let him know we will not be going." Madeline crossed fingers behind her back and turned slowly as if to leave.

"I will go." Eleanor looked toward the hallway and lowered her voice. "I don't suppose I need to ask Mama's permission. After all, we will be well-chaperoned."

Madeline felt like singing her answer. "Yes, we will. I'll let Mr. Remington know we'd like to go tomorrow."

Eleanor laughed as the brightly colored puppets pummeled one another with puppet-sized boards, smiles pasted incongruously on their hideous faces. This was the first time Madeline had seen her sister laugh out loud. She looked over Eleanor's head at Bennett, and he winked.

Just then a surprise gunshot exploded on stage and Madeline jumped. Eleanor, startled, grabbed Madeline's arm, but pulled away in laughter the next moment as both puppets flew through the air. Madeline thrilled to the trace of her sister's touch.

Later, as they strolled together, Madeline suspected this day had been equally enjoyable for both of them. She'd seen a buoyant side of her sister that was normally stifled under the weight of Mrs. Pickett's shadow. Eleanor gleefully begged their leave when she spotted a tiny sweets cart with red-striped awning. Standing in the shade, watching her sister waiting to make a purchase, Madeline thought once again about matching Eleanor and Bennett. Bennett was so kind; he'd be a much better influence on Eleanor than Mr. Emerson.

"Bennett—do you despise matchmakers?"

Bennett turned from watching the juggler. "What a noose of a question! Better tell me whom you have in mind."

Madeline looked at Bennett with innocent eyes and a teasing smile. "I was thinking about a certain young Remington man and a certain young Pickett maiden."

Bennett pulled a finger around the inside of his collar, as if in need of a little more air. "I . . . I'm flattered, but I don't think my brother would approve."

Madeline harrumphed. "I don't give a fig whether Mr. Jace Remington approves or not. And why should he care?"

Bennett looked uncomfortable.

Madeline looked over at Eleanor. "Though I suppose he's right . . . just this one instance. She is already engaged after all."

"Who is engaged?"

"Why, my sister Eleanor. Isn't that whom we are discussing? Eleanor and yourself?"

Madeline was dwelling on what a success the day had been as Bennett drove them home in his smart carriage. Bennett was right—Vauxhall had been the perfect outing for Eleanor. Even the picnic at the end of their visit had been an excellent suggestion, knowing Eleanor's love for eating: they'd emptied their wicker hamper of pickled salmon, bread, Wiltshire cheeses, a bit of ham, honey cakes and a bottle of champagne.

"Hyde Park! Isn't that Hyde Park?" Eleanor's eyes glowed,

and she snapped her attention to Bennett. "Oh, please, please may we take a round in your carriage, Mr. Remington? Oh, do say we may, please?" Eleanor turned full round in her seat to stare at the equestrian scene.

Madeline had never seen Eleanor this vivacious. Perhaps that champagne with their picnic lunch had been a mistake. Madeline tried to recall how many fluted glasses her sister had consumed.

"Bennett," Madeline tilted her head toward Eleanor and whispered, "I think someone may have had a little too much—"

"Yes." Bennett was grinning. "Yes to both of you. Eleanor, let's take that spin." He expertly maneuvered the two-horse team onto the crowded public trail, quickening their pace to a trot. Eleanor's mouth was open as her eyes swallowed the crowd of elegant solitary riders and open curricles.

Eleanor squealed. "There are two of Mama's friends!"

Eleanor leaned out to wave, and Madeline grabbed her sister round the waist as she leaned a little too far in her exuberance. The ladies being waved at brought their curricle close to Bennett's, forcing his team to stop.

"Isn't that Miss Eleanor Pickett?" One of the ladies, a woman in a voluminous gray satin dress, lifted her lorgnette.

"Miss Pickett, what are you doing out without being escorted by your fiancé?" asked the vehicle's companion, another stout lady dressed in mauve.

Eleanor appeared to sober quickly. "But, I am with his cousin. This is Emerson's cousin."

"Is that proper? To be out with an unmarried young man who is not your fiancé?" Gray Dress focused her quizzing glass on Bennett, and then back on Eleanor.

"Oh—but he is married." Eleanor looked around at the two shocked faces sitting beside her. "And . . . and this is his wife."

Madeline was too shocked to deny it. This creative imagination was a dimension the quiet Eleanor had never before revealed. The two women nodded, their heavy bonnets looking about to topple forward onto the ground.

"Very proper, then," said Mauve Dress. "Pleased to meet you, sir."

Eleanor spoke quickly. "Oh, he doesn't speak English. He is from Brussels." Brussels escaped with a lisp.

Madeline's eyes were frozen into shilling-sized circles. She elbowed her sister and whispered, "Eleanor, we must be on our way."

"We must be on our way," parroted Eleanor with a ghost of a slur.

"So soon?" asked Gray Dress.

"Yes," said Eleanor. "You see, their nanny is watching the little one. The little one is sick. We really shouldn't be out."

"Sick? Then you must leave. What is your little one's name?" This was directed by Mauve Dress to Madeline.

Madeline wasn't sure she should answer. As Bennett's wife, did she speak English, or . . . or was it Belgian they spoke in Brussels?

"Little Nelly," called out Eleanor, as Bennett did not waste any time nudging their horses back onto the wide path.

"Bothersome old nosy biddies," stated Eleanor, unfortunately not *sotto voce*.

"What was that, Miss Pickett?" called Miss Mauve Dress as they began to separate.

Madeline leaned past Eleanor, blocking her from the ladies' view. "She said, 'Botheration we have to go—such a pity!' " Madeline suppressed her giggles until they were well on their way, then she and Bennett laughed out loud.

By the time they reached the thoroughfare approaching Gresham Park, Eleanor was asleep, softly snoring on Madeline's shoulder. As if she were the most precious of children, Madeline patted Eleanor's halo of hair, and returned Bennett's smile, mouthing "thank you." Passing the great iron sweep-gate, Madeline gently roused her sister.

"Thank you, Mr. Remington," Eleanor said meekly, almost stumbling on the gravel drive. "That was the most wonderful outing I've ever been on."

Madeline hastened to her support, steering Eleanor by her elbow. If she hadn't been looking down at the path in front of them, she might have seen Mr. Jace Remington reclining against a porch column.

"Good evening, brother. I came to call upon Miss Madeline. And what are *you* doing here?"

Bennett opened his mouth to answer, but Madeline interrupted as she reached the porch steps. "Excuse me. I'd like to pass."

Jace did not step aside. "Miss Madeline, I need a moment of your time. This is rather urgent."

"I am sorry, Mr. Remington. Or—is it Mr. Duncan, or some other name today? But I must assist my sister to her room." The icicles in Madeline's gaze nailed Jace, but when she turned to Bennett they twinkled. "Besides, I believe I hear little Nelly crying." She touched Bennett gently on the forearm. "Thank you, sir, for a wonderful day."

"Excuse me," she said to Jace coldly, pushing past him and escorting Eleanor into the house.

"Rupert, I am toying with the idea of having a houseguest during the Season." Glynnis stroked the cat in her lap.

She'd already made up her mind, and of course dear Rupert would agree, but he need not know that yet.

"That's nice, love."

His chair angled toward hers, both warmed by the hearth, but he never glanced up, his nose pointing at his book.

She rubbed the cat under its chin until it purred. "Rupert—did you attend what I said, darling?"

"Yes, dear. A capital idea. Suit yourself."

"Rupert! Aren't you even interested in whom this houseguest will be? I don't mean to nag, but if you do not pay attention, I shall take that as direct approval, and shall make all the arrangements on the morrow."

If she were lucky, he would not pay any notice, and afterward she could tell him it was his fault—after all, he'd not been interested in listening at the time.

But he closed his book, marking the spot with his hand as he reached for his marker. Sliding it between the pages, he set his book on the side table and studied his wife over the top of his reading spectacles.

With eyebrows raised innocently, he inquired, "Dearest, I've found in the past that by the time you approach me with one of your schemes, it is already too late. I'm sure that, in your usual efficient fashion, you've already begun hatching this egg of an idea, and you do not really need me to agree. Am I right?"

She blushed, knowing he'd hit the mark a bit too closely. And by her blush, he had his answer. Rupert smiled and picked up his book once more.

"Well!" she replied tartly, as she stood. "Well," she repeated, as she approached her husband, placed her hands on the arms of his chair, then quickly bent and placed a kiss upon his forehead. And, with a laugh, she left the room.

"Score one for the male of the house," muttered Rupert, his nose already bent to the book.

Glynnis went directly to her room and pulled a pastel note card from a pigeonhole of her writing desk. She would invite Madeline to join them immediately. The poor orphaned girl needed a family while in London.

She hadn't mentioned anything to Rupert about walking in

on Madeline and that weasely cousin of Mary's. What was his name? Oh, yes—Mr. Edwards. He'd introduced himself as Eleanor's fiancé.

Something had felt terribly wrong in that room when Glynnis walked in—Madeline had appeared pale and frightened. While Mr. Edwards had recovered his composure so quickly and smoothly. It made one suspicious. No, something was not quite right. Madeline hadn't wanted to talk about it, though.

Glynnis's instincts about strangers were uncannily perceptive, and this Mr. Edwards made her uncomfortable. Speculating on what her niece might be hesitant to discuss, Glynnis shuddered and picked up her quill. The sooner Madeline was here, the better. The Pickett residence was neither a happy home nor a safe haven, Glynnis was sure.

Glynnis pictured that odious Mary Pickett commanding their country relative to do household chores. She was convinced Mary would use the girl as a servant. Why, Madeline had most likely already been consigned to the downstairs world, grime on her dress, chimney soot on her chin. And only porridge and water for sustenance!

Glynnis was indignant. She could not scrawl hastily enough.

The others left the breakfast room, leaving Eleanor and Mrs. Pickett at the table. Eleanor dished up another poached egg while her mother delayed over coffee, studying her daughter.

"Eleanor, I don't think you should be having seconds. You need to think about fitting into your trousseau."

Eleanor ignored her mother, and took another bite of toast. With her food half chewed, she said, "Is this why you linger, Mama—to count my servings and to criticize?"

"No, but the thought did just occur to me, sitting here watching you. No. I have something I wish to discuss with you, daughter . . ." Without making eye contact, she instructed their footman, "You may leave us for a few minutes."

Mrs. Pickett waited until he'd left the room. "Have you noticed, Eleanor, how Emerson watches Madeline?"

"That is evil of you to say, Mama. You say that to hurt me."

"I say it because I see it. You are blind if you haven't seen it as well, miss. It's what I wished to discuss with you."

"But . . . why? Why would he be interested in her?"

"That's for you to find out, Eleanor. One wonders what has been happening right under our noses. Of course, I haven't trusted her since the day she stepped over our threshold. But, whatever is going on, if I were you, Eleanor, I would not put up with it."

"But, what can I do? What would you do?" Eleanor's whine was short-lived, as she took another bite.

"I'd think of something. There are only a few possibilities, Eleanor. Use your head. Either you get your Mr. Edwards to commit to an earlier marriage date, or . . . dream up something to make *him* jealous. Or . . . what if our guest was caught in a compromising situation?"

"With Emerson? I won't hear of it!"

"Not with Emerson, you ninny. No. If you want to keep Mr. Edwards for yourself, then Madeline must be caught with another gentleman."

Eleanor looked blankly at her mother.

"Good God, I can't believe you're your father's daughter. Think, Eleanor. Think like your father. Surely you can think of something. Else, don't come crying to me when Emerson cries off the engagement and winds up with Miss Goody."

"Can't we just make her leave, Mama?"

"No. We'll be the talk of the neighborhood if we throw her out on her ear. She'll only be here another week or so. But you must keep a closer eye on Emerson." Mrs. Pickett sniffed. "I daresay you'll be best served to keep an eye on him the remainder of your married life, Eleanor. He may be my cousin, but the man has a lewd eye."

"Mama, don't be crude."

"And don't you be so prissy. I didn't raise a sheltered daughter to hide her head in the linen closet. Men want an eyeful of other women besides their wives. And that's to be expected. Lord knew your own father had a wandering eye. But that's as far as you allow it, Eleanor. The rest of his body your father kept to himself. I insisted."

"She must be leading Emerson on. He'd never pay attention to her unless she's leading him on."

"I may not care for her airs, and I may not believe she's Harold's daughter, but you're a fool if you think your Mr. Edwards needs some prodding and coaxing. He's a man. They're all alike."

"My father wasn't base like other men."

Mrs. Pickett held her daughter's eye, but said nothing.

CHAPTER SIXTEEN

Clutching her reticule tightly, Madeline stood before the pair of oak-paneled doors and closed her eyes. She inhaled deeply, twice, willing herself to be composed.

Opening her eyes, she was dismayed to find the door now open, and a large gentleman with sooty gray hair staring at her. She tried not to blush, but was unsuccessful, and smiled ruefully.

"Come in, come in," he said. "Or, would you prefer to meditate for another minute out in the hallway?"

"Rupert!" said his wife with a great show of exasperation. "Can't you see she's already embarrassed?"

"Embarrassed!" he barked. "Why ever should she be?" He took Madeline by the elbow and led her into the room.

Glynnis glided over to place a kiss on her niece's cheek, and to give her a quick squeeze of affection. "Madeline, dear, this is your uncle Rupert."

"Sir," Madeline curtsied, and her uncle executed a stately bow.

"Come, sit by me, Madeline," Glynnis said, moving gracefully over to the striped-satin settee. She seated herself and reached a hand to Madeline, who clasped hers warmly and settled on the cushion next to hers.

"You sent a message. You wanted to see me, Aunt Glynnis?"

"Actually, we both wanted to speak to you, dear." Glynnis

glanced over at Rupert, who had moved to stand before the fireplace.

He smiled at his wife, and she returned his look of affection.

How different this household was from her stepmother's, mused Madeline. This room had warmth to spare, and not all of it from the fire that roared in the corner.

Glynnis turned back to her niece. "We have something to discuss with you—but first, will you have some tea?" she asked, on seeing Dexter enter with the cart.

Madeline nodded, mulling over what her aunt and uncle could possibly have in mind.

The cart stopped in front of Glynnis, who spooned two teacakes onto a rosebud-edged plate that she handed to Madeline. "Tea, Rupert? Or, would you prefer something a bit stronger?"

"I'll join the two of you," he said, crossing the room. He dished up his own savories as Glynnis poured the aromatic tea into matching cups. Rosebuds wrapped artfully in vines climbed the small handles.

"Humph. Barely enough room to pinch the handle," complained her husband as his wife handed him a cup. The tiny handle did look ludicrous in his large hands.

Madeline set her cake plate on the pedestalled tea table at her elbow. Her aunt held out a steaming cup on a saucer.

"This smells wonderful. Is it an Oolong?" asked Madeline.

Her aunt beamed appreciatively. "My own blend. An Oolong with a little orange."

"I think inhaling the aroma is as enjoyable as sipping it."

"I'm pleased you like it. Sugar or cream?"

Madeline shook her head. "No, thank you. This is perfect."

"Your sister and your stepmother usually drop a whole cow and a larder of sugar into their tea." Glynnis watched Madeline for a moment, speculating as she stirred. "My dear, how do you get on in that house?"

Madeline set her cup on its saucer, and thought about how to answer honestly without being *too* honest. "They certainly believe I am odd. But at least they've given up on trying to correct me constantly." She forced a bright smile.

Her aunt exchanged looks with her uncle. He nodded.

"Madeline." Her aunt touched Madeline's hand. "Rupert and I would like to invite you to move to our home for the duration of your stay in London."

Madeline brought her other hand up to cover her mouth. Small tears quickly filled her eyes.

"Oh, my dear, please don't be upset!" Glynnis squeezed Madeline's hand. "If you'd prefer to be with your sister, we understand. It was my idea. It was a bad idea. I . . . I thought Mary might be hard on you. She can be. It was a bad idea—"

"No!" Madeline waved her hand in the air, then began fanning her eyes with it. "I'm . . . I'm honored. I'm so very honored. I'm getting weepy, because . . ." She shook her head, unable to speak.

"Dear, don't worry—we don't need to pursue—"

Madeline struggled for composure. "No! I'm just . . . so happy." She didn't realize she could laugh and sob at the same time. "I've dreamed so of meeting my family in London. But—you're the first ones who've made me feel welcome. Aunt Glynnis, I'm so very happy! Uncle Rupert—thank you, sir."

In spite of her words, she began crying again. Glynnis began crying as well, and they hugged each other.

Rupert cleared his throat and looked up at the chandelier.

Madeline told Mrs. Cork of her invitation the moment she returned to Gresham Park.

"I can't say I'm sorry to hear we'll be leaving here, miss. The servants are friendly to me, but they say both mistresses are sour and difficult. And, from what you've said, they don't seem none too happy to have you here."

"I think that's true, Mrs. Cork. Though I'm worried this will be difficult news to break. I would have imagined a few days ago that they would be ecstatic to see me go. Yet everything my stepmother thinks is screened by what she suspects the neighbors will say. She's obsessed by a fear of gossip. If she perceives her friends and neighbors expect me to be happily residing in this house, she'll demand I stay, happily or no. I fear I'm like a bad painting to them. They don't want to see me in their house, but they're not willing to let anyone else have me, either."

"Humph. Then let's just sneak out, shall we? How about while they're out tonight doing their social engagements?"

Madeline opened her jewelry box and selected a finely carved cameo of ivory on amber. She looked in the mirror, securing the pin at her collar, and caught Mrs. Cork's reflection.

"I don't think that would be right. Anyway, I shall be attending a dance with them tonight." She poked around her jewelry and found two emerald-cut amber earrings to match her pin. "Not that they want me to go with them, understand. It's all for appearances, as usual. Mary Pickett says I must go because her friends will expect to see me there." Madeline sighed and turned around to face Mrs. Cork.

Mrs. Cork stood with arms akimbo, fists dug into her hips. "Now suppose I were to have you all packed while you were out tonight? And, what if I misunderstood and had your bags removed by one of the servants, and delivered to your aunt's address while you're gone? You inform them sometime this evening at the dance—you know she won't dare make a scene in public—and then you hire a carriage to take you home tonight. Straight to your aunt's." She raised her eyebrows, looking for affirmation from her mistress.

Madeline crossed over and hugged her friend and companion. "You are so good to me, Mrs. Cork."

"Then we'll do it?"

"No. Much as I wish I could go along with your excellent plan, I cannot in good conscience do so to my stepmother. But, tonight, I'll think about what to tell them, and I'll do so first thing tomorrow morning. I promise."

"Then I'll have your trunks all packed, miss, other than a morning outfit. Don't you worry. By tomorrow afternoon you'll be gone from here, and good riddance to bad memories."

Madeline was in the middle of a dance step, and her partner across the line disappeared from the set. To her further surprise, Mr. Jace Remington stepped in to replace him. When the pair came together, he reached to link his arm in hers. She jerked back, away from him.

"I do not care to cause a scene, Miss Pickett, but I need to talk to you."

"And I have no need to talk to you, sir." They parted again. As the circle moved, they next met on the outside of the crowd. She peeled away from the dancers, deserting him on the floor. He was next to her in a trice, following her toward the potted plants that lined the ballroom.

"Please. This will be very brief. Have you told anyone who your father is? Your real father?"

"No." She spun to face him, the wall at her back. She affirmed no one was close enough to overhear. "But I assume *you've* told everyone, since you were paid to spy on me."

"That's unfair. I wasn't paid; I was simply repaying a debt to my cousin. But that was before I got to know you. And they'd led me to believe you were an adventuress, posing to retrieve a piece of a fortune."

"That's absurd. I told you when we were in the forest that I came to London to meet my family. To meet my sister. The only reason I am attending the reading of the will is in the hope my mother may have left me a small trinket. I am not anticipating there will be any money involved."

"Can you possibly be that naive?"

She turned to leave, and he grabbed her wrist. "If you do not let go," she said, "I shall *indeed* cause a scene."

He continued to hold her narrow wrist in his strong grip. "The reason I don't wish a scene is that it will harm you, not me, Miss Pickett. I don't give a fig for what these matrons think of me."

"And why does that not surprise me?" Madeline turned her head as far to the side as she could. Pretending to study the crowd, she would not give him the courtesy of looking at him while she spoke. "Whether you believe me or not, Mr. Remington, money is not what I'm hoping for. Now remove your hand, and leave me."

"We're talking about a large fortune, Miss Pickett. Is it truly possible you didn't know?"

"How should I know? Or care?" Now, she turned to study him. "And, how is it that you know?"

"My cousin Emerson told me what was discussed with your stepmother in the lawyer's office. Mary Pickett already has a fair idea of what the legal papers will reveal."

"Are you saying you kidnapped me in order—"

"Stop saying 'kidnapped!' I'm trying to help you, blast it. I simply came to advise you."

"Why? I don't understand why you are trying to help me."

"Lord knows. I don't know why myself. Look, you must not tell them who your real father is. Let them believe it's Harold Pickett."

"Why?"

"Because they are already suspicious of your relationship to the family. Legally, you truly are Harold's daughter. You must leave it at that, and things will proceed more smoothly."

"But I *am* Jeannette Pickett's daughter."

"I know that. Are you listening to a word I'm saying? Legally, you *are* the daughter of Harold and Jeannette Pickett. Just don't repeat the story about the gentleman who sired you. It can only fuel the fire of their suspicions. Say nothing more about your real father until after the reading of the will."

"So . . . you are suggesting I renounce my true father."

"No. I mean yes. What I mean is—if they ask you whether Harold is your father, simply say 'yes.' "

"Lie about my real father? No."

"No?"

"No. I won't do it. I at least owe that to my grandfather."

"You're a little fool! I can't believe this."

"Well, I'd prefer being a fool to being a kidnapper. Good evening to you, Mr. Remington." She was able to yank her hand from his grasp and moved quickly through the crowd.

Madeline had hardly slept for her anticipation of leaving Gresham Park—and apprehension at telling her stepmother she was doing so. She'd lain awake practicing what she would say to Mary Pickett until it became part of a half-waking dream.

She peeked into the dining room. Only Cousin Emerson waited within, and Madeline pulled back around the corner and closed her eyes in relief that he hadn't seen her. Only one more day of avoiding him. Only one more meal with him sitting uncomfortably close. Only one more hour of his leering at her. Her palms were sweating. Why was she so nervous? She was packed and ready to go. All she had to do now was tell her stepmother, and she would be free of this funereal home. She'd be with Aunt Glynnis and Uncle Rupert until the reading of the will. And then, home to Grandfather.

The happy events to come gave her a new sense of determination.

"What are you doing?"

Madeline spun away from where she'd been leaning against the wainscoted wall. Mrs. Pickett and Eleanor looked quite annoyed that she was blocking their ingress to the breakfast room.

"I . . . I was waiting for you." It sounded lame to her own ears, yet the two women didn't question her excuse. Madeline followed them in. One more meal. Just one.

The usual silence ensued, punctuated only by Emerson's droning lectures. Would he ever take a breath? Her chance came when he stuffed a honeyed biscuit past his greasy lips.

"Aunt, I have something I must say," ventured Madeline quickly.

The three turned to her in surprised expectation.

"I . . . I don't wish to appear ungrateful, for I'm truly appreciative of the time you've allowed me to spend with you in your home."

"You're not going home so soon?" Mrs. Pickett commanded; it was not a question.

"Oh, no. No. I still plan on staying for the reading of Fath—of the will." Madeline thought she was going to choke, her throat was so tight. She took a sip of water. "But my aunt Glynnis has asked me to spend a few days with her." There. That didn't sound so bad. More like a temporary visit, really.

Silence.

Finally, Mrs. Pickett set her china cup down very deliberately on her saucer; a gavel on a judge's bench. "You shall remain here. What would my friends think?"

For a full minute, the clinking of silverware was the only sound to follow her edict. The tinkle and scrape of cutlery against china; occasionally, the sword swish of a knife against a fork.

Madeline took a drink of water, then a deep breath. "I . . . I beg your pardon, but . . . but you cannot force me to stay. I plan to spend a few days with my aunt."

Madeline took another swallow; her mouth was dry, as if all the moisture had abandoned her body and was pooled in her palms. She wiped them on the napkin in her lap. "My mind is made up. My maid has already seen to the packing of my trunks and valises. I shall be leaving after breakfast." She pushed her chair back. "If you'll excuse me?"

She placed her napkin gently upon her plate, and made herself look up at her stepmother. The woman glared. "I'm . . . I'm sorry. Please try to understand."

"Get out, you ungrateful—just get out of my sight."

"Yes, ma'am." Madeline stood. She stole a peek at the others. Eleanor had her usual dull look; no expression of surprise or curiosity. Emerson, however, continued to stare . . . at her bosom, of course. Madeline escaped the room in a mixture of disgust and giddy relief.

Eleanor retreated to her room. Perhaps she'd write a scathing letter to Emerson. She couldn't bear to face him after breakfast, the way he'd stared at Madeline. She'd dismissed him curtly, pleading a headache.

Besides, it was so much easier to put one's thoughts in a letter. She took out a quill, and poised her pen above the parchment. No. She'd write a nasty letter to Madeline, warning her to stay away from Emerson. Or perhaps she'd write a letter to Aunt Glynnis, warning her what a spider she'd soon have hiding in her house.

Of course, there remained the possibility that her mama was wrong. But Eleanor had watched him closely since her mama had told her she should. She noticed him peering down Madeline's dress whenever he had the opportunity. In fact, now that she studied Emerson, she saw his little piggy eyes darting back and forth like a hog at a feast. She'd watched him talking to other women; he looked at their bosoms, not at their eyes.

"But he loves me," she wailed to the empty room.

She was engaged to Emerson. She wanted a house of her own, so Mama wouldn't always be ordering her around. Emerson promised she would have a house with lots of rooms. And lots of maids.

No, she could not give up Emerson. She hated her sister; did Madeline think she could take Emerson away from her? Emerson and Eleanor. Even the names fit together. He'd carved them on the willow tree drooping over the pond. "E & E." Mrs. Emerson Edwards. Hadn't she practiced writing it a thousand times?

Emerson had promised she could go to Bath to take the waters. He'd described the fancy hotel where they would be staying. He'd whispered about how they would bathe together in a private bath.

No, he might look at Madeline, but it was likely because he found the resemblance so striking. This was why he watched her sister.

Anyway, it didn't matter. It was Eleanor he loved. And he was hers.

CHAPTER SEVENTEEN

"A Mr. Jace Remington has presented his card at the door, my Lady. He is asking if Miss Madeline Pickett is accepting visitors." Dexter waited for instruction.

Glynnis raised expectant eyebrows at her niece, and a flash of pink crossed Madeline's face.

"Do you know this Mr. Remington?" asked Glynnis, pausing her needle as it poked through her embroidery.

"He—we—yes. I mean . . . I'm not sure how well I know him, aunt. He is a cousin of Mr. Edwards—you remember Mr. Edwards, Eleanor's fiancé? I . . . I met Mr. Remington . . . on the way to London." Madeline sighed. "No. That's not quite true. It's a long story."

"Shall we send him away?" Her aunt's hands stilled on the oval hoop.

"I don't know. I *suspect* I should. He approached me at the dance last night, but I shunned him. Perhaps he is here to apologize." Madeline frowned as she closed her book. "I see he wasted no time in finding my whereabouts."

"Have you been formerly introduced to him, then?"

"My stepmother introduced him to me at her house. But I'd already met him, when he was Mr. Duncan. Not the Mr. Duncan I've told you about. Mr. Remington changed his name."

"I'm not sure I'm following you, dear."

"Mr. Remington was . . . um . . . sent to my village, and to my grandfather's home, to spy upon me."

"How extreme! Did that odious stepmother of yours set him up to this?"

"No. That is, I don't know for sure. He claims he did it as a favor he owed to Mr. Edwards. However, when he returned, my stepmother was most interested to hear what he had to report."

"Is this why he is apologizing? Did you run into him while he was in the vicinity?"

Madeline twisted her fingers in her lap while she considered what to tell her aunt. "I fear I must tell you the truth, Aunt Glynnis, and . . . I want to confide in you, but it's quite embarrassing."

"You needn't tell me anything you're not comfortable with . . . though I must admit you have me curious."

"Mr. Remington showed up at Grandfather's door as I was waiting for Mr. Duncan—the real Mr. Duncan, from Scotland. Mr. Duncan is a trusted friend of my grandfather's, and was called upon to escort me to London due to Grandfather's illness. Well, never having met Mr. Duncan, I mistakenly assumed Mr. Remington to be my grandfather's companion from Scotland."

"But surely your grandfather could have pointed out that this man was a stranger?"

"Grandfather was quite sick, and asleep at the time. And I was anxious to be on the road. I asked . . . no, that's not quite true . . . I suppose I ordered . . . Mr. Remington to load my bags and to get us on the road. He didn't deny it. He just did as he was told."

Aunt Glynnis chuckled. "That's an unusual trait in a man, dear. You may not want to let him escape." Her laugh trailed off abruptly. "Never tell me he went along with it."

"Yes, he did."

"The scoundrel!" Another thought struck Glynnis. "You were not unchaperoned, Madeline, were you?"

"Oh, no. Mrs. Cork was with us."

"And you believe the young man wishes to apologize?"

"Why else would he be following me around town?"

"Do you want to see him?"

"I think I would, but I don't know that I should. What would you suggest, Aunt Glynnis?"

Glynnis hesitated. "I would suggest we send him away, dear. At least today. If he is determined to see you, he'll be back. I'd like first to know as much as you can tell me about him, and then we can decide whether you should see him another day or not."

"Yes, that makes sense. Thank you."

"I'm glad you agree. Especially since I cannot *wait* to hear the rest of your story. Let me send him away, and then we'll have a long chat over tea, shall we?" Glynnis turned to Dexter, instructing him to deliver Miss Pickett's regrets.

Madeline could not understand the desire she felt to see Jace again. She simply must get over this.

The clock chimed the hour as Madeline began her story, and chimed once more to signal its end, reminding the two ladies it was time for tea.

"So," concluded Madeline, "he still claims he's not a kidnapper."

"Dear, there is no in between. One either kidnaps or one does not kidnap. It isn't like taking marmalade with your toast."

Madeline had the impression her aunt was teasing her. "I suppose he's not a kidnapper. He was dishonest, certainly. And he led me on—allowing me to believe he was Mr. Duncan when he was not. I have asked myself many times if he was justified in what he did, if I would have done the same thing in his shoes." She contemplated for a moment. "He has assured me he deeply regrets the masquerade." Madeline chuckled. "When Mr. Duncan caught up to us in the forest, I'm positive he regretted it."

The next afternoon, both ladies sat in the parlor entertaining Mr. Jace Remington. Madeline served tea while Aunt Glynnis made small talk with their guest.

Mr. Remington was remarkably at home, noted Madeline. One long leg was leisurely crossed over his other knee, and his arm stretched almost to the opposite end of the tiny settee.

Madeline served her aunt, and then Mr. Remington. When she resumed her seat, a brief silence descended.

"So, Mr. Remington, to what do my niece and I owe the pleasure of your visit?"

"I came to formally apologize to Miss Pickett, for certain misunderstandings that have occurred between us."

"Very commendable." Glynnis's eyes belied her serious countenance as she nodded. "Madeline? Shall you accept his apology?"

Madeline was suddenly unsure how to proceed. "What would you recommend, aunt?"

"I think I would suggest a small penance for Mr. Remington. And, if you judge in your heart that he is sincere, you should then follow your instincts, my dear."

Jace and Madeline both said, "A penance?"

"Yes. My husband insists that having tea with two women is the worst form of punishment for a civil gentleman, Mr. Remington. Would you agree that would be a suitable penance?"

Jace inclined his head to Madeline's aunt. "On the contrary. I would consider it an honor."

"Do be careful, Mr. Remington. Do not forget my niece is to be judging your sincerity."

Madeline enjoyed their guest's visit. She'd forgotten how easy it was to talk to Mr. Remington. Someday, perhaps she would confess to him what a wonderful time she'd had on their adventure.

They were finishing their second cups of tea, accompanied by a moment of companionable silence. Madeline remembered something her sister Eleanor had mentioned.

"Oh. By the way, I understand Mr. Remington is a student of mesmerism, aunt," offered Madeline into the silence.

Jace was about to take a drink, but paused with the teacup chest-high. "I'm not sure I understand, Miss Pickett. Or, is this a jab at my amateur investigation efforts in the country?"

"Your modesty does you credit, sir."

"Well, while I've never been accused of being modest, in this case you are quite mistaken, I fear. I've never had any interest in Dr. Mesmer's claims."

Her brow wrinkling prettily, she pressed on. "But . . . I thought . . ." Focusing her gaze somewhere between them, she tried to remember exactly what she'd been told. "Do you mean to say you do not dabble in the powers of suggestion?"

"Hardly," he said. "Where on earth did you hear such a thing?" He smiled as he took a sip of hot tea, watching her over the top of his cup.

"From my sister Eleanor. She was quite adamant I inquire the next time I saw you. She said you are quite famous among the ladies of the *ton* for your impressive powers of penetration."

At that, Jace choked on his drink and spat a good mouthful out.

"Are you all right, sir?" Madeline jumped up to assist him, giving his back a good thump.

"I'm fine. Please. I'm sure it was simply a swallow taking a mis-turn." He cleared his throat repeatedly.

"So, do you?" she persisted. "Do you have impressive powers of—"

"Miss Pickett!" he interrupted, at the exact same moment

Aunt Glynnis exclaimed, "Madeline—"

"Let us change the subject, Miss Pickett. I have never been involved in mesmerism, and I daresay the other is an exaggeration as well."

"What other—"

"Miss Pickett—your sister Eleanor was playing a trick on you. Quite a mean trick, I would add. It appears she is having a little fun at your expense, by asking you to question me."

Madeline frowned. "But I don't see the humor in the question."

"Believe me, neither do I," he confided with a bit of disgust.

Mr. Remington furiously concentrated on his teacup, and her aunt Glynnis watched her with the look of one about to comment, but she didn't.

Madeline looked at the remaining biscuits, trying to think of another topic.

Jace enjoyed watching the clouds of expressions that flashed across Madeline's face, one after another. My God, he thought, did she have a single expression that was not utterly charming?

"Why are you smiling, Mr. Remington? Does my discomfort give you entertainment?" asked Madeline, with a note of pique in her voice. "Perhaps I shan't accept your apology after all."

Aunt Glynnis's eyes widened, but she said nothing to her niece.

"No, no." He held up his hands in apology. "It's that your honesty gives me pleasure."

"My, my, the time has flown," said Aunt Glynnis, checking the silver watch pinned to her spencer. "You will excuse us, Mr. Remington? Perhaps you'll stop by another time?"

With that, he was dismissed.

As she escorted him to the door, Glynnis held a palm toward Madeline, implying she should stay where she was.

When the two women were once again alone, her aunt suggested, "Madeline, dear—perhaps we should have a quick discussion, woman-to-woman, about gentleman callers and suitable topics . . . especially before we trust any more of your sister's suggestions?"

The quiet parlor was punctuated with the crackling of the fire and gears clicking as clock chimes began to mark the hour.

"Madeline, I've been thinking . . ." said Glynnis.

Madeline paused, her needle poised to dive through the homespun. "Yes, aunt?"

"Mr. Remington has been appearing regularly of late."

Madeline nodded shyly.

"Please do not think I am chastising, but . . . perhaps it is not seemly that, as an eligible young lady, you are seeing one gentleman so much. I fear it is not proper that Mr. Remington appears as he chooses and monopolizes your time. I've invited him to our party tomorrow evening, as well as his brother, but I'm hopeful you will assist me by hostessing."

"Oh, of course," Madeline said.

"But that means you shall have to socialize with all of our guests, Madeline, and not show favor toward one. Besides, I think it will be good for Mr. Remington to see you dancing with others. We've invited a number of eligible young men. I guess what I'm trying to say is that there is a whole orchard to pick from, Madeline."

Her niece looked blank.

"Have you considered having a Season, dear?"

Madeline shook her head. "Before I came to London? No. I wanted to see the city, of course, but . . . no, I knew nothing about young ladies and their Seasons and such. I never gave it a thought." She laughed, looking outside at the mizzling afternoon. "The seasons in the country were all I ever considered . . ." Her needle still hovered above her work.

"My first Season was magical," Glynnis said. "I dreaded it, mind you. I told my parents I refused to have a Season. They ignored me, thankfully."

"Is that how you met Uncle Rupert?"

"Goodness, no. Your uncle would not have been caught dead at a soiree for young ladies just out of the schoolroom. Rupert's parents were neighbors of ours. Our families attended the theatre together regularly, and . . . well, I suspect they orchestrated that Rupert and I always sat together."

Glynnis set her embroidery hoop on her lap and gazed at the hearth with a smile; what she saw was not visible to Madeline. "I know the night I decided I wanted Rupert. It was *A Midsummer Night's Dream.*" Glynnis laughed. "Oh, dear, I ramble. This was not what I meant to discuss with you—"

"No, please, continue. I want to know. I love hearing romantic stories."

"And what of your own? Don't you wish the chance to live one?"

Madeline thought of Mr. Jace Remington, and tried to control the redness from peeking through her cheeks. The warmth of her skin told her she was not entirely successful. "Tell me more. Of you and Uncle Rupert."

"Actually, having a Season helped me catch Rupert."

Glynnis looked around toward the parlor door, to be sure they were alone. Then she stood and sat again, tucking her slippered foot beneath her, and leaned toward Madeline.

"I was sure he'd never propose. I became infatuated with him, but he gave no indication he even noticed me. I began looking forward to those nights at the theatre with such expectation. But no response whatsoever, though he was an excellent listener. And witty. And those eyes—such expressive eyes." Glynnis sighed. "But no hint that he found me any more fascinating than the velvet on the chairs, or the drama on the stage."

Madeline looked confused. "Then why did you love your first Season? That is so sad! And, how did he ever come up to snuff?"

"Ah, but that's where the Season came in. Toward the end of my first Season, my papa made it known to Rupert's mother that he'd received three offers for my hand. Told her he couldn't decide which to accept. He suggested perhaps Rupert could be of assistance to our family. My father asked if her son would be willing to vouch for the different gentlemen, as they were of the same age, and surely were known to Rupert." Glynnis raised an eyebrow. "Can you imagine?"

"How awful. To think the man you loved would help your papa choose a husband for you. What happened?"

"The next night, Rupert came to our door to see Father. I saw him about to enter Father's library, and he gave me a very cold look. He appeared quite angry. I was devastated."

"Angry? But why? Did you find out why?"

"Indeed. Papa summoned me to the library, exactly one hour later. I'd been crying in my room, and begged Mama not to make me go downstairs. But she insisted. She helped me fix my face, and sent my maid to tell Papa I would be down shortly."

Glynnis shuddered, then continued. "I was so nervous as I entered the library. I stared at the carpet until I was halfway into the room. I looked up to see if Rupert was still there . . . and the idiot was smiling!" Glynnis put a hand on her waist, elbow sticking out. "Well, I should have been relieved. But, do you know, I decided to be angry. Here I'd been crying out my heart, because of those evil looks earlier from the only man I loved, and the devil now stood there grinning."

Glynnis looked to the door, to ensure they were still alone. "Papa explained that Rupert was *very* concerned about my prospects."

"Oh, goodness. All of them?"

"*All.* It appears he told Papa *none* of them was suitable. Not in the least. The only safe solution, Rupert told my father, was that he should marry me himself."

Madeline's eyes widened in delight.

"My papa had appeared shocked. He deliberated, grilled Rupert on his logic. Then, hesitantly, Papa said he must agree."

"That is wonderful. Thank goodness your father finally agreed. Was Uncle Rupert happy?"

"Your uncle Rupert was grinning in self-satisfaction, having orchestrated a solution to his liking." In a dry tone, Glynnis added, "I didn't have the heart to tell him he'd been expertly manipulated by my father."

Madeline clapped her hands together. "I love it. That is so romantic, Aunt Glynnis."

Glynnis gave Madeline's hand a squeeze. "And you, Madeline? Is there a man who's captured your heart? Perhaps a neighbor near your grandfather's?" fished her aunt.

"Well, I do—" She stopped abruptly at the clearing of a throat.

Lord Chesterton stood in the doorway. "Good evening, ladies. May I join you?"

"Of course," echoed both women, though Glynnis looked a little disappointed, having anticipated her niece's exposition.

"I thought I might interest the two of you in a game of whist?" asked Rupert.

"Yes," Glynnis said. "That would be enjoyable, dear. Madeline?"

Madeline set aside her needle and threads. "I should love nothing better than to give my pitiful needlework a respite."

"I must warn you, my Lord," Glynnis said. "Two ladies against one gentleman—two excellent strategists, rather. You are already doomed."

"Remarkable. That was the very same thought I had as I sat that night in the library with you and your father," Rupert said with a wicked gleam in his eye.

Glynnis gasped, then jumped up to slap him softly, playfully, on the arm. "Oh, you—you were listening, you cad!"

Madeline smiled, pretending not to notice as Uncle Rupert placed a quick kiss upon her aunt's cheek.

Madeline glanced down the hallway the next morning and saw a man standing in the entry, backlit by strong daylight. In spite of the bright sun against her eyes, she knew of only one man whose size could rival that of the sun's radius through the glass panes.

"Why, Mr. Duncan! What a surprise to see you here. A nice surprise," Madeline added, taking his hand in hers.

"Miss Madeline." He nodded stiffly.

"Is everything all right, Mr. Duncan?" Madeline noticed a slight hesitancy in the giant's manner.

"Why, yes, miss. Nothing wrong at all. I hope all is well with you? Here and all?"

"Yes. Very. But, I didn't send for you, Mr. Duncan. Not that I'm not happy to see you."

He smiled briefly, then pivoted his eyes to look down the hall.

"Mr. Duncan, exactly why are you here, if you are fine, and I am fine?"

His eyes swiveled back to hers. "Well, I'm here to . . . to see a friend." He cleared his throat—a deep base rumble. He blushed and his eyes turned to search the hall, seeking . . . Of a sudden, his life preserver appeared.

"Albus." Mrs. Cork practically cooed his name as she scurried around the corner.

His face shaded one level deeper and his fingers reached to pull at his collar, though it didn't look a bit tight to Madeline.

"Meg and I are just tidying up from our tea," Mrs. Cork said. "If you'll excuse me, I'll be back in a wink."

The big man dipped an awkward half bow, but Mrs. Cork had already disappeared around the hallway.

"Al-bus?" Madeline's eyebrows almost touched her hairline.

"That's me name," he muttered.

"Ah," said Madeline with a nod and a smile.

Mrs. Cork rescued him from further embarrassment, arriving with Meg just behind.

"Meg, how nice to see you again," Madeline greeted the maid warmly, and Meg returned a quick curtsy.

"It's me afternoon off, miss, and I do love having tea with Mrs. Cork. We all miss her at Gresham Park."

Mrs. Cork patted her friend's arm. "We're just about to head off for an excursion with Albus—I mean with Mr. Duncan."

"I think that's wonderful," Madeline said. "Do enjoy yourselves. And take your time, Mrs. Cork. I'll be out this afternoon myself, so please don't feel rushed to return."

"Thank you, miss." Madeline saw the pleasure in her maid's eyes, boasting to Meg of her wonderful relationship with her employer.

They moved toward the door, amid a busy arranging of shawls and hats.

"Have a good time. Are you going to Vauxhall?" Madeline asked, pleased with her new connoisseur's knowledge.

The three stopped their motion and turned as one.

"Oh, no, miss," Mrs. Cork said. "That's a little common, don't you think? We were planning on seeing that new sculpture exhibition you and I discussed."

They waved as they turned to be on their way.

"Too common . . . I see," repeated Madeline, but the three friends had already closed the wide doors behind them.

Mr. Jace Remington appeared with his customary regularity the following morning, inquiring if he might see Miss Pickett. Aunt

Glynnis directed him to the arbor, where Madeline would be found reading a book.

Madeline never heard him approach, she was so absorbed in her novel. When a shadow fell across the page, she jumped.

"I'm interrupting. Once more, I find myself owing you an apology, Miss Pickett."

She was inwardly pleased to see it was Mr. Remington. She closed her book. It felt natural to place her hand in his when he reached out to assist her to her feet.

"Would you care for a turn through the gardens?" he inquired.

She nodded, and he drew her closer, but she pulled her hand free and led the way through the arbor, noticing Mr. Remington had to duck to avoid the pendulous clusters of wisteria blossoms. The walkway widened, and Madeline and Jace strolled side by side along the paved path. Neither spoke, but it was not an awkward silence.

"There is something I've been wanting to say to you, Mr. Remington."

Jace inclined his head toward her, his hands clasped behind his back, as they continued walking.

"I want to tell you I had a *wonderful* time on our outdoor adventure."

He laughed. "I find that hard to believe, Miss Pickett. Nothing went as it should."

"But I realized how lucky I was after Mr. Duncan—the real Mr. Duncan," she said, giving him a knife-edged look, "appeared. Do you know, I suggested the same plan to him . . . that we take advantage of the time remaining, and spend another day in the forest."

"Aha. And, of course, he was the perfect outdoorsman, surpassing all your expectations?"

"No. I mean—he *may* be the perfect outdoorsman. I wouldn't know, as he absolutely refused even to consider it." Madeline stopped and faced Jace. "If I hadn't been with you, Mr. Remington, I never would have had my adventure. And I never properly thanked you."

Jace took her hand, and brought her wrist to his lips. "You are welcome. I enjoyed myself as well, Miss Pickett."

She was aware of the flush brought on by his touch, and it sent a shiver through her. She stood still, enjoying the feel of her palm against his warm hand.

Focusing her gaze on the gazebo ahead, Madeline spoke softly. "I remember how I anticipated both adventures. I could not wait to go into the forest, and then I could not wait to meet my sister in London . . . and my stepmother. They were to have been like the family in one of my novels—loving and laughing. I would walk in, and they should all surround me, embracing the long-lost daughter."

She turned a rueful look to Jace. "If it weren't for you, Mr. Remington, I should never have realized any of my dreams. This trip would have been all for naught." She squeezed his hand. "Thank you."

He reached for her other hand. "I can't believe your Mr. Duncan didn't take you where you wished. How was he able to resist those gray eyes of yours? Plus, you ordered me about so sweetly."

Madeline looked down at her slippers. "I was a bit of the commander, wasn't I?"

"Well, and I was trapped to play the role of the dutiful servant. I suppose I deserved it."

Madeline chuckled. "I was fortunate after all. It was fun being kidnapped."

"Miss Pickett! You must stop using that word."

"And I couldn't believe it when I stepped out of my tent, and there you were on the ground, and there Mr. Duncan was towering over all of us like the old tree of the forest." She paused in thought. "Why didn't you explain to him, instead of fighting?"

"Explain? To a tree? To tell you the truth, I never even got a look at the man. All I saw was an anvil attached to an arm, about two inches from my face."

"Oh, but he's so gentle. He's just an oversized puppy. You should get to know him."

"Humph. That's all right. If I never see the Scotsman again, I think that will be fine."

Madeline was never sure who stepped closer first. Of a sudden, her skirt was brushing the tops of his boots. He leaned toward her, and she realized he was about to kiss her.

She put her hands against his chest, holding him away. "Tell me about your escapade."

"What?" His expression was unreadable. He looked half asleep.

"Tell me what happened after we left you."

"Why?" He moved closer, if that was possible.

Madeline stepped back. "I'm just curious."

"Would you like to go to the gazebo?" he asked softly. "Then we can both satisfy our curiosity, Miss Pickett."

She slowly shook her head no. "I think it's time for tea. I . . . I need to go back. My aunt must be wondering where I am."

Jace held her gaze before answering. "All right. We shall go back, if that's what you wish."

Hypnotized by his eyes, she made herself shake her head yes.

Jace linked her arm in his, and they walked back the way they'd come.

"Nettles." He broke the silence.

"Nettles?"

"Stinging nettles, to be precise. As I walked back toward the highway, I cut through some bushes, and realized—too late— they were stinging nettles."

"Oh, poor Mr. Remington. I am so very sorry for you, sir."

She chuckled once, but pretended it was a cough.

"What was that? That didn't sound like a sorrowful, sympathetic sound, Miss Pickett."

"I was just wondering—what else could possibly have gone wrong? When I saw you at my stepmother's, you looked as if you'd walked the inner circles of hell."

"Well, Dante never had to deal with a bee's nest, either, Miss Pickett."

"Oh." She mouthed the word in sympathy, but the laugh she tried to stifle cancelled all her good intentions.

CHAPTER EIGHTEEN

Meet me in the conservatory at midnight. J

Madeline read the note again, experiencing the same re-action: her pulse raced; her stomach fluttered.

Who else could it be other than Jace Remington? She made herself calm down and slowly tick off all the guests at her aunt's party; did anyone else have a name that began with J?

She chuckled aloud as she recalled Lord Quizzen's first name was John. An image of the eighty-two-year-old man tottering to the conservatory with his rounded back hunched over made her smile. No, there were no other Js, and she doubted very much it was that octogenarian gentleman.

She brought the paper closer to her nose; strange—the note-paper had a trace of something cloying. She couldn't place the scent though it tickled her recollection. Odd how smells could bring back the strongest memories. Perhaps it was something the maid had been handling as she delivered the missive.

She crumpled the letter and deposited it in the fireplace. It seemed best not to leave it lying where other eyes might see it. The dark ink smoldered, dark cinder bands striped the paper, and it was gone in a flash of flames.

Now: the decision. Would she be at the conservatory tonight?

She recalled Mr. Remington's strange behavior at the late supper table. She'd turn suddenly from conversation with a neighbor, and he'd be looking at her. Of course, he was on the other side of the table and several guests down, so perhaps it only seemed he looked in her direction.

For in truth, every time her eyes went to his, he looked elsewhere. Was he making a show of ignoring her in public as a distraction from tonight's rendezvous?

And when the party retired to the parlor for tea and claret, he'd certainly avoided her . . . other than one instance. She'd stopped at a corner window while making her round of the guests. As she looked out at the night and the scattered coach lights, Sir Peter Willoughby had joined her. He was such a charming young gentleman. Just as Sir Peter had leaned in to whisper a piece of light gossip in her ear, Mr. Jace Remington had appeared out of nowhere, with a cough. She glanced up to find him glowering—first at Sir Peter, and then at her.

Sir Peter had smiled bashfully and, nodding to Mr. Remington, backed away. She'd frowned at Jace, not understanding what was transpiring. But he did not even deign to say anything; had only held her eyes for a moment.

When his brother Bennett called to him to resolve some silly argument, he leaned forward. "Later," he promised in a serious whisper—or was it a threat?—and turned away.

Ah! Now it made sense—he'd obviously been referring to the meeting they were to have tonight. But—she remembered that frown, and his chasing Sir Peter away. Perhaps he wished to scold her further for some imagined transgression? Perhaps she would not be in the conservatory at twelve, she thought coolly.

But she knew she would be.

Looking in the mirror, Madeline chastised herself for tying the ribbons under her bodice so tightly. What was she trying to do, entice the man? Besides, she could hardly breathe with the satin strings cutting into her rib cage. She tugged until ties fell loose, then retied them carefully, a bit more loosely.

Peering at her reflection by candlelight, she felt herself flush and put her fingertips to her cheeks to affirm they were indeed warm. This seemed such an evil thing to be doing. What would Grandfather have said?

Oh, Lord—she'd never done anything so daring before. She couldn't even imagine what fury would have thundered in Grandfather's eyes. That made her smile—even imagining Grandfather at his most crotchety made her miss him.

Should she wear a hat? She had no idea what a lady of the night should wear. A veil? She had a clever maroon hat with a matching veil. Of course, she had no black veil; she'd not expected to attend any funerals . . . her own funeral? How angry could Mr. Remington possibly be? She tried the maroon hat upon her head, tipping it seductively.

Her reflection looked back at her in the soft light. How ludicrous her pert little hat looked in the dark. She was about to commit an improper act, and she was worrying about dictates of fashion and modesty. Blast it—forget the hat. She removed it. A few wisps of long hair escaped from her careful arrangement.

Unless—what if he meant to chastise her, as she feared? Then, wouldn't he be doubly incensed if she were not dressed properly? She shuddered, dug around in her armoire, and pinned on a small modest peacock-feathered hat.

Her reflection frowned at her. How dare he chastise her for impropriety. He was the one who had invited her to this clandestine meeting! She pulled the pin out so forcefully a thick lock of hair spilled in a long curl along her face. *This is all his fault,* she snapped to herself, coaxing the stray lock behind her ear.

And yet . . . Mrs. Cork always said the way a lady dressed dictated her actions. If she intended to keep a modicum of coolness, being properly dressed in this improper situation would certainly give her the upper hand. She resolutely grabbed two more silver pins from the small ivory dish, and secured a soft yellow confection of a hat in place.

Hmm. . . . it was a little too confectionary. Looked more like she was going to tea than to an assignation. She yanked it off in disgust, freeing several additional stubborn curls.

She threw the hat across the room with the others, and checked the clock. Drat! Time to go, and none to spare to repair her hair arrangement; haphazardly, Madeline hooked loose curls behind her ears.

She grabbed her wrap to ward off any chills. Even though the conservatory was kept softly heated around the clock, the moisture collecting on the glass walls might put an unhealthy air in the room at night.

She would be late, and it was his fault she was not impeccably attired. He had caused all this indecision with his too-cryptic note. Couldn't he at least have given a hint of what this was about? Would it have wasted too much of his precious ink to have jotted one sentence more? Make that two, she thought angrily.

Looking around, she memorized where the doorknob was, and leaned forward to blow a soft puff of air that extinguished the candle. It took a moment for her eyes to adjust. She started toward the door, taking small safe steps in the dark. With hands extended, she touched the smooth wood of the door, and quietly groped for the key, pulling it out of the lock.

She pulled the door open a few inches, as slowly as possible. To her relief, no jarring squeaking of hinges or creaking of wood announced her transgression to the world, or at least to those rooms immediately surrounding hers.

Madeline peered through the crack, then continued edging the door until she could peek her head out to look the other direction. No one in sight. She stepped out on slippered feet, then locked her door by feel, afraid to take her eyes from the hallway they scanned.

Her heart pounded like a drum. She feared the drumming would be a reveille to those in rooms nearby, who'd come bursting into the hall at any moment.

The brass key slid out of the lock. She began to drop it into her reticule, and nearly dropped it to the floor, gasping. She'd forgotten her reticule. She felt practically undressed, without a hat and without a hand purse. She closed her eyes in mortification, but opened them and decided quickly to move on about her business.

Tiptoeing along the hall, she was grateful for the soft carpet running the length of the hallway. She debated whether to use the main stairway or the servants' stairs. She opted for secrecy, and padded softly toward the back stairs.

Yet—wouldn't she be more likely to meet a servant at this hour than to meet a guest? Turning, she retraced her steps, and shuffled quickly toward the main stairway.

And which would be the more damaging? To be discovered by a guest, or by a servant? Drat, how did one have an affair? She was wearing a rut in the carpet from her indecision. Doing an about-face, she sidled back toward the servants' stairs. Her hand along the wall helped her descend the narrow steps. She made it safely to the landing below without spying the telltale sign of approaching candlelight.

Madeline began toeing the next flight of narrow steps. She'd not brought a candle, counting on the soft moonlight through windows to guide her. Yet with no windows in the service stairwell, she had to proceed slowly in pitch dark.

What seemed like hours later, she tested with her toe for the next step and discovered only solid landing. Cautiously, she slid her slippered feet along, in case an unexpected step or two should lie ahead. Along the corridor, she found a little more light, and at last reached an intersecting hallway.

If memory served her correctly, the hallway on her left should lead to the conservatory. Ancient clerestory slits showed just enough light to discern two French doors at the end of the wing. Those glass doors should mark the entry.

No one was about. Willing her slippered feet to silence, she successfully reached the entry, her heart beating against her chest. She stopped at the edge of the glass cavern and peered into the eerie dark, taking deep breaths until her heartbeat slowed.

Inhaling the earthy smell was a comfort to Madeline. Gardening usually calmed her spirit, and the humidity filling the air with the richness of damp soil drew her. Calmed and determined to proceed, she slipped through the doorway. Well, she thought smugly, perhaps assignations were not so difficult after all.

But now, where to go? Should she follow the brick pavers between benches? It might be too noisy to walk down a side gravel path. She stepped into a circle of light cast by the moon through the peaked glass ceiling. Not comfortable standing in the ghostly beams, she moved on toward a path of Amazon palms. The palm fronds arched above her, blocking the moonlight and throwing the path into darkness. This walkway was paved; only a few errant pieces of gravel crunched underfoot.

She closed her eyes, and listened to her breathing. This was intoxicating. Was it the tinge of humus from the potted earth, or the thrill of a midnight rendezvous? She glided further along the path, with a delicious sense of danger. However, it was but a gesture, as she knew the doorway was not far away.

From the direction of the glass doors, she heard voices. More than one voice, which was somewhat surprising. At the tittering of female voices, she realized it was not Mr. Remington. Panicking, she wasn't sure if she should hasten back and reveal herself, or stay hidden among the giant ferns.

The decision was made for her, as an arm shot out of the

bushes, wrapping around her waist. At the same time, a hand clamped on her mouth, stifling her scream.

A command whispered softly into her ear: "Do not make a sound, Miss Pickett."

She recognized Jace Remington's voice, and was grateful for the darkness. The intimacy of the whisper in her ear, the closeness of the man, made her close her eyes in surrender to her senses.

She nodded and moved slightly, expecting him to release his tight grasp. But his arms continued to enclose her, and she could even feel his muscles tighten in response to her movement.

This was too much! She lifted her right foot, and swung her heel back into his leg, giving him a bit of her mind.

"Do that again, and you'll regret it," he growled against her face.

She froze at the threat in his tone, but steamed in helpless anger at the tightness of his arms.

The voices chattered in a gossipy tone. She couldn't recognize any of them, but there seemed to be at least two distinct tones, and perhaps a third. All were female, she thought, listening. Of course, she had nothing better to do than to stand entrapped beneath the potted palms, listening to the chattering.

After what seemed forever, the door of the conservatory opened again, and the voices trailed away as the occupants exited.

She expected to be released, but as if reading her mind, he whispered one word, "Wait." Another minute or so passed, and his grasp relaxed.

She spun around. "How dare you!"

In spite of the dark, she could make out the whites of his eyes as he widened them in disbelief.

"How dare *I?*" he parroted. "And keep your voice down! They may yet return. I was merely saving your reputation, you harebrained twit."

She gasped in indignation. "Saving my reputation? From what? If you'd left me alone to join them, no one would have been the wiser that you were even here. I am quite capable of looking out for myself, thank you."

"Obviously, you are *not* capable of any such thing," he said. "Inviting me to join you here was not only irresponsible, it was taking a risk that we might have been seen together. At this late hour, your reputation would have been stained, to say the least."

"Inviting you to join me!" she said loudly, causing him to shush her. "Don't you dare shush me," she continued in the same loud squeal, causing him to clasp his hand over her mouth while pulling her close. She bit the edge of his palm, and he immediately released her, swearing.

Pulling away, she had every intention of marching off to her bedroom, but his hand snaked out and grabbed her upper arm.

"We need to have a discussion, but it is *not* going to happen this close to the door." With that dictate, he began striding down the path even deeper into the potted jungle, dragging her along.

He didn't stop until they almost collided with the back wall of the greenhouse. She could see their reflections in the glass, but nothing outside in the darkness. All she noticed was her hair, which was in even worse disarray.

"I knew I should have worn a hat," she muttered under her breath.

"What?" he asked in disbelief. "What on earth is that supposed to mean?"

Embarrassed by her disclosure, she looked obstinately over at the orchid beds, refusing to meet his eyes.

"I am sorry I manhandled you," he said softly, "but surely

you understand the risk." His voice became hard again. "I can't believe you took it upon yourself to initiate such a harebrained scheme!"

"Would you stop saying *I* initiated it? It was *your* idea. You are driving me crazy." She stamped her foot in the darkness, even though the gesture would be lost on him. "Ow!" The gravel cut into her heel.

She could see his narrowed eyes in the dark. "What do you mean it was my idea?" he asked.

"You are the one who sent the note asking me to meet you here. I was simply responding. Not that I should have. And certainly not without my hat," she complained, patting the stray curls back behind her ear.

She could see a brief flash of teeth, but didn't know if it was a smile, or a gritting of teeth. Lord help him if he was smiling, she determined. And—Lord help him if he was baring his teeth at her in anger.

"I did not send a note, as well you know," he said. "You were the one who scrawled out a hasty invitation and sent it to me. I have it here with me," he finished, reaching into his vest pocket and flourishing the note under her nose.

"Ugh, it's that same smell." She backed away. "How can I possibly make out anything in this dark? And, anyway, I don't need to, because I never sent a note to you! You sent one to me, sir, and do not deny it."

"Oh? And I suppose you can prove that? I have shown you the note you sent. Where is this imaginary note that I am supposed to have sent?"

She sputtered before replying. She was so angry it was hard to arrange her thoughts coherently. "You doubt my word? Then you are a liar, sir, and *not* a gentleman."

"I've been told I'm not a gentleman," he grabbed her face in one large hand, "and I'll be glad to prove it to you in other

178

ways. But"—he moved his face close to hers—"I've never been called a liar, and if you weren't female, you would pay for that remark."

Jerking her head to the side, she pulled her face away from his grasp. And found herself with her cheek up against his woolen vest. She was aware of his wonderful scent; it was not that of the note.

Pay attention, she reminded herself, and rediscovered her angered indignation. "So—yet you are allowed to imply that I am a liar, as I've already told you I wrote no note."

"And where is the note I sent to you?"

"I happened to have burned it in the fireplace."

"Ha! A convenient story," he barked in a half laugh.

That was it. She reached up, and grabbed his chin, exactly as he had grabbed hers. However, her hand certainly did not encompass his face, or even a small part of his cheek, so the gesture seemed less threatening. Still, she stood up on her toes, put her face inches from his, just as he had done. "And if you, sir, were not a male, I would make you pay for implying that I am a liar." Her eyes flashed.

She didn't know how he would react, but found to her embarrassment he did not react at all. He stood quite still, allowing her to cup his stubbly chin, and held her eyes.

Slowly, he reached his own hand up to cover hers, and then he leaned towards her the last few inches, his lips beginning to part.

Something snapped inside her, and she grabbed her hand out from his, and brought it across his cheek in a resounding slap.

Laughter was not the retaliation she'd expected.

"Truce, Miss Pickett? I deserved that, as you read my intention correctly." He took her hand, the one that still smarted from the slap, and turned it over, as if to ensure he hadn't injured her palm. "You continue to amaze me. A truce?"

"I . . ." She looked away from his dancing eyes, not understanding her frustration and confusion. "Perhaps I should apologize. I don't know what's come over me tonight. Meeting you here is the most improper thing I've ever done." She was close to tears.

"And without a hat."

She snapped her eyes to his face, sure he was making fun of her. "I suppose *you* have midnight assignations on a regular basis." She tilted her nose a bit higher. "Forgive me, but I am not familiar with what a proper lady should wear to a nocturnal rendezvous."

"I believe the point is for them to wear nothing."

She flushed furiously, hoping he could not see her in the dimness.

"Though," he continued, "I must admit that the idea of a hat, by itself, is a bit appealing."

She closed her eyes in mortification, and spun on her heel.

"Please." He did not grab her. "One more minute, Miss Pickett. We have a mutual problem."

She turned back. "We do?"

"Yes. If you did not send me the note—" He held up his hands in peace. "And I believe you now. And if I did not send you a note . . ." His voice trailed off.

A terrible coldness shot through her stomach. "Then, someone was setting us up to be discovered." He was right, of course.

He nodded. "But why?"

"What exactly did your note say?"

He pulled it from his pocket again. "Simply to meet you in the conservatory at twelve tonight." He squinted at it in the soft moonlight. "It doesn't have your name. Just initials: Miss M.P. And yours?"

"The same. Signed with the initial J."

"Just one letter? How did you know it was me?"

"I went through the guest list . . ." She chuckled. "If I'd thought it was Lord Quizzen, I'd have preferred to stay in my bed and read." Realizing her admission, she pinked, thankful for the dark.

"Ah, but assuming it was me, you did prefer to leave your bed?"

There were those teeth flashing again. She'd forgotten how annoying he could be. "And you? You could have stayed in bed reading as well, sir," she pointed out.

"That was never an option. As you said, I have nothing to do each night but go for assignations."

"That was unkind of me to say. I did not mean it."

"I am teasing you. Do I detect a truce then? Come, Miss Pickett. As we will not be able to solve this mystery tonight, let us each retire separately. I shall wait here while you go to your room. You have your key?"

She reached for her familiar reticule dangling from her wrist. "My reticule!" She looked around, but recalled the key was in her pocket. "Oh . . . never mind. I . . . I forgot. I put the key in my pocket."

"Miss Pickett, am I to believe you came to the conservatory at midnight without a hat, *and* without a reticule?"

Madeline didn't deign to respond to the odious man. She headed swiftly down the paved path toward the entrance.

CHAPTER NINETEEN

Madeline hadn't been able to sleep well after the midnight debacle. Filtered light painted her room, and she stretched on tiptoes at the window. The sunlight bumped against a stubborn layer of fog. Dismal weather for gardening, but working outside would clear her mind, she decided.

She patrolled the raised beds of roses, pruning tools and basket in hand. Perhaps this was not the best of ideas—the rich loam of the rose beds kept bringing back memories of the conservatory. She'd begun in a pensive mood, but anger seeped through her thoughts, like the fog that seeped and curled among the rosebushes.

Was the note written by her half sister? Was Eleanor's voice one of the whisperers in the conservatory last night? Who else would wish her such ill? Madeline was sure the cruel trick had to be another act of her sister's. She pinkened in memory of Mr. Remington's visit two days ago, and Madeline's naive *faux pas*.

And if her half sister's plan had succeeded, Madeline would have found herself ruined this morning. Compromised beyond recovery—she might have had to accept a hasty proposal from Mr. Jace Remington. That gave her pause. She picked the rose snips from the straw basket on her arm, but wasn't looking at them. She stared inward, analyzing the mixed feelings roiling inside herself. Marriage to Mr. Jace Remington? Her stomach clenched.

What if she'd been found alone with him—compromised? He'd almost kissed her. Would a marriage to him be so distasteful? Else, why this sudden discomfort thinking about him?

Of course, if he'd been forced to wed, she'd soon feel his resentment. He'd shown himself to be one who didn't bother to hide his feelings—no social graces there; no manners. Humph! Given his reputation, his wife would no doubt sit at home while he spent his evenings with his mistress. No, make that mistresses, if the rumors were correct.

She fumed. The very idea of that man leaving her at home surrounded by babies while he . . . she stopped cold. Surrounded by babies . . . his babies. She felt warm and pink, embarrassed by this line of thought, even though the air was chill. *Oh, this is ridiculous!* she chastised herself. *Nothing happened, and here I am imagining myself having his babies!*

She smiled and reached out to snip a faded rose.

The sun had weakly banished the fog as she rounded the last rose bed. She bent to smell another open bloom, a delicate apricot blush. This was her favorite time of the day to be among the roses—their colors intense in the early light, their heady scents slightly warmed by the sun.

So calming—until she recalled the dangerous note. She didn't want to admit it, but the note must have been from Eleanor. And that reminded her of her sister's prank about Mr. Remington and mesmerism. Madeline's blush mirrored the peaches and pinks of the blooms. After he'd left, Aunt Glynnis had explained the nuances of Eleanor's statement. Just wait until she saw Eleanor!

Madeline snipped a bloom a little too sharply, and it went flying through the air. She had to reach between two branches to retrieve the blossom. "Ouch!" As she withdrew the soft cushion of petals, a deep thorn nicked her thumb. Pulling back quickly had scratched a thin line above her wrist. It was red, but didn't look as if the blood would break the surface, other than where the thorn had snagged her. There, a ruby ball of blood quickly rose.

This was all her sister's fault. She'd been thinking about Eleanor's prank, and was distracted. She turned to grab rose petals or a leaf to stanch the tiny cut. Instead, she screamed as she turned right into another body.

"I'm sorry," said Jace, catching at her upper arms to steady her. "I was about to announce myself, when you spun around."

Her eyebrows rose.

"Well, I planned eventually to announce myself. But, you know, you stood there for the longest time—just standing and staring somewhere. It was enchanting, so I watched you. There, I've admitted it. But I'd give a doubloon to know where your thoughts were, Miss Pickett."

Her eyes opened wide. She'd been thinking of his visit, and of their conversation. She stared at his vest, where she'd put her hand at impact. He'd felt so warm and hard beneath her palm, right there where the tiny red spot was. Madeline gasped, jumping back. "I'm so sorry! I've got blood all over your vest."

Jace looked down. "I hardly think it's 'all over my vest,' " he said with a laugh, "it's just a spot. And," he added dismissively, "it's just a vest."

She thought about other gentlemen she'd met in London. She was sure they'd have run indoors hollering for their valet. She tipped her head, rather liking this cavalier disregard of his wardrobe.

"However"—he fished in a pocket for his handkerchief—"let's stop that bleeding so you don't soil your own beautiful dress."

Madeline looked down at her dress and smiled. Beautiful? Hardly. She was wearing one of her oldest muslins for gardening.

"Have you ever been told"—he pressed the white linen against the red trail—"how very transforming your smiles are?" He held the handkerchief firmly to the tiny cut. "When you're not frowning, that is."

Embarrassed by the contact, she shook her head. "I suppose you could flatter a woman in gardening boots and a potato sack."

"Are you implying, Miss Pickett, that my compliments are insincere?"

She gave serious thought to his question, and looking him frankly in the eye, responded, "Yes."

"I am mortally wounded, Miss Pickett!" He put a hand over his breast.

Laughing, she moved his hand aside and touched the stain she'd left on his vest. "Why, yes, I see you are indeed wounded. However, it doesn't appear to be mortal."

Her smile disappeared as he moved his hand to cover hers. It reminded her of a dance: facing one another, her hand captive in his.

"I must go now. Back to the house," she explained unnecessarily.

Jace didn't reply; didn't move.

She looked away. "It looks like the rain clouds may be returning. Would you like to join us for tea?"

"Of course." He released her. "After you, Miss Pickett."

She turned, and heard him mutter behind her. She chose to ignore it, but it sounded like, "Coward."

Bennett took the wide steps two at a time, and nearly ran down the doorman at the club on St. James Street.

He slid to a stop in the marbled foyer, just long enough to shrug out of his cloak, which was then efficiently handled by the liveried staff. He offered his topper and gloves, and was off to the carpeted rooms in a rush.

Beneath the ornately carved lintel separating foyer from the front den, he collided with Baron Bleachford. "Jeremy, so sorry. Have you seen my brother?"

"Can't recall that I have, but I've come straight from the gaming room. Good luck finding him in that crowd, Bennett."

Bennett nodded thanks and looked around the reading room. A marked difference from the lively back rooms—a few older gentlemen sat reading newspapers, a drink by every elbow. Bennett squinted at a long pair of legs extended toward the fireplace. The owner's face was hidden, buried in the news. Bennett stalked across the room and peered over the paper wall.

"Jace! I came as quickly as I could."

Jace looked up, then snapped his paper closed. "Good timing, Bennett. Have a seat." Jace signaled a nearby waiter and sent the man for a bottle of port.

"What's wrong?" Bennett pulled up a nearby armchair, and dropped down.

"I need to talk to you. I'm in the deuce of a dilemma, little brother." A frown line cut a cleft between Jace's brows.

"What is it?"

Jace studied his brother. "Isn't that collar a little high?"

Bennett stared back and chose his words with care. "Surely you didn't summon me here to inquire about my collars?"

"No, no." Jace shrugged one shoulder. "Just hadn't noticed before."

The waiter arrived, and Jace paused until the man had left again. "Bennett, I need your advice."

"It's quite straightforward, Jace. *Your* collar cut is old-fashioned, as is the cut of your jacket, *and* don't get me started on your cravat."

"All right. I deserved that." Jace's words smiled, but he didn't.

He drummed his fingers on the arm of his chair. "It's about Miss Pickett."

"Which Miss Pickett are we discussing?" Bennett noticed his brother's surprise, and suspected Jace had long ago dismissed Miss Eleanor Pickett from his thoughts.

"Why, I refer to Miss Madeline Pickett, of course."

"Of course." Bennett's smile also remained hidden in his eyes; no betrayal of mirth touched his lips.

"She is vexing me." Jace swallowed, and ran his thumb over the base of the snifter.

"The devil you say. Have you seen her then?" Bennett looked over the rim of his glass as he took a drink. "Last time we talked you'd been avoiding her—"

"I wasn't avoiding her; I just hadn't the time to make social calls. I was in bad shape, if you'll remember."

"Ah, yes. How's the limp?"

"I'm fit. All that's behind me."

"How's the hard head?"

"I beg your pardon?" Jace said.

"Well—and have you seen her yet?"

"Yes, you scoundrel. And I'm not stubborn. In fact, I've seen her several times."

"Do you still think she's innocent? You said so the first time she arrived in town."

"She *is* innocent. Emerson and his future mother-in-law are fools." Jace twirled his glass slowly, contemplating the ruby depths. "I only wish she weren't."

"Weren't what? A fool?"

Jace sighed. "Innocent."

"You've lost me, big brother." Bennett gave his head a rapid shake, and looked at his glass. "And I'm still on my first drink, so don't bother to blame it on the Portuguese."

Jace stared at his drink abstractedly. "If she were not innocent—if she had not been Harold and Lady Jeannette's legal daughter—there would be no inheritance. If there were no inheritance, it would make things less sticky."

"Less sticky for . . . ?"

"For me. Can't you see that?" Jace squinted at his brother. "Bennett—have you attended anything I've said?"

This smile did slip from Bennett's eyes, and landed on his face. "I shall try harder, big brother. Suppose you start from the beginning, and I promise to listen carefully."

Jace seemed appeased. He cleared his throat and looked down, tracing the fleury pattern in the hearthrug with his eyes.

"As I said, Miss Pickett—" He glanced up at Bennett. "—Miss Madeline Pickett—is in fact innocent. Harold Pickett might not have been her real father, but legally she is Harold and Lady Jeannette's daughter."

Jace drained his brandy. Without glancing over, he set it on the tripod table at hand and continued. "Since she is, indeed, their daughter, she will stand to inherit a good-sized fortune." He began drumming his fingers again. "If she inherits a fortune, she will doubt my sincerity when I profess my interest in her."

Bennett sat up. "Jace! Are you saying what I'm hearing? You plan to offer for Miss Pickett?"

Jace shook his head. "No. That's not what I said. I said I was interested." Jace looked confused. "I am interested in her. I perhaps do wish to court her, yes. But . . . no. I said nothing about marriage."

"Of course. I misunderstood." Bennett had promised to listen. He waited, watching the comedy of the tragic mask on his brother's face go through shades of change and awareness.

Jace ran his hand through the hair over his ear. "Don't you see the problem, Bennett? She will think I am of a sudden interested because of her damned money."

"That's absurd. You have plenty of blunt of your own."

"It doesn't matter. Aren't all men looking to increase their fortunes, no matter what size?" Jace stood and paced close to their chairs. "Not that I am looking to marry her, mind you. She, however, may suspect that is my intention."

"Not, I'm sure, if you make it clear you are simply 'professing interest.' " Bennett's eyes glittered with humor.

Jace never noticed. "Thank you. Yes, I must make my intentions clear. Or, rather, make clear my lack of intentions." Jace stopped pacing, and dropped into his seat. "That sounds ridiculous." He put his head in his hands.

Bennett studied the slumped figure across from him. "Brother, have you considered telling her the truth? I mean, tell her you would like to . . . to get to know her better . . . as friends. And that you are not at all interested in her money, as you already have plenty of your own, and . . . why should friends be interested in one another's money?"

"Yes." Jace was nodding. "Yes. Ingenious." He looked thoughtful, then nodded decisively. "Of course. Thank you, Bennett. I knew you could help me think this through. I am indebted."

Bennett wondered if Jace was drunk.

Not smelling any sour drunken smell on his brother's breath, he assumed the man must be love-bitten. Bennett's friends told him it was a kind of temporary insanity; quite contagious, evidently, and grown men of any age could catch it. They told Bennett not to laugh—cynicism was not a talisman against this disease.

And here sat the mighty Jace, making no sense. Bennett's invincible big brother, weakened by lust, or love—perhaps both? And it would be the first crisis of many, if his friends' predictions were correct. Ah, well, Bennett had simply done what any friend or brother would have done. He'd listened sympathetically.

And he now did what any brother would do in his shoes. "So, big brother, since we've solved that dilemma, would you order me another bottle on your account? A little food as well, perhaps?"

The butterfly china gleamed, reflecting the soft light from the wax tapers. The afternoon had remained overcast, and Glynnis requested the candles be lit to chase away the gloom during their early dinner.

On Mondays, they dined on Glynnis's favorite tableware—butterflies fluttered across the plates, their wings edged with pearlescent nacre. On Mondays, they had stew and partridge.

Glynnis loved traditions. Her friends declared they also had routines of their own: as little lovemaking as possible, and only on rarely scheduled nights. Hypnotized by the shimmering dinnerware in the candlelight, Glynnis shuddered at that thought. Cuddling with Lord Chesterton was much too enjoyable to assign to a routine, like Monday's soup.

"Why do you shiver, dear? Is there a draft?" Her husband twisted his large frame halfway around, to see if the door were open, or the dining-room windows.

"No, my Lord, it was nothing. Just the grayness outside."

Both smiled across the candlelit table.

"And where is our niece? She disappeared rather quickly after cards."

Glynnis dabbed her lips with a pink napkin, and sighed. "I think the poor child still believes she shall have a relationship with her sister. She excused herself, as she's gone to call upon the Picketts. I only hope they don't rebuff her; Eleanor seems to be as petty as her stepmother."

She sipped her white wine, then set it down and studied her husband. "But, do tell me your news, Rupert."

Sir Rupert lifted brows in honest surprise. "How the devil

did you know I have news?"

"Because you've appeared very pleased with yourself since you entered, husband. Well?"

"I swear, I think you are a witch sometimes, madam." Unexpectedly, he reached over and wrapped his large hand around hers where it rested on the stem of her goblet. "I can attest you've bewitched me with your beauty."

She turned a shade of pink and ducked her head, smiling her contentment.

Releasing her hand, he picked up his spoon and dipped it into the thick broth, casually mentioning, "I ran into Barrister Hollis this morning."

"And? How is his wife?"

"Damned if I know," said Rupert. "I certainly didn't think to ask."

"Did he say how their new offices are suiting them now that they've moved farther west?" she prompted.

Again he frowned and grimaced slightly. "Damned if I didn't neglect to ask. It's a shame you weren't with me, dear. You always remember those little things about everyone."

She laughed. "Then I won't ask how his new son-in-law is faring in the practice with him, shall I?" She took a spoonful of soup, an innocent smile on her face.

Lord Rupert wagged his finger at her. "Now perhaps I won't even tell you my news," he said in a mulish tone.

Grabbing his finger, she clasped it tightly in her hand and cooed, "Please, my Lord, don't make me beg."

Now it was his turn to turn a slight shade of red, as he glanced over to where the footman stood, then raised an eyebrow at her. She sat back, but grinned mischievously.

Clearing his throat, Rupert reached for a slice of warm bread and took a large bite. His mouth half full, he mumbled, "Add-addin iz an airz."

"What was that? I have no idea what you said."

"I said," he chewed past the mouthful of bread, "Hollis tells me our niece Madeline is already an heiress."

"What! Do tell."

"According to Hollis," he began, fishing in his soup bowl for more succulent pieces of lobster, "though she came to town for the reading of her father's will—which we both know, of course—it turns out she already stands to inherit her grandfather's estates as well."

"That is news. Though I'm not sure I know her exact relationship to the gentleman she calls Grandfather. No sons, then?"

"No. There are no sons. Hollis knew a little about it— evidently, the man adopted her as an infant. Found her on his doorstep, is the rumor, when her mother died." He mopped the remaining juices with his bread. "The man is quite wealthy. Keeps to himself in the country. Almost never seen in London. Believe Hollis said the gentleman made his fortune in trade as a young man, in the West Indies. Delicious bisque! Believe I will have more."

Glynnis contemplated. "Rupert, now I am even more determined that our niece should have a Season. And, she'll need a sponsor—a female relative. Don't you agree?"

"Wouldn't know. Don't believe in Seasons all that much myself. We didn't need a Season, after all, to get to know one another."

"Still, she is an heiress, and stands to inherit from both sides, it appears. Perhaps I should start corresponding with her grandfather. Surely he would see the necessity of seeing his ward properly introduced into society." Glynnis broke a roll. As she reached for her butter knife, she glanced at her husband. "Rupert, I think it would be great fun to escort Madeline, and to have her staying here as a guest during her entire Season. I should love to be her sponsor. What do you think, sir?"

"As long as those men don't ogle you, dearest. You're still young and beautiful—what if they think you're on the market?"

She laughed prettily. "I promise I'll just sit on the shelf with the other matrons, and give stern, no-nonsense stares."

"Are you making fun of me, my dear? You know I cannot help but be jealous."

"Well, Rupert, then I'll be sure to invite you to each and every recital and soiree."

"My mother is not in, Madeline. And I'm busy. What is it you need?"

Madeline sat rigidly on the settee in the Picketts' parlor as her sister swept into the room, impatient tone mirrored by her body. Madeline also did not fail to notice that Eleanor said "my mother." Not "our mother." Not "Mama." If there had been prior doubt of Madeline's birthright in this family, she'd forfeited any claims in the eyes of her sister and stepmother by choosing to desert them.

Sitting very still, Madeline inhaled as inconspicuously as possible. The fragrance was slight, but it was enough. Its familiarity was now certain.

"I came to see you, Eleanor, not our stepmother." She studied her sister's stance carefully, watching for any subtle revelations. "It is probably just as well she is not here—I can't imagine you'd want her to know about the invitation."

Eleanor didn't blink. "What invitation?"

Nice recovery, admitted Madeline. "The invitation you sent to me during Aunt Glynnis's party—to meet in the conservatory, Eleanor."

"I don't know what you're blathering about."

"Oh? I think you do. The smell of your perfume was on the letter. Did you think of that?"

"That's absurd," Eleanor said. "Lots of women wear similar

perfume. Even my mother wears this blend." Of a sudden she was back on solid ground. "And how would you know my handwriting?" Eleanor's smile was smug, as she drew out, "I've never written anything to you, sister."

Madeline flinched. She'd never heard Eleanor use the word *sister.* But the sibilance was evil. Madeline would not have been surprised to see a tiny forked tongue slither across Eleanor's lips as she uttered the endearment.

It shocked Madeline that such a beautiful word could be turned upside down and ugly by the twist of a mouth. She refused to show hurt. She'd not expected a confession, and certainly not an apology. She'd come to confirm the perfume, and had done so.

"Your jest about Mr. Jace Remington being a mesmerist was not funny either, Eleanor. But, at least it was not dangerous."

Eleanor strolled to the desk, picking up a paperweight. That smile again, but she aimed it at the inanimate object. Wouldn't give Madeline the courtesy of eye contact. "Is this all you came to say? As I said, I'm busy."

Madeline nodded her resignation, though Eleanor didn't look at her. "So. That's how it's to be between us."

"That's how it's to be."

"I will see you at the lawyer's in three days."

Eleanor closed her eyes and shrugged. "It matters not to me whether you are there or not."

Time to leave this house for good, thought Madeline. It could not get any worse.

She was wrong.

Madeline swept around the corner and into Emerson. She recoiled off his chest, but he reached out his hands and locked them onto her arms.

"Well, well, Miss Madeline. Throwing yourself at me again?"

"Remove your hands."

He slid his hands from her arms, slowly, a caress that matched his eyes as they slid down her neckline.

"You are despicable." Madeline breathed the last word in a forceful whisper.

"Ah, still playing your tigress games?" he whispered. "I told you I like that. I think you're the type who'd enjoy being tamed. Slowly." He reached out and touched a lock of hair.

Madeline stiffened, then saw his eyes look over her shoulder. He dropped his hand, and slid it into his pocket as he stepped past her and moved on.

Eleanor stood at the doorway watching.

CHAPTER TWENTY

Eleanor slouched further, folding her arms across her chest. "I don't want to hear about Emerson's gambling."

"Well, young lady, you are going to hear about it—when I think of how very embarrassed I was at cards today—I am so, so mortified. If that man were here in this room I swear I would give him a good sound slap across the face. How dare he make me the object of ridicule among my friends?"

"I'm the one engaged to him, Mama. If anyone would be ridiculed, it's me."

"Yes, you stupid girl, it's about time you realized that. We are both being talked about behind our backs, and all because of your fiancé."

"He's *your* cousin, Mama. You introduced—"

"And I rue that, believe me."

"But lots of men gamble. You said yourself that Papa was always off gambling."

"I did not learn of your father's gambling until after we were married."

"So, if—"

"And," Mrs. Pickett spoke loudly over Eleanor's interruption, "he never caused me embarrassment because of it. He only gambled at the Cocoa Tree, which is a respectable gentleman's lounge. While Emerson—and I had to hear this from Mrs. Hedgewich, that gossiping, two-faced biddy—Emerson is known to frequent very disreputable establishments."

Eleanor huffed, sinking lower into the couch and crossing her ankles. "All right, then. I'll talk to him. I'll tell him he must frequent the Cocoa Tree, or some other such gambling house."

"You're not listening to a word I'm saying! He is known to be suffering heavy losses. He's counting on your fortune to subsidize his habit, Eleanor. But men like that don't stop at losing a fortune. I *won't* visit my future grandchildren at the Fleet Street Prison. And, more importantly, I *won't* have my friends laughing at us behind our backs."

Eleanor pouted. "Very well, very well. I will tell Emerson he is not to gamble anymore. At all."

"No, you won't," said Mary Pickett. "You will tell Emerson you are crying off this engagement, is what you will tell him, Eleanor."

Eleanor screeched, and shot up to a sitting position. "No! I won't! You can't make me."

"Eleanor, either you will break this engagement, or I will break this engagement. But it will be broken. That is my final word."

Eleanor jumped up, wailing, and with a parting "I hate you!" she ran from the room.

CHAPTER TWENTY-ONE

"I don't understand," Madeline said, but there was no one to hear.

She stood in the middle of her bedroom, holding the small ivory sheet of paper in her hand. She read it again.

Miss Madeline,

Forgive my penmanship; I am writing this letter hastily, under duress. My dearest Eleanor is being blackmailed. I have not told her yet. You are aware of her weak heart? I fear the strain may kill her.

I know how important she is to you. If you love her as much as I believe you do, I beg your immediate help.

The blackmailer has agreed to meet with Eleanor and me, alone. I am hoping you will take Eleanor's place, as you could easily pass for her, if you cover your hair. We must find out what this person wants in exchange for silence.

I implore you—meet me at the Pork and Pigeon Inn, off Elderberry, as soon as you receive this. But you must tell no one. He threatens to disclose all if we are not alone.

I realize I have not been proper in my treatment of you; I beg your forgiveness, as we must now unite as family for Eleanor's sake.

Your sister's future happiness—nay, perhaps her very life— depends upon it.

Emerson Edwards, Esq.

What horrible scandal could Eleanor possibly be involved in? Was Mrs. Pickett aware? Or . . . perhaps it didn't involve Eleanor at all; perhaps it was something scandalous in Mary Pickett's past.

Madeline didn't know what to do.

Should she go to Mrs. Pickett? No. Her stepmother would not believe her. Mrs. Pickett wouldn't believe Eleanor capable of anything that would stain Eleanor's name or the family's.

Unless Mary Pickett already knew exactly why the blackmailer was threatening. But, if that were true, why was the blackmailer approaching the daughter, and not the mother?

Madeline glanced at the tiny porcelain watch pinned to her dress. By the time she could convince Mrs. Pickett—she'd show her Emerson's note—it might be too late.

She hadn't known of Eleanor's weak heart. The news brought tears to her eyes. She couldn't bear to think she'd finally found her sister, and now might lose her as they lost their mother. Had mother also had a weak heart? Was that why the journey to Grandfather's killed her?

No, they couldn't risk telling Eleanor.

How caring of Emerson to shield his fiancée from such horrible news. But for how long could they keep this from her? Would the blackmailer continue to return to their doorstep?

And should Eleanor find out someday . . . well, she already acted out her hatred for Madeline, in spite of the outing they had shared. What would Eleanor think about her sister's meddling? If Emerson and Madeline were not successful, would Eleanor accuse Madeline of driving the scandal to its conclusion? It didn't matter. Madeline knew she would risk everlasting hatred, if in doing so she could save her sister's reputation and perhaps her life. It was a small sacrifice to make for sisterly love.

She considered contacting Mr. Jace Remington. He would know what to do. But she couldn't tell anyone. Her instructions were most explicit. She must make this decision on her own.

Yes, she could disguise herself as Eleanor. Everyone claimed they looked like twins, except for their hair color. If Madeline were to hide her hair in a snood, and then wear a great cape tonight, the blackmailer would assume it was Eleanor, as Emerson suggested.

Madeline folded the note, then crossed the room to ring for her maid.

"Mrs. Cork, I . . . I've received distressing news. It's about my sister."

"About Miss Eleanor? What is it, miss?"

"I was told not to reveal it to *anyone*, Mrs. Cork."

"But surely you can trust me, child! I won't tell a soul. But you're so distressed. Are you all right? Is she ill?"

"Ill? Oh, no! But it is even more serious, Mrs. Cork. It is news that will surely ruin her reputation. It could even be life-threatening to her weak heart."

"Oh, dear! And her about to be married! How did you hear about it?"

"A note was just delivered. I'm beside myself, Mrs. Cork. There's a blackmailer involved." Madeline held up the folded paper. "This note insists I meet him tonight, at a tavern."

"No! Of course, you won't. It's too dangerous. Getting involved with blackmailers! Oh, no, no. Miss Madeline! You must tell Mr. Jace Remington at once. He'll know what to do."

Madeline rubbed her hands anxiously. "I wish I could, but I cannot."

"Where are you to meet at this late hour?"

"The Pork and Pigeon. The note says it's near Elderberry." Madeline made a decision. "Mrs. Cork, I am going to give you the note, but I must order you to hide it in your pocket."

Mrs. Cork reached for the note, then started to unfold the corner.

"No! Don't open it. I only want you to have it in case . . . in case anything should happen to me."

Mrs. Cork's eyes filled with tears. "No, miss. No. You can't go. Don't say—"

"I must, Mrs. Cork. Please don't try to talk me out of it. Time is of the essence. If I am not in time, I dare not think of the consequences for my sister." Madeline curled Mrs. Cork's fingers around the note. "Put it safely away, Mrs. Cork. And wish me Godspeed."

Mrs. Cork pulled at the neck of her uniform, and tucked the note into a secure spot within her bodice. "I'll guard it with my life, miss."

Madeline rushed to the wardrobe and grabbed a heavy maroon cloak.

Mrs. Cork sobbed. "Please don't go. Let's find Mr. Remington. Or Mr. Duncan."

Madeline had already donned the cloak, but visibly drooped. "I can't, Mrs. Cork. The note states that if anyone else should come, or find out about this, then the scandal will be revealed at once. I must find out what the blackmailer wants. Besides, I'll be with Mr. Edwards."

"Mr. Edwards! What does he have to do with this?"

"I can't stop to explain more, Mrs. Cork. But I promise I'll be back as quickly as I can." She opened the bedroom door, but turned. "Mrs. Cork?"

"Yes, miss?"

"If . . . if I should not return . . . please tell my sister Eleanor I love her."

Mrs. Cork wailed loudly now, but Madeline quickly left, closing the door against the tears.

Madeline shook with fear; she was close to crying herself.

Mrs. Cork's eyes were puffy and red as she yanked the door open. "Mr. Remington, Mr. Remington. I knew you'd come, sir."

"What is it, Mrs. Cork? Where's Madeline?" Jace looked around the entry. Not seeing her confirmed his greatest fear. "Is she sick?"

"No, sir. She's gone."

"What do you mean, gone? This late? Where did—"

"And I fear for her, Mr. Remington! I told her not to go. I begged, and warned her—"

"Mrs. Cork! Please! Where is she?"

"She left this note." Mrs. Cork reached into her apron pocket. "Wait. It must be in the other pocket." She groped deeply with her other hand and said, "Oh, dear."

"Just tell me!" roared Jace. "I don't have time to see the note. Don't you know what it said?"

"Yes . . . yes. You must go to the inn."

"What inn?" His eyes pleaded; she was pushing him to insanity.

"It was . . . yes, it was the Pork and Pigeon. Or, was it the Elderberry?"

He spun and grabbed the large oak door handle, almost knocking down the footman.

"Mr. Remington!" called Mrs. Cork.

"Yes?" He looked over his shoulder.

"I fear there is danger. I was told not to tell anyone, but there is a blackmailer!"

"I won't let anything happen to her, Mrs. Cork," he said in a growl.

She saw him disappear with speed amazing for a man his size.

As the carriage slowed to a stop in the inn's courtyard, Madeline kept her face averted from the lamps shining dimly through the coach's window.

The stable lad opened the door and handed her down onto wet flagstones. She hurried through the rain to the inn's entrance, her half-boots splashing through small puddles on the walkway. She slipped once, but caught her balance, remembering to grab the side of her hood so it would not slide down.

As she entered the large room, Madeline pulled the hood further forward, shadowing her face. She must make sure her hair didn't show, if she were to maintain the guise that she was Eleanor.

She spied a woman planted with an air of authority behind the polished bar, and hurried to her. "Please, I am to meet my—my fiancé, Mr. Edwards?"

The woman looked her up and down, and Madeline flushed. She was aware not having a maid with her made her appear most improper. However, the innkeeper's wife evidently saw more of this type of affair than interested her, for she sniffed with boredom and jerked a thumb toward the stairs.

"Mr. Edwards is in the second parlor on the left."

"Thank you," whispered Madeline, then ducked her head and hurried toward the stairs.

"Mr. Duncan, Mr. Duncan! I knew you'd come, sir." The last word broke on a sob, as Mrs. Cork grabbed the Scotsman by the arm, pulling him in the door.

He reached for her shoulder and she broke down crying, leaning against his large chest. He cocooned her in his hairy arms. "What is it, lass? What's wrong?" He looked around the entry. "Is it Miss Madeline?"

"She's gone! She's gone! And at this time of night! I fear for her, Mr. Duncan! I fear—"

"Stop ravin', woman! Where is she?"

"She left me this note." Mrs. Cork reached into her pocket. "Wait. It must be in this other pocket." She twisted her body round to reach deeply.

"Who did she go with? Why aren't ye with her?"

Mrs. Cork continued to fish in her large pocket. "She ordered me to stay and protect the note."

"Yer not makin' any sense, woman. Who is she with?"

"A blackmailer, Mr. Duncan! And, she said a life could be at stake." She looked incredulously as her hand came up empty.

"Forget the damned note. Do ye know where she went?"

"An inn. The Pork. And the Pigeon. The Pork and the Pigeon. And something about Elderberry."

Mrs. Cork looked up from her apron pocket, but Mr. Duncan was already halfway down the stairs.

"Mr. Duncan!" said Mrs. Cork, running out the door.

"What!" he roared, and she backed away.

"I fear foul play. I fear she will be abducted . . . again."

"Not on my watch."

She saw his kilt flying in the wake of giant steps.

"Mr. Remington! Thank you for coming, sir."

Bennett did not take off his hat or cloak. "I just got your note, Mrs. Cork. What is it? Is it Miss Madeline? Or Jace?" He looked around the empty entry.

"It's Miss Madeline, sir. She's gone."

"What do you mean? Where did she go, Mrs. Cork? Is my brother with her?"

"Oh, Mr. Remington, I can only hope he's found her by now. You see, she went to meet a blackmailer—"

"*What?* She left here on her own? Does Jace know about this?"

"Yes, yes, she went on her own. She left me this note." Mrs. Cork reached one hand in each pocket, fishing in frustration. "And, Mr. Jace came by, but then he flew out the door to follow her."

"Can you tell me where they went, Mrs. Cork? Don't worry about the note. Just tell me where they are."

"At an inn. The Elderberry."

"I'll go." He spun around.

"Wait! Pigs! Pigeons!"

"What?" He turned back.

"The inn! It's the Pork and the Pigeons. Or, the Pigeon and the Pigs."

"Right, Mrs. Cork. I'll find her, before . . . Well, I'll find her before anything happens. Don't worry."

Mrs. Cork grabbed his hand in both of hers. "You'll find her before the blackmailer harms her?"

"I was more worried about my brother's throttling her." At Mrs. Cork's look of horror he squeezed her hand. "Don't worry. I jest; of course he wouldn't harm your mistress."

Mrs. Cork did not look convinced. Now she had a new worry. Had she sent the wrong hero?

"Mrs. Cork! I must go. They could both be in danger."

"Of course. Thank you, sir. And . . . and Godspeed."

CHAPTER TWENTY-TWO

"Mr. Edwards! I came as quickly as I could." Madeline caught her breath from the dash up the stairs. "Has the blackmailer arrived?"

Emerson sat at a pine table occupying the center of the room. Behind him a fire was lit, but its paltry warmth failed to light every corner of the room adequately.

"No. Not yet, though he should have been here by now, and that makes me uneasy. Would you like a drink, cousin?"

Madeline observed several empty bottles on the table. He poured himself a full glass while waiting for her reply.

"No, thank you." She examined the small private dining parlor. Other than the table with its two chairs, little else filled the drab space: a set of worn shelves under the window, and a door that led to another room. A bedroom?

"Take off your cloak. Or, is it too cold? I can put more wood on the fire."

Madeline couldn't believe how relaxed he sounded. Was that a hint of a slur? She approached the table, pulling off her gloves. Yes, she could smell the liquor on his breath.

"What do we do, Mr. Edwards? Do we simply wait here until he arrives?" Madeline's voice was strained with tension. She looked at the remaining chair. "Shouldn't we call for another chair?"

"Of course. How could I have overlooked it? However, it's

just you and I at this time, so—you might as well sit and get comfortable."

She remained standing. "What can you tell me about this before the man arrives? Is it my sister who is being blackmailed for something in her past, or is our stepmother the object of the scandal?"

He considered her words, and took a half minute to answer her. "This is not Mrs. Pickett's scandal." He shook his head. "No, not hers at all. You'll soon learn enough about it."

"But don't you know anything? What if this man is making something up? Don't you have any idea of why he approached *you*, Mr. Edwards, instead of my sister or stepmother?"

She watched him look at his glass in surprise, as if wondering how it had become empty again. He picked up the bottle and swirled the liquid at its bottom, not looking up. Had he heard her? What was wrong with him? How could he be in his cups, when it was critical they keep their wits about them this night?

Emerson pushed back his chair, stood, and crossed to the door. "Let's see if he's nearby and listening." He opened the door and leaned out. He had to catch his balance by grabbing the doorjamb. "No. Not here yet." He slid the latch quietly. "Why don't you take off your cloak?"

"If I do, he will see the color of my hair." Madeline was confused. "Didn't you say I needed to disguise myself as Eleanor, Mr. Edwards?"

He laughed a short bark. "Oh, so I did. Forgot."

They both stood in silence.

"Do you think we missed him?"

"No." He looked at the fire as he spoke, as if she weren't even in the room. "I knew you'd come, Madeline."

"Please don't call me by my given name, Mr. Edwards." Even if he was drunk, she must maintain decorum, as ludicrous as it seemed.

He turned his head and leered. "Do you know why I knew you'd come? Because you're more honorable than Eleanor and her stepmother combined. And you've got spirit. I'd even wager you're enjoying this late-night adventure." He nodded appreciatively. "You're a woman with pluck."

Her skin crawled. "You're drunk, Mr. Edwards. Please remember yourself."

"Are you afraid of me, Madeline?"

"Of course not," she lied. "However, I must insist you call me Miss Madeline, sir."

"Don't you correct me. I'll call you as I please."

She flinched at his whiplash tone. She must change the subject. "How long do you think we shall be required to wait?"

"For what?"

"Mr. Edwards! Get hold of yourself. For the blackmailer, of course."

Of a sudden, his eyes focused. He watched her narrowly. "And what if I told you there was no blackmailer?"

"*What?* What are you talking about?"

"Perhaps the scandal is closer than you think. Here is a hint: it's not Eleanor. And it's not your stepmother."

"What are you saying?"

"Think of it, Madeline." Emerson wormed closer. "A young woman at an inn, unchaperoned. With a man who is not her husband. Sadly, she won't be home tonight. By the time they realize she is gone, she will have been compromised. An unfortunate tale, but it happens. Perhaps *you* are the cause of this family scandal, Madeline."

Madeline was thinking furiously. "Why would you jeopardize your engagement to my sister? I don't understand."

"So you haven't heard the news. I suspected not. Eleanor broke our engagement this afternoon."

Madeline started. "Then there truly is no blackmailer?"

"No. Just you and I, Madeline dearest."

Madeline spun to leave, but he grabbed her by the arm.

"Unhand me!" She pulled away, and he dropped her arm, but still he stood too near, blocking her path to escape.

"Don't you see?" His silky voice nauseated her. "You're the one who came to me, Madeline."

Her tightened throat made a whisper of her voice. "I came to save my sister."

"You know, I banked on that. You and your desperation to be accepted into the family. I knew you'd play the heroine and meet me here, perhaps even if you knew about the estrangement. Playing the role of a loving sister." He made it sound sordid.

"I do love her."

"No one can love Eleanor. I've tried. Just as Eleanor and her mother love no one except themselves." The corner of his mouth met his nostril in a sneer. "They'll never accept you as one of them. You know that, don't you?"

Her chin came up. "That's—that's not true. My sister and I just need time to get to know one another."

He barked. It was a nasty half laugh. "That's rich. Your sister despises you; and Mrs. Pickett despises you even more, if that's possible. You may be inheriting half the fortune, but they'll want you out of their lives after you see the lawyer, mark my words. You're a constant reminder of their financial loss."

Madeline glanced around. Her eyes wandered to the adjoining room. Would there be a lock on the door?

Emerson grinned, unfocused eyes staring at the table. "This will teach them both, with their airs. They think I'm not good enough to marry into the family. Won't they be shocked to find out I'm going to be a son-in-law anyway, once you and I are wed?"

"What—"

"The joke will be on Mrs. Pickett, when she finds out I get my half of the inheritance anyway, by marrying you."

"That's absurd. I would never marry you."

"Oh, I think you'll look at it differently by time you realize you've been compromised. And I don't mean by being away from home, unchaperoned, overnight with me, Madeline. I plan to compromise you truly well this night."

She shuddered, and took a step back. "My grandfather will kill you if you touch me."

"He may wish to, but when he realizes the situation, he'll insist we wed."

"No. He won't. You don't know him." She pleaded, "Mr. Edwards, my grandfather would never make me marry a man I didn't love."

"When you've been compromised, he'll be grasping at anything he can. I know these so-called country gentlemen. They won't want soiled goods dirtying up their parlor."

"No. You're wrong." She sidled toward the entry door, but he was there, blocking it, in three strides. She had hoped his reaction would be slowed by the drink.

"Don't even think about leaving, Madeline. If I have to tie you to the bed in the next room, I will." Emerson licked his already wet lips. "Well, well. Now that I think about it, it's an appealing idea, you know?"

He stalked her, and she moved behind the table.

Madeline played to his greed. "But . . . but I won't have any of the fortune, Mr. Edwards. I've already planned on disowning it, and leaving everything to Eleanor."

"But you won't!" He struck the heavy table loudly with an open palm. "You won't disown it, Madeline. And, as your husband, I won't allow it."

"I'm . . . I'm not Eleanor's true sister." Her only hope was to convince him there would be no inheritance.

His expression turned ugly. Doubt ran visibly across his face. "My cousin Jace vouched you were indeed the daughter of Harold and Jeannette Pickett."

"You heard me correctly, Mr. Edwards." She nailed him with a cold stare. "I lied. My true name is Madeline Halvering. I am the daughter of Adrian Halvering. Granddaughter of Sir Arthur Halvering. And Jeannette Pickett wasn't my mother."

Emerson looked confused and angry. His pinched red face had a lowered brow.

"You . . . you're an imposter! Is your sister Eleanor aware? No, not your sister. You're not related. That was all a ruse. You thought to take their money, exactly as they suspected."

She could see the gears turning in his pecuniary mind. He was only just realizing what he'd lost. A fortune—Eleanor's fortune, to be precise.

"Yes. I am an imposter. But no longer. There is nothing for me here. I won't ever come back to London again, Mr. Edwards. And I won't tell anyone you kidnapped me. I promise."

She could tell the moment he gave up the inheritance. But the game now had different stakes.

"I've wanted you all along, Madeline, since we first met. Eleanor is a dull little thing, but you—you have an aura that pulls me. It makes me want to fight that spirit within you, and dominate it."

She was having trouble breathing. *Please, please, don't let me faint,* she prayed.

She scanned the room for a weapon. The finely turned candleholder on the table looked too delicate to use in self-defense, and she didn't think she could wield a glass bottle at such close quarters. She spied the heavy tools tucked next to the hearth. Yes. She knew she'd get only one chance.

She must keep him talking; must somehow distract him. Shivering, she turned toward the fire. She pulled her cape closer and rubbed her hands together.

"Take off your cape."

"I . . . I can't. I'm too cold. Perhaps if we stoke the fire?" She inched closer to the chimney.

"Ah, yes. And while I do so, you'll run for the door? I think not. Let's tie your wrist to the chair first, and then I know you'll stay put like a good girl. I don't think you'll get too far with a chair bound to your wrist. Do you?"

He moved toward her, extracting a length of hemp from his pocket.

Madeline felt a bubbling in her throat, like bile. She would either scream or throw up. Too late to reach the poker, she must dash for one of the doors. Now.

Anticipating her rush, Emerson caught her cape and jerked her back into his arms. He grasped her from behind, and locked her in his arms like a vice. His side-whiskers tickled her jaw as he laid his head on her shoulder.

"You smell delectable, my dear Madeline. I am so looking forward to our long evening together." He kissed her ear, then her cheek. She struggled, but was locked in the steel bands of his embrace. He turned her toward his body, and she fought to avert her face from his. One hand pulled her tighter, and the other grasped her jaw roughly. He jerked her head to face his, and slid his sloppy lips across her mouth.

Through her silent scream, she heard a log crash in the fireplace. No. It was the wood around the latch splintering as it was kicked in. The door banged open against the wall. Emerson released her face, and she snapped it toward the entry, ready to scream for help.

Jace stood there. No carving of an avenging angel ever looked more fierce.

Madeline saw the look in Jace's eyes: hatred. Hatred of

everything he'd told her he despised: dishonor, greed, betrayal.

Her breathing became difficult, as Emerson snaked his arms tighter about her, crushing her lungs. Or perhaps her breathing had already stopped altogether, as the threads of Jace's hatred spun across the room and wound tightly about her heart, squeezing any remaining life.

How could he condemn her so quickly? She'd grown to trust him as a friend and confidante, yet he could believe the worst of her: that she was stealing her sister's fiancé.

"Jace." She could barely speak. She must explain. And quickly.

Jace turned his stare from his cousin to her. He opened his mouth to speak. And he was jerked back violently, a marionette on the strings of a giant puppet master.

"You!" roared Duncan, with one huge fist wrapped in Jace's coat. "I should have known!"

He swung Jace around, and planted a solid blow to his temple. Madeline screamed.

"Mr. Duncan! *No!*" She broke free from Emerson's hold and ran across the room, but it was too late. Jace dropped like a rock to the floor.

"Are ye all right, lass?" asked Duncan. He reached out his arms, a welcoming tree.

Madeline stumbled into the protective arbor. Nodding her head "yes" against his broad chest, she choked back a sob. "Thank you for coming, Mr. Duncan."

Her head snapped back and she looked up to the giant. "Oh, but you've got the wrong man! It wasn't Mr. Remington this time; it was . . ." She spun around, her finger like a compass that couldn't find north. Emerson was nowhere to be seen.

"But he's the lad who kidnapped ye before," Duncan said.

"Yes, yes, but you know he apologized for that, Mr. Duncan." The big man grunted.

"Truly. This time it was his cousin, Mr. Edwards. Emerson

Edwards. But . . ." She looked around again, as if he might materialize from under a table, but he did not. "He's gone."

"His cousin, did ye say?" repeated Duncan.

"Aye," Madeline answered, absentmindedly imitating the Scotsman.

"Well. That's quite a determined family," was all that Duncan could add.

Madeline was weak and nauseated. She'd barely averted a harrowing situation with Mr. Edwards. She couldn't think about it. If she did, she would faint. She fought the dizziness and focused on Mr. Duncan's solid arm supporting her.

Jace's face was turned toward her accusingly, but thankfully his eyes were closed. She could still see his look of hatred and disgust, as if it were a permanent mask lying transparently over his face.

Blood trickled down his face, joining the red rivulet from his bleeding lip; she watched the shallow rise of his dark vest. He wasn't dead.

But she was. Inside. Part of her wanted to kneel next to him and clean the blood gently from his face. But she was afraid. He might wake up, and the mask would come alive again—that mask of contempt. A knot of ice sat in the pit of her stomach, its cold entrapping her heart. Wiping tears she hadn't even known had fallen, she turned and put a hand on Mr. Duncan's arm to steady herself.

"Are ye sure yer fine, lass?" The big man anchored an arm about her waist. "Ye don't look too steady. Yer pale. Let me get ye some smellin' salts, or a mug of ale."

"No," she said in a soft voice. "Just take me home, Mr. Duncan. Home to Grandfather. Please."

She smeared the wetness where her tears ran onto her upper lip, and wiped her nose with her hand.

Duncan half carried her along, out the door to the coach.

Bennett jostled through the crowd of revelers at the noisy inn. He leaned forward on the bar, interrupting a discussion between the innkeeper's wife and a portly guest inquiring about dinner options.

"I beg your pardon, please. There was a young blond woman who arrived to meet with a gentleman?"

The bored woman finished her menu-bargaining with the customer, and then turned slowly to Bennett.

"Yes. Seems everyone wants to join that party. Must be a lively one." She winked lewdly. "Up the stairs; second door on yer left."

Bennett took the stairs two at a time.

The upstairs hallway was forebodingly quiet, after the noisy barroom downstairs. He walked softly to the door and found it slightly ajar and in need of repair. Peering through the narrow crack, all he could see was the glow of firelight. No voices were heard. He pushed gently. The door barely squeaked as it edged open.

"Miss Madeline?" he called softly, pushing the door wide.

Bennett slid into the room, but saw no one. Until he almost tripped upon his brother's body.

"Jace!" His brother's face was striped with rivulets of blood. Alarmed, Bennett dropped to a knee and put his fingertips against Jace's neck. A pulse. His eyes closed briefly as he slumped with relief.

"Jace, it's me. Bennett. Jace . . . Jace, are you all right?" He put his hand on Jace's shoulder and gave it a soft shake.

Jace's eyelids opened, and his eyes rolled as he struggled to focus. "Madeline?" It was all he could croak.

"It's Bennett." Bennett shook his head. "Madeline's not here, Jace. What's happened? Do you know where she is?"

Jace struggled to sit. "I saw her. When I first arrived. Just before I was knocked out."

Bennett supported his brother as Jace raised himself on one elbow. "Did the blackmailer do this to you? Madeline's maid mentioned a blackmailer. Was he armed? Do you think the blackmailer has her?"

"I . . . no, I don't think so." Jace touched the side of his face.

"Then who did this? Did the man have an accomplice?"

"No. At least . . . it felt like that damned Scotsman. It appears I've become his personal punching bag."

"That Duncan fellow? What was he doing here? And, why were you here? I'm confused." Bennett shook his head again. "Mrs. Cork said Madeline was in danger. Come to think of it, I'm sure she didn't mention anything about Duncan being here."

Jace swiped an arm across his bloody lip, but winced and swore. "And I don't suppose she told you Cousin Emerson was here either?" he asked in a dry tone.

"Emerson? The devil you say."

"Very appropriate, brother," Jace said as he rolled onto hands and knees. "That devil abducted Madeline against her will."

Bennett reached under his older brother's arms, and aided him in coming to his feet. "Are you steady? Can you stand?"

"I'm fine. Thanks."

"Abducted her, did you say? Our cousin abducted Miss Pickett?"

Jace dusted off his body. "Yes," he said with disgust. "At least, that's how it appeared. As I entered the room it was obvious she was struggling against his grasp. Though why the bird-brained Miss Pickett was here unescorted is still a mystery I expect to get to the bottom of."

"Abducted," mused Bennett. "Damn, what is it about our family and kidnapping Miss Pickett?"

Jace smacked him on his arm. "Don't. Don't pursue that, brother."

Bennett smothered his smile behind a fist, and helped Jace limp from the inn.

CHAPTER TWENTY-THREE

Duncan delivered a disheveled Madeline to her aunt's home within the hour. He opened the coach door, setting the step. His face mirrored his concern at seeing her pale face.

"Would ye prefer to rest a moment? I can go fetch Mrs. Cork, lass."

Madeline sat quite still, as lifeless as the blanket she clutched on her lap. When he moved to leave the carriage, she stirred.

"No, please don't bother, Mr. Duncan. I'll be fine." Her trembling belied her calm voice. She rose and stepped down from the carriage.

He took her hand in one of his, and placed his other on her elbow, assisting her as if she were made of porcelain. "Now, take yer time. There's no rush." He took hobbling small steps with his large feet. If Madeline hadn't been so miserable, she might have laughed at the sight.

The entry door was thrown open, and Aunt Glynnis came flying down the steps, barely touching the brick pavers.

"Madeline! Oh, Madeline, are you all right?" She ran to Madeline and clenched her, wetting her niece with her tears. This broke the dam of Madeline's reserve.

"Oh, Aunt Glynnis." Madeline buried her face in her aunt's shoulder. "I've been so foolish."

"Hush, dear." Glynnis held her close, but studied Duncan over her niece's head. "Mr. Duncan . . . is Madeline . . . was she . . . is she . . . unharmed?"

"Yes, ma'am. I arrived just in time. I ran into a scoundrel I recognized, so I cold-cocked him. But it weren't him this time. It were his cousin. And the coward ran away."

"Whose cousin?"

"Mr. Remington's cousin." Madeline's voice was muffled against her aunt's shoulder.

"Do you mean Bennett? That nice young man you told me about, Madeline?" Glynnis was clearly shocked.

"No." Madeline lifted her head. "No, it wasn't Mr. Bennett. Bennett is Jace's brother." Madeline wiped her eyes. "It was *their* cousin who was behind this. Mr. Edwards."

Glynnis gasped. "You cannot mean Emerson? Eleanor's fiancé?"

"Yes. Emerson."

"But . . ." Duncan stammered out the word. "Shouldn't we notify the authorities? Before this Mr. Edwards gets too far?"

Madeline turned to explain to her aunt. "He slipped out when Mr. Duncan . . . um . . . socked Mr. Remington."

"Socked Mr. Remington!" echoed Glynnis. "Mr. Bennett Remington?"

"No. It was Jace he . . . socked," supplied Madeline.

"Oh, my!" Her aunt Glynnis looked around. "I cannot believe we're standing in the courtyard discussing this. Come inside, please, where it's warm."

Glynnis wrapped an arm around her niece and turned her toward the manor. Duncan hesitated, but Glynnis looped her other hand around his tree-trunk of an arm, and tugged him along. "You, too, Mr. Duncan. I'm sure you could use a drink. I certainly could."

The trio trudged toward the open door, just as Mrs. Cork came flying down the steps, shrieking happily. They proceeded into the parlor, Mrs. Cork fussing busily about her mistress.

"Shall I see about some tea, ma'am?" Mrs. Cork looked at

Glynnis as they eased Madeline onto the settee.

"That would be wonderful, Mrs. Cork. And brandy as well, please."

Madeline was visibly reviving by the minute. "But, Mr. Duncan, how did you know where I was?"

Duncan looked over at Mrs. Cork, who coughed and muttered, "I'll just see about that tea," as she scooted out the door.

"Of course. I told Mrs. Cork about the note." Madeline closed her eyes in relief. "Though I also instructed her to tell no one. Thank goodness she ignored me, as usual."

"Aye. That Mrs. Cork is a treasure of a woman," said Duncan, contemplating the empty doorway.

Madeline's eyes met her aunt's, and both raised eyebrows. *Well,* thought Madeline, *we shall remember that tidbit for discussion with a future tea.*

"Madeline, tell me everything," encouraged her aunt. "Oh, I wish Rupert were here. He'd know what we should do about that awful Mr. Edwards."

"I know what I'd do with him," swore Duncan. "I'm only sorry I didn't get my hands on the right man."

"Oh, yes. And what of Mr. Jace Remington?"

Mrs. Cork bustled back in. "Sorry to interrupt, my Lady. Just wanted to let you know the tea is on its way."

"Thank you, Mrs. Cork." Glynnis turned again to Madeline. "But I don't understand. How was it Mr. Jace Remington came to be there as well?" Answering her own question, Glynnis turned back to Mrs. Cork, who stood in the doorway, watching with round, innocent eyes.

Duncan and Madeline also turned questioning looks upon Madeline's maid.

"Why don't I just fetch that drink for Mr. Duncan?" she suggested, her voice trailing off as she hurried away down the hall.

Glynnis and Madeline laughed tiny laughs of relief.

"Thank goodness for Mrs. Cork." Madeline's lips curved up. "I'm so glad I told her not to tell a soul."

Mrs. Cork came back in, following the butler with the tea set. She carried a silver tray with brandy snifters, and set it on a credenza.

"Mrs. Cork, did you tell anyone else besides Mr. Duncan and Mr. Remington?" Madeline asked.

Mrs. Cork busied herself with the drinks. "Uh . . . well, now, which Mr. Remington would you be referring to?"

"Are you saying you told *both* Mr. Remingtons? Jace *and* Bennett?"

Mrs. Cork kept her back to Madeline, concentrating on pouring brandy as if her job depended on it. "It might have slipped out, miss." She turned and blurted out, "I was so afraid for you!"

Madeline got up and moved quickly toward her maid. "Thank you, Mrs. Cork." She had to stoop a bit to hug the shorter woman. "Thank you so very much. You saved my life."

Mrs. Cork hugged her back, and then leaned away so she could pull her handkerchief from her apron pocket. She was wiping her eyes as she crossed to the door, but her steps faltered when she reached the Scotsman. She hesitated, then grabbed his large hand in both of hers.

"Thank you for rescuing her, Mr. Duncan. You're a true hero."

"And yer a brave lass as well, Mrs. Cork."

She turned red and hurried from the room.

"You say Emerson broke off his engagement with Eleanor?" Glynnis leaned forward, gently swirling the brandy in her glass.

"I believe he said Eleanor is the one who broke the engagement."

Glynnis shook her head. "I still can't believe his outlandish behavior. He appeared to be such a milque-toast of a gentleman. But I did not like something about him from the moment I first met him in the Pickett library with you."

"I . . . I should have been honest with you earlier, aunt." Madeline looked down at her interlaced fingers, and then back up. "May I have a glass of brandy?"

"Oh! Of course. I didn't even think to offer you one, Madeline. I don't think we should stand upon the propriety of age. Especially after what you've been through."

Duncan was up and pouring a generous amount into a third snifter. It amused Madeline that it took him only three giant steps to reach her.

"Thank you." She swallowed and made a face, but ducked her chin and forced herself to swallow a second time. "Ooh, it's warm." Her eyes widened. "I can feel it moving down my throat. What a delightful sensation."

"Well, wait until Rupert hears I've made a drunkard of my niece. Go on, Madeline, you were about to say?"

"I'm ashamed I did not confide in you sooner, aunt. The day you came to see me at my stepmother's house . . . well, I can't tell you how relieved I was to have you enter. You see, Mr. Edwards had just made a rather . . . inappropriate . . . advance."

"The devil he did!" thundered Duncan.

"Child, why ever didn't you say so?"

"I . . . I don't know. Part of me was embarrassed—"

"Why so?"

"I was afraid you might not believe me. Or worse, you might not want me to come visit, if you suspected I was a loose woman."

Glynnis reached over and picked up Madeline's hand. "Oh, dear, I'm so sorry. How frightening for you."

"Also," Madeline continued, "he's Eleanor's fiancé. I mean, he *was* Eleanor's fiancé. I didn't want her to know. I didn't know if you would tell Mrs. Pickett."

"Certainly one of my closest confidantes." Glynnis smiled to make a lie of the words. "But I suppose you and I know each other well enough by now for you to have guessed."

"I'm sorry I didn't trust you sooner."

"Nonsense," Glynnis said. "I am sure I would have done the same in your situation, Madeline." She peered closely at her niece. "Madeline, did he . . . did he harm you . . . in any way?"

Madeline could see her aunt was embarrassed even to phrase the question. And Duncan moved to the edge of the chair, a tiger ready to pounce should Madeline but say the word.

"No." She closed her eyes. "Fortunately, neither then nor this time was he able to carry through his vile threats."

"But . . . if he had accosted you in the past, why did you agree to join him at the inn?"

"That was very stupid on my part. Very stupid. He sent a note saying my sister was being blackmailed. If we were to save Eleanor's reputation, he wrote that we must meet with the blackmailer." Madeline looked at Duncan and her aunt, anticipating their next question. "He said Eleanor mustn't know, because of her weak heart."

"What? That's poppycock. That child has an iron constitution. The only thing sturdier than her heart is her stomach."

"I didn't know." Madeline couldn't seem to stop shaking her head in self-disgust. "As I said, it was very stupid of me."

"No, Madeline. Stop." Glynnis gave her hand an extra squeeze. "It was very noble of you. Very. And I shan't hear another word of self-blame. Do you understand?"

Madeline nodded slowly.

Duncan stood to take his leave, and said, "I'll be back in the mornin', Miss Madeline, when yer packed."

"Packed?" a slight hysteria made the word come out as a squeak from Aunt Glynnis.

"I told Duncan I'm ready to go home, aunt." Madeline

looked down again, picturing the scene with Jace at the inn.

"Let's discuss this, shall we?" Glynnis rose, and took Duncan's elbow as she walked him to the door. In a low voice, she said, "Mr. Duncan, I'd like to talk to Madeline about staying. Shall we give you an answer late tomorrow morning?"

Duncan looked over his shoulder at Madeline. She hadn't heard them. Her head was hanging. "Yes, perhaps ye can cheer her up, my Lady."

"I'll try," whispered Glynnis. "Thank you for bringing her home, Mr. Duncan."

He bowed. Closing the parlor door behind him, he left the two ladies alone.

"Madeline." Glynnis spoke her niece's name gently, determined to tackle Madeline's low spirits.

"Yes?" Madeline looked up. Her eyes looked haunted.

"What haven't you told me, dear? Do you swear that evil Mr. Edwards did not touch you?"

"Yes." Madeline nodded distractedly. "I swear it."

"Then, what is wrong? It's obvious something is still weighing heavily on your heart."

Madeline smiled ruefully. "Yes, you have that right. It is my heart. I fear it broke tonight."

Glynnis waited for her niece to continue.

Madeline stood and drifted to the fireplace. "I have lately come to the realization that I have feelings for Mr. Remington. Mr. Jace Remington, that is," she hastily added.

She paced back toward Glynnis. "But he hates me, Aunt Glynnis. And I don't know if I can bear it that my heart is so full for him, but he looks at me with such contempt."

"But, Madeline, every time he has been here to visit, I have remarked to Rupert how very companionable the two of you are. Really, dear, I would even say well suited, if you must know. One can't fail to notice the gleam in Mr. Jace Remington's eyes when he watches you."

Madeline shook her head sadly, in denial. "Oh, aunt, if only you'd seen him tonight at the inn. When he walked in and saw me in Mr. Edwards' arms . . ." She shuddered. "I've never seen such a horrid look of disgust. He despises me. He must have believed I was returning Mr. Edwards' affection. Or, perhaps he believed I was betraying my sister Eleanor." Madeline put her hands over her face.

Glynnis rose and went to comfort her niece. Both women stood in the center of the carpet as Madeline's shoulders shook with her soundless crying. Glynnis eased her back to the couch, and they sat together.

"Perhaps if you talk to him, and explain?" her aunt asked.

Madeline shook her head remorsefully.

"Madeline, don't leave. Not like this. Stay with Rupert and me, and let yourself heal."

Madeline stopped crying, and wiped her swollen face. "I don't know. I think I want to go home." She saw that her words had stung her aunt. "I'm sorry. How rude of me. I know you've made this a second home for me, Aunt Glynnis, and I love you and Uncle Rupert for that. But I think I want to go home to Grandfather. I miss him, and I worry about his health. I want to see him getting better every day. If I stay here, in town, I'll see reminders of Mr. Remington everywhere."

"I understand, dear." Glynnis sat up at a recollection. "But, when is the reading of the will scheduled? Isn't it coming up shortly?"

"Yes. In two more days. But I no longer care about that, Aunt Glynnis."

"Listen to me, Madeline. You're worn out right now, emotionally and physically. You need to sleep on this. I think you should stay, just for the reading of the will. I'll accompany you, if that would help. And you can leave immediately afterward. I won't try to keep you, as much as I'd love to have you with me longer. Recall what you told me. You said your dream is that your mother may have left a token for you. Don't cheat yourself of that, Madeline."

Madeline sniffed, but sat up straighter. "You're right, aunt. Yes." She nodded to herself. "I'll go through with it."

To Glynnis, it sounded as if Madeline forced a false note of determination in her voice. But Glynnis chose to say nothing more. In her heart, she believed it would be best for Madeline to appear at the lawyer's office.

Madeline took a deep breath as she stood looking up at her stepmother's house. Gresham Park held nothing but bad memories. Its gaping shutters laughed at her. To think she'd thought to find a loving family here.

She approached the door as a criminal would approach the gallows. It was time to let Eleanor know about Emerson's plot the previous night. But if they were no longer engaged, did she need to inform her sister? *Yes,* said her conscience. *If he tried that with you, he might do the same to her: kidnap her, and have her as wife after she'd been compromised.* Eleanor needed to be warned of the possible danger.

Madeline knocked at the door, hoping to dispatch this duty quickly. The footman went off to find Eleanor, then returned and instructed Madeline she was to wait in the lilac parlor. Madeline remembered this room. It was drafty, furnished poorly—the room where Mrs. Pickett met undesirable guests.

"You wished to speak to me?" Eleanor's voice clearly gave the answer as well: I don't wish to speak to *you.*

The cold room became colder with her sister's frosty entrance. Madeline shivered and wrapped her arms about herself. "Eleanor, how are you?"

"What do you care? You now live with our aunt Glynnis."

"That's not fair, Eleanor. You know our stepmother has no desire to have me under her roof. I'm sure it pleased her to have me take Aunt Glynnis's offer. And it does not prevent you and me from visiting with one another."

"Obviously. You are here, aren't you?"

This would not be easy. Eleanor was already in a snippy mood. Of course, she was always irritable when she first woke. Perhaps Madeline should return later. "Am I calling too early, Eleanor?"

"No. And whatever is that supposed to mean? Are you criticizing my morning outfit? My hair?"

"Oh, no!" Good Lord, Eleanor probably hadn't had her hot chocolate yet. Madeline definitely should have called later. "Have you had your morning chocolate?"

"If you would like refreshments, Madeline, say so. Stop beating about the bush. That is most annoying."

Yes, her sister definitely needed a relaxing, hot drink. "You are so right. Could we please ring for some chocolate, Eleanor?" *And, a little sherry to dump into yours as well?*

"Very well." Eleanor picked up the silver bell at her elbow and swung it vigorously. A servant was soon dispatched to the kitchen.

"May I sit?" Madeline asked.

Eleanor was already seated on the chintz armchair, and waved a hand impatiently toward a chair. Madeline took a seat, and returned her sister's stare. She'd rehearsed what she would say the entire drive here, but the rehearsed words took wing and flew out the window and out of her memory.

Eleanor drummed her fingers on the wooden arm frame.

"I . . . I don't suppose you know why I'm here, but . . . there was a rather startling incident last night." Madeline watched for any sign that Eleanor might already know about the evening's events.

Eleanor continued to stare, two blank eyes already unfocused in their boredom.

"I received a letter last night." Madeline unpinned her chip bonnet, and placed it on her lap. "The letter implied you were in trouble."

"I was in trouble?" The disbelief was clear in Eleanor's voice.

"Yes. I didn't know at the time that the letter was a trick. You weren't in trouble, of course." Madeline began twisting the blue ribbons of her bonnet. "But I was worried about you."

Eleanor lowered her eyelids, to look disinterestedly at a spot beneath Madeline's chair.

"The letter informed me that a blackmailer had some information about you—"

"That's preposterous."

"I . . . please, Eleanor, let me finish. Though you are correct. Now that I am telling you, it does sound impossibly ludicrous." Madeline found her mouth twisting in an acknowledgement of humour she certainly didn't feel. "The author of the letter said that a blackmailer had information about you, and if I were to meet with the blackmailer, then perhaps your reputation could be spared."

"You are offending me more and more by the minute. You imply that you assumed the worst of me. You were ready to believe I had a scandal hidden in my closet."

"I'm sorry." Madeline ducked her chin in chagrin. "Yes, I see that is how it is sounding, Eleanor. I'm ashamed, but . . . I didn't know. I simply wanted to help you, to protect you."

"So . . ." Eleanor focused her gaze on Madeline. "Continue. This is actually more entertaining than the latest serial in Mama's papers."

Madeline blushed. She felt a fool. How differently the world looked in the morning light. "Well, to sum up this tale, I was foolish enough to believe you were at risk, and then I was foolish enough to make the rendezvous—"

"With whom? Exactly who was waiting for you to appear?"

Madeline closed her eyes, so as not to see her sister's expression. "Mr. Edwards."

"Emerson! My Emerson, my fian—" Eleanor caught the word about to fly from her lips, and snapped them shut like a purse. "You are telling me . . ." Her pursed mouth had a decided down-curve. "You expect me to believe that my—that Emerson sent that note to you about a blackmailer?"

"It's a fact, Eleanor."

"I don't believe you."

"It doesn't signify whether you believe it. The truth is I received a note from—"

"Show me."

"I beg your pardon?"

"Show me the note. Surely you have it? Surely you brought it?"

Madeline flushed again, and began stammering. "No. No, I didn't. I gave it to Mrs. Cork."

"Of course. That's what I would have done with a blackmail note," drawled Eleanor. "Give it to the maid."

"Eleanor! Please. There is a reason I am telling you this."

Eleanor forced a yawn. "I hope so. Oh, here are our beverages. Do hold your story." She turned to the pastries and chocolate with three times the enthusiasm she had shown thus far.

Madeline sagged with defeat. Perhaps she should leave now, before Eleanor was told the worst of the tale. She resignedly took the cup of chocolate that was handed to her.

Without taking a sip, she set it down on the side table. "Eleanor, it gets worse."

Eleanor watched the maid leave before she answered. "What could possibly be worse than my Emerson sending you a letter to meet a blackmailer?"

"There was no blackmailer."

"Of course not. I already told you there could not be."

"Emerson sent the note to lure me to the inn."

Silence.

Madeline continued. "He wished to compromise me, Eleanor."

Eleanor screeched. "How dare you!"

"Is it true you broke the engagement?"

"How would you know?"

"I am trying to tell you. I met with Emerson last night. He told me you had broken the engagement."

"Mama made me break it, if you must know. I suppose everyone will soon be aware of it, and I shall be a laughingstock."

"Why did she make you break it?"

"That's none of your business, Madeline," her sister warned.

Madeline picked up her cup and took a sip, debating if she should pursue the reason, but discarded that path. "All right. I don't need to know. But Emerson was very angry about it. Very resentful. And I believe he was using me to get his revenge."

"That's absurd. Emerson is a gentleman—was a gentleman—I mean, of course he is still a gentleman."

"No, Eleanor. He's not. He's the worst sort of man. He planned to compromise me, and to force me to wed him. He believed that by doing so he would get half of the inheritance you cheated him out of by breaking your engagement."

"I think you should leave." Eleanor's voice dripped ice.

"But you must hear me out."

"You tried to steal Emerson away from me."

Madeline was puzzled. "I thought you were no longer engaged."

"So you admit you couldn't wait to snatch him from me."

"Eleanor, wait. Emerson is the one who kidnapped *me*."

"You said you met him at the inn. That hardly sounds like a kidnapping to me, Madeline."

"I told you, he lured me to the inn. He made me believe *you* were in danger."

"Mmm . . . And you expect me—"

"Damn you, Eleanor!" Madeline slammed her cup onto the table, and saw Eleanor jump. "I don't give a ripe fig whether you believe this, but I came to tell you that Emerson may try to abduct you as well. He is angry, he is desperate, and that makes him dangerous." Madeline stood. "So be careful." She shoved her bonnet over her curls. "That's all I came to say, Eleanor. Just be careful."

Her hands were busy tying the ribbons in a hasty bow, but paused at Eleanor's cold accusation.

"You tried to steal Emerson. Just as you've stolen every other person I've cared for."

Madeline tilted her head to the side. "What are you talking about?"

Eleanor stood and brushed imaginary crumbs from her skirts. Without looking up, she said, in a choked voice, "Just go away."

Yes. It was past time to leave. This would most likely be the last conversation she'd have with Eleanor . . . with her sister. They'd sit in the lawyer's office together, but Madeline knew they wouldn't talk. Eleanor would snub her, as she'd done that very first day. Eleanor disliked her, and Madeline still didn't understand why.

She'd seen softness on occasion in her sister, when Eleanor was with Emerson, or when Mr. Bennett Remington teased her. And their day at Vauxhall together. Yes, she could be soft. In fact, when Eleanor chose to be gruff, it didn't sound natural. It sounded more like their stepmother's voice, a parroting of Mrs. Pickett's opinions and attitudes.

But Madeline saw no softness toward herself. She gazed at

her sister, to capture this one last memory. As if to foil her, Eleanor turned to the window, her back firmly to Madeline, her arms folded. She'd already closed the door of her mind on Madeline. She'd already shut her firmly out of the rest of her life.

Madeline spoke her thoughts aloud, unaware why she did so. "Why do you hate me so? Just tell me that before I go, Eleanor. What have I done to earn such hatred? All I wanted was a sister. Why?"

"Oh, please. Don't act the martyr. And don't play ignorant. It turns my stomach."

"But I'd never met you until this month. It's as if you've always hated me." Madeline heard the whine in her own voice. She couldn't help it. She was so frustrated, and now she would leave, never knowing the truth.

Eleanor wrapped her arms tightly about herself. She studied the wisteria vine outside the window, refusing to turn and face her visitor.

Madeline blew out a loud sigh, picked up her reticule, and wrapped her shawl about her shoulders. She looked at the stony back Eleanor turned to her. "Good-bye, sister. I'm sorry. I do love you, whether you like it or not. I love you, and I'm sorry for whatever I did to you." She moved toward the door, and heard a soft sob.

"Why? Why did she pick you?" asked a small voice.

Madeline paused. "What?"

"Why didn't she take me? Why did our mother pick you? I hate you."

Madeline stood frozen. "What do you mean? Why did our mother pick me? For what? I don't know what you're talking about."

Eleanor turned a red face to Madeline. Tears spilled from her eyes. "Why did she take you instead of me, Madeline? Why didn't she want *me* with her?"

It struck Madeline then. How could she not have guessed? Eleanor hated her because Lady Jeannette took one child with her. Only one. Eleanor had been deserted by their mother, who took baby Madeline with her when she made her escape to the country.

"Eleanor, she was coming back for you. She was coming back to get you, and to take you away, too."

"That's a lie."

"No. No, it's not. I swear it's true," said Madeline, moving back into the room.

"Mama told me. She told me Father confided that our mother didn't want me. Our mother didn't want *me*," she repeated the ugly words she'd obviously been told so many times.

"No! Eleanor, that's not true. Our mother talked to Grandfather the night before she died. That's not what she said. That's not what he told me."

Eleanor's shoulders collapsed. "Tell me. I need to know. Before you leave. Tell me what she said . . . what our mother said to your grandfather."

Madeline took slow steps, setting her reticule back on the chair.

She began the story, the story that seemed like a fairy tale. "Our mother was escaping to save my life, Eleanor. You see, Harold Pickett was not my real father. Mother fell in love with another man. His name was Adrian Halvering, and he was my grandfather's only son.

"Our mother claims that Harold Pickett killed Adrian, but it was never proven. Harold Pickett threatened to murder me if I was not his child. When mother realized the truth—she discovered I had my father's white-blond hair—she ran away.

"She planned to leave me with my grandfather, Adrian's

233

father. And then she was coming back to you. She told Grandfather that after I was safely hidden away, she was coming back here. To you. That means she would desert *me*. She chose *you*, Eleanor. Grandfather said our mother was devastated at the idea of leaving you behind. It killed her, Eleanor. It wasn't only the journey that killed her. She could not bear the thought she'd left you alone."

Eleanor's tears were streaming, and she buried her face in her hands to try to stop them. Perhaps to hide her sorrow. Perhaps to hide her relief?

Madeline continued. "I'm sorry you never knew this, Eleanor. I should have told you when I first met you. I . . . I wanted to find my sister so badly. I didn't think of your needs, only mine." Madeline took another step closer to Eleanor, whose face was still buried in her hands. "I'm so sorry our mother was never able to come back for you, Eleanor. She wanted to. She wanted to come back, Eleanor, but she died."

Madeline began to cry also as she confided her own sorrows. "I never knew our mother, Eleanor. At least you knew her for a few years. You had her to yourself. You got to know her voice, her face. Her touch. She was sending me away to live with my grandfather, but she was coming back to you. And she died, trying to save me. I'm so sorry."

Madeline reached out a tentative hand to her sister's shoulder. Eleanor didn't shrug it off, but leaned in to Madeline. The sisters held one another, rocking together as Madeline stroked Eleanor's back, soothingly repeating, "I'm sorry. I'm so sorry, Eleanor. Mother loved you. I love you. You're my sister."

Chapter Twenty-Four

Mr. Bartlestaff, of Redigen, Bartlestaff and Porter, cleared his throat. "I believe all concerned parties are here, and we may get started."

Mary Pickett sat on the couch next to her daughter Eleanor.

Madeline sat in the matching armchair facing them. She now regretted not taking up her aunt's offer of accompaniment. This morning it had seemed a simple matter to attend the appointment alone, but Madeline was no longer feeling so brave.

"We are here to review legal proceedings pertaining to the death of Harold Aloysius Pickett." Mr. Bartlestaff peered over the top of his half spectacles. "Mrs. Mary Marple Pickett?"

Mrs. Pickett made a disgusting sound. "You know who I am, sir. We've met before."

"Indeed. I recall that with distinct pleasure, madam." He turned his head slightly, and Eleanor was in the scope of his gaze. "Miss Eleanor Harriet Pickett?"

Mary Pickett elbowed Eleanor, who sat up and raised her hand in the air. Mr. Bartlestaff then turned to Madeline. She couldn't see his eyes, for the bright morning light glinted off the small spectacles.

"Miss Madeline Elizabeth Pickett?"

Madeline nodded. "Yes, sir. I am Madeline."

Mr. Bartlestaff nodded twice. "I see your mother in you, Miss Madeline. This office remembers her with fondness. Her father was a friend of—"

"How interesting. But we're not here to discuss the former Mrs. Harold Pickett." Mary Pickett concentrated on rearranging her skirts. "*I* am Mrs. Harold Pickett, and I'd like to get this business done with. That is . . ." She skewered the lawyer with her sharp nose. "If you have no objections?"

"As you wish, Mrs. Pickett. As you wish." He picked up a sheaf of papers from the left-most stack on his desk. "This firm has been entrusted with overseeing a trust that was set up by a clause in the will of Harold and Lady Jeannette Pickett. It specifies that upon the deaths of both Lady Jeannette and Harold Pickett, the aforementioned trust monies shall be split evenly among all living children of Lady Jeannette Pickett. In this case, two dependents have been identified: Miss Eleanor Harriet Pickett and Miss Madeline Elizabeth Pickett. The money shall be—"

"No."

Mr. Bartlestaff looked up from the papers he held above the desk, waiting to see why Mrs. Pickett had interrupted.

"No. There are not two daughters," Mrs. Pickett said loudly. "That young woman—" She pointed at Madeline, but continued to stare at Mr. Bartlestaff. "—is a fake."

"Mama!" Eleanor was shocked by her mother's assertion.

"Hush, Eleanor," Mrs. Pickett said. "I will not see your inheritance split in half. It is yours, and she is an imposter who does not deserve to have a penny. And I shall see she does not get one crumb more from this family."

"Please, Mama. I now believe Madeline is my sister." Eleanor looked shyly at Madeline. "I think she is entitled to half."

Mrs. Pickett looked at her daughter as if she had slapped her mother in public. "You will have nothing to say about this." She turned to Mr. Bartlestaff, and said, "That young woman has no proof. Surely the law says she must have just cause for her claim?"

"Mama," Eleanor said, "I told you I believe Madeline is my sister. And . . . and, if you deny it, I shall support her with my inheritance. I shall give her half my money. It will be mine to do with as I wish." Eleanor turned to Mr. Bartlestaff. "I am claiming her as my sister. Isn't that proof enough?"

The lawyer set the papers on his desk, then removed his glasses, methodically wiping them. He looked at Madeline. "I'm afraid it is true there should be some proof. Surely you have some way of proving your claim?"

"I . . . I didn't come here for money," Madeline said. "I came to find my sister. And . . . and I was hoping my mother might have left something, said something in her will about me?"

"Aha! You see, she admits she cannot prove it." Mary Pickett's mouth still turned downwards, but her eyes smiled in triumph.

"But the resemblance is obvious—surely you will admit that," Mr. Bartlestaff mused.

"Half of London's by-blows happen to have their relatives' features," scoffed Mrs. Pickett.

Madeline was devastated. She hadn't anticipated that by coming here she would suffer further humiliation at Mrs. Pickett's hand. She looked at Eleanor, who returned her look with kindness. A special corner of Madeline's heart was warmed by Eleanor's sticking up for her.

Perhaps that was reward enough for this trip to London.

Should she bow out, and allow Eleanor to keep the fortune? She'd never planned on an inheritance; didn't really care about it.

"Mama—" Eleanor started to rise.

"Sit!" Mrs. Pickett grabbed her daughter's elbow, and yanked her back down. "And I forbid you to say another word."

Madeline stood as well. "No, Eleanor. Please. It's all right. I . . ." Madeline turned toward Mr. Bartlestaff. "I have no proof.

I *am* Lady Jeannette's daughter. That is the truth." She considered saying more, but stopped. "I have no proof. I . . . I shall leave now."

"No!" Eleanor jumped up before her mother could stop her. She wheeled to face the lawyer. "Mr. Bartlestaff, I don't understand. If I tell you I *know* Madeline is my sister, isn't it proof enough?"

Mr. Bartlestaff looked from Eleanor to Madeline.

He looked about to speak, when Eleanor continued, "Wait! Wait. I remember something. Madeline! The brooch."

Madeline looked blankly at her sister.

Eleanor's eyes pleaded with Madeline. "Don't you remember? You told me you had a brooch our mother left with you before she died. It matched the brooch I was given. They were part of a set."

Turning again to Mr. Bartlestaff, Eleanor asked, "Would that be proof enough, Mr. Bartlestaff?"

Mr. Bartlestaff looked expectantly at Madeline. "Well, yes, I believe it might."

Eleanor ran across the room to where her sister stood frozen. "You must show it now, Madeline. Before it is too late."

Eleanor grabbed Madeline's reticule, and pressed it to her sister's hands. "Show them," she begged. She eased the top open, and pulled the satin gathers apart. "Show them what you showed me." She looked into Madeline's eyes as she handed her the purse. "Please," she whispered.

Madeline looked down into the open mouth of her silken purse. Winking up at her was an ice-blue pin. She reached in and lifted it out reverently.

"See, Mama?" Eleanor said. "It is a twin to the one my mother Jeannette left for me. Do you see it, Mama? You cannot deny the resemblance, nor call it a coincidence. It is a most unusual color and carving."

Mrs. Pickett's eyelids narrowed. But she said nothing.

Mr. Bartlestaff said, "Well, I do believe your daughter has made her point, Mrs. Pickett. Ladies, please be seated, so we may, as your stepmother requests, complete this session quickly."

Eleanor returned to her seat, sitting as far from her mother as possible. Madeline sat, stunned. She clasped the brooch so tightly, the needle-sharp point bit into her palm.

It was not hers. She'd never seen it before. Her sister Eleanor had planted it there.

Madeline's trunks were packed, and the footman had already taken them downstairs. She looked around the bedroom. This had become a second home to her. She loved Aunt Glynnis so very much. Uncle Rupert, too. She would miss them, but it was time to return to Grandfather.

Madeline descended the stairs, and looked down to see Aunt Glynnis waiting at the bottom step in a buttercup morning gown. The sun shone in from a clerestory window. "You look like an angel standing there in the sun, Aunt Glynnis."

"I'm the *avenging* angel, Madeline. I've been dying to hear about your visit to the lawyer's, and you've kept me waiting while you oversaw the packing. Will you join me for tea?"

Madeline reached the foyer floor. "I'm sorry, I was rude. I didn't see you when I came in."

"Tut, tut. I'm teasing you. I was busy with correspondence, and didn't hear you enter as well. But, come along, come along, I can't wait to hear! Did all turn out to your satisfaction?" Glynnis appeared anxious.

Madeline smiled inwardly a moment before she answered. "Ever so. You were right to advise me to go, Aunt Glynnis. I'm very glad I went." She nodded to herself as they entered the parlor. "I'll miss this parlor, Aunt Glynnis." She waved a hand. "Especially the palms, and the parrot." She glided over to Sammy's cage. "Yes, little Sammy." She made tongue-clicking noises. "Hello, little Sammy. I'm going to miss you." She added kissing sounds, and the colorful bird cocked his head up and down, as if enjoying her antics.

"So, let me see if I understand." Aunt Glynnis was already seated, studying her nails. "You will miss this parlor. You will miss the palms. You will miss the parrot. Hmm . . . how unfortunate my name does not began with the letter P."

Madeline turned from Sammy's cage and laughed. "I deserved that. I've not yet told you how much I'll miss you and Uncle Rupert. I shy away from good-byes, if you must know." She came to join her aunt on the settee.

"Capital! Then, we won't have a good-bye. You'll give me your promise to come back to me for the Season, and this won't really be a good-bye. In fact, I just may come out to the country to pick you up, and meet this wonderful grandfather, and escort you back myself. Now, tell me about this morning's adventure."

"Well, Mrs. Pickett tried to have me thrown out as an imposter."

"Oh! That insufferable woman. Yet somehow I'm not the least bit surprised." Dexter arrived with the tea, and the two ladies busied themselves with the service.

"But Eleanor stood by my side. My sister, Eleanor," said Madeline with a twist of pride, and a quick lump in her throat.

"So am I now addressing the heiress, Miss Madeline Pickett?"

"I suppose so. But, I'm planning on disowning my share." Madeline took a sip of tea, watching her aunt's reaction over the rim.

"What! Why ever would you do so?"

Madeline set down her teacup, and began slowly massaging her knuckles, but didn't answer right away.

"When you do that, you're nervous, Madeline," observed her aunt.

"When I do what?"

"Pull on your fingers like that. I've noticed you only do it when you're nervous about something. Come. What's on your mind?"

"You've been so good to me . . ."

"And you've been wonderful company to me." Glynnis waited, watching her niece.

"What if you discovered . . ." Madeline stared at her hands, and massaged a bit harder. "What if you found out I was not really your niece?"

"Considering you are a mirror of your mother, I don't think we have a worry there."

"But . . . yesterday, when I told you Eleanor and I had finally reconciled? I had to reveal something to her." Madeline looked at her aunt and made a decision. "Something I should have told you, Aunt Glynnis, when you first asked me to come here to stay with you. I'm not *truly* your niece."

She couldn't read Glynnis's expression, so she hurried on, wanting to have the revelation behind her. "I didn't realize I should have refused your offer. Truly. I was just so overwhelmed with the idea that I had a relative in town who didn't hate me. I so wanted to find a mother, and a sister, and an aunt. You were the only one who made me feel wanted. I felt close to you immediately."

"It was mutual, dear."

"But I'm not your brother Harold's daughter." She held her breath.

Glynnis took a sip of tea. "Drink your tea, Madeline, before it cools."

"Did you hear what I said, Aunt Glynnis?"

Glynnis shrugged. "That you are not my brother's offspring.

241

Well, by name you are. And no one looking at you could deny you are Lady Jeannette's daughter." She placed her delicate teacup down as well. "Madeline, you've shown me more affection in this fortnight than Mary Pickett or Eleanor have in the almost twenty years since your mother's been gone. Rupert claims you're the daughter we were never able to have."

Madeline fought the tears marching to the corners of her eyes.

"What I'm saying is that I don't care, Madeline. You *are* my niece, and I shall only stop loving you if you insist on denouncing me as your aunt."

Madeline sighed, but the expulsion of breath was closer to a sob. "Thank you."

"What was that?"

"Thank you."

"Thank you . . . yes?"

"Thank you, Aunt Glynnis!"

"You are most welcome, niece."

A long while later, the clock struck noon. Madeline had told her aunt everything about the appointment with the lawyer, her stepmother's outburst, and Eleanor's ruse.

"Do you have the pin with you?"

Madeline reached gently into a pocket. The stone glittered in the bright light of the parlor as she laid it in her aunt's hand.

"It is beautiful. And, it truly was Lady Jeannette's?"

Madeline nodded. "And Eleanor told me to keep it." Glynnis handed it back to her, and Madeline smiled as she reverently placed it back into her pocket.

"I'm so happy you have the keepsake you desired." Glynnis took another sip of tea. "However, Madeline, I'm thinking about your intent to disclaim. I find it noble, but the money really did come from Lady Jeannette's family. You said the lawyer stipulated it was for Lady Jeannette's offspring, and you are her child. None of the inheritance came from my brother, though he was your legal parent as surely as he was Eleanor's. Trust me. Harold gambled and drank away his portion of the allowance on a most regular basis. Your mother's family was overly generous to him."

"But—"

"Madeline, it really should belong to both you and Eleanor. I'd like to give you some advice, and you can choose to ignore it, but at least don't do anything until you've thought on it. I would advise you to talk it over with your grandfather. I understand from Rupert this is a sizeable fortune, and though I am not at all surprised by the nobleness of your intent, it is a decision a woman could come to regret over the years. Just promise me you'll think on it."

Madeline nodded. "All right. I can at least promise to wait until I've talked it over with Grandfather." She lit up. "I am so looking forward to seeing him. I believe it is time I was on my way."

"And, you will promise to talk to him about coming to spend a Season with me? Your *aunt?*" She emphasized the word with a dimple.

"I will. I promise." Madeline stood, and picked up her reticule and bonnet. "Thank you, Aunt Glynnis. For everything. I love you so, and shall miss you and Uncle Rupert."

"We'll miss you too, dear. Hurry back."

They clutched each other in a hug. It must have been a bit too fierce, as it squeezed a little water from both their eyes.

As Madeline stepped up into her uncle's traveling coach, a bead of water touched her outstretched hand.

"Did you feel any drops of rain, Mrs. Cork?" she asked the only other occupant of the carriage.

"No, not at all. Just look at that bright sky. I do note a few clouds, but they're very high. And they're white, too. No, there won't be any rain today. My arthritis guarantees it."

Madeline craned to see the sky, then waved to Aunt Glynnis and Uncle Rupert on the porch as the coach rolled forward. "Good. We'll make much better progress if this good weather holds."

They were about five miles from the estate when the downpour hit.

"I thought your arthritis never lied?"

Mrs. Cork's blue eyes were innocently round. "Imagine that. It must be tuned to your grandfather's county, do you think? I mean, it makes sense, as that's where I've lived all these years. I suspect it cannot predict London weather."

"Makes perfect sense to me, Mrs. Cork." Madeline hid her smile behind her glove as she turned her face toward the window.

Thankfully, her uncle Rupert's coach was cozier than her grandfather's older vehicle. The seats were plush velvet, not cold leather. The window coverings were thick, and if pulled would keep the cold winds from whistling in. The rain fell in sheets, drumming across the carriage in a regular beat.

Madeline could feel the carriage slowing to a safer pace.

"Are we stopping?" asked Mrs. Cork.

"I think we're slowing down due to the rain. It's harder for the driver to see, and the roads are hidden when it's pouring."

"Ah."

"Though, there's another possibility. Perhaps highway robbers are surrounding our coach."

Mrs. Cork reacted in shock, and craned her neck this way and that at her window. "Do not say so! My heart could not stand it."

"I'm sorry. I was teasing, Mrs. Cork. Anyway, you'd be in no danger. They'd only be intending to kidnap *me*," Madeline said in a tone bespeaking her boredom.

"It *is* an interesting fact that you've been abducted twice in your life." Mrs. Cork counted on her pudgy fingers. "Once on our trip to London. And then by that evil Mr. Edwards."

Both women silently contemplated the last few weeks.

Mrs. Cork leaned across and put a hand on Madeline's. "Did you have a tendre for him, miss?"

"Good heavens! For Mr. Edwards? I despised the little ferret."

"Oh, no, not for Mr. Edwards. I was referring to Mr. Remington."

Madeline's cheeks warmed, but she turned to look out the window, hoping Mrs. Cork hadn't noticed. She shook her head to the negative. "No. No, not especially. He—he was a little bossy, didn't you think?"

"Why, I'm sure I never noticed. But, I did notice he was always watching you."

"Was he?" Madeline noticed her own voice had a touch of anticipation when she had intended boredom.

"Oh, yes, miss. The other servants and I were always commenting on it." Realizing what she'd just said, Mrs. Cork froze. "I mean, the other servants commented on it. I myself chose never to participate in that sort of house gossip."

"Very worthy of you."

Another minute passed in silence.

"What was said about Mr. Remington and me? By the other servants, I mean?"

Mrs. Cork squinted one eye and looked heavenward, a habit that meant she was reaching into her memory. "They said you two were a most handsome couple. But they also said there would be too many folks wearing pants in the house if you were its mistress."

"Mrs. Cork! What is that supposed to mean?"

Her faithful maid realized she'd been a little too honest.

"Who knows what idle chatter means? Especially from a London crowd. It's obvious the soot gets to their brains, if you know what I mean."

Madeline frowned. Whatever did they mean by that? She was not the forward one. He'd been the one who tried to kiss her. If the servants were going to gossip, they could at least get their facts straight. "What else did they say about Mr. Remington?"

Mrs. Cork gave it a moment's thought, and said, "They thought he'd make a much better husband than his brother Mr. Jace."

"What? Are you speaking of Mr. *Bennett* Remington?"

"Yes. Isn't that whom we were discussing all along?"

"Oh, yes. Of course. I just wanted to be sure. When there are two Mr. Remingtons, one could easily get them mixed up."

Mrs. Cork laughed. "Oh, no, not those two. One would be more likely to disbelieve they were brothers at all as to mix them up."

Madeline ran the past few minutes' conversation through her head. So, the staff had talked about her and Bennett, not her and Jace. How interesting, especially since it was Jace who made her pulse beat faster. So Mrs. Cork did not know.

Mrs. Cork chuckled again.

"What is so funny, Mrs. Cork?"

"Oh, I was just thinking about what that silly upstairs maid said about Mr. Jace."

"Yes?" Drat. Madeline meant to sound disinterested.

"She said if Bennett's wife displeased him, Bennett would try to change himself. But if Mr. Jace's wife displeased him, he'd haul her out to the stables and use his riding crop on her."

Now why on earth would someone think that was funny? wondered Madeline. "That's ridiculous. He is a modern thinker and would do no such thing."

"Well, that same maid said as long as she was guaranteed a

tumble in the hay afterwards, she might not—"

"Mrs. Cork! That will be enough of this topic, I think."

"Of course, miss." Mrs. Cork looked out the window, and grasped a new topic. "My, I wonder how long it will take us to get home in this kind of weather?"

"Well, since it won't be raining in our own county, according to your arthritis, I'm sure we'll make up the time once we cross the border."

"Mr. Jace Remington is here. He was inquiring whether Miss Madeline was receiving visitors, my Lady."

Glynnis looked up from her book. "Yes? And, did you inform him Miss Madeline is no longer in residence here?"

"No, my Lady. I thought it best to check with you first."

"Very wise. Please show Mr. Remington in here, and bring refreshments."

Her butler started to leave.

"Oh, Dexter."

"Yes, my Lady?"

"I hear Mr. Remington has quite an appetite. Please request servings for three."

"Right away, my Lady."

"Dexter! Better yet, make that servings for four."

Glynnis untucked her slippered feet from under her, and set her marker in the book. As she set it on the table at hand, she wondered why Mr. Jace Remington would be calling here. According to Madeline, the man now despised Glynnis's niece, and was quite a bully as well.

She did not have long to wait for her answer, as she heard the urgency of long strides approaching.

Glynnis eyed Mr. Jace Remington with reluctant appreciation. She noted he cut quite the thoroughbred figure in his morning coat outlining wide shoulders. His hair, a little longish for the current style, was shiny and still a little damp from its recent washing. Good lord, she thought, I'm not at Newhall, and he's not a horse. "Mr. Remington," she inclined her head.

Jace had started on not seeing Madeline present, but recovered himself and crossed the room to take the hand proffered by Madeline's aunt.

"Won't you have a seat?"

"Thank you." He sat, and turned expectantly toward the door. "Miss Pickett will be joining us?"

"Mr. Remington, may I ask your interest in my niece?" She saw a flash of impatience. Madeline was right. This man did have odious manners when crossed. Well, this was her house, and he was her guest. She'd be hell-bound if she'd be intimidated by him. He was not much taller than Rupert, and she'd learned to ignore Rupert's masculine bluffs years ago.

"As you know," Jace said, "I . . . I am a friend of Miss Pickett's."

The refreshments arrived, and both waited until the servant had left before continuing their conversation.

"You were saying?" asked Glynnis as she handed a plate of biscuits and frosted teacakes to Jace.

He took the plate, and the first teacake disappeared in one bite. "We are friends," he said after a swallow.

Glynnis looked down to stir her tea. "That's not what my niece tells me, sir." She looked up into his shocked eyes. "My niece has left, Mr. Remington."

"Left? Shopping?"

"No. Left to return to the country."

Jace stood. "Then I won't waste your time, madam. I was not informed Miss Pickett was no longer in residence with you."

"Do you intend to kidnap her again, Mr. Remington?"

She noted the hardening of his jaw muscle.

"It was not a kidnapping, Lady Chesterton. I fully intended

to escort your niece to London."

"Sit, Mr. Remington. Sit, sit. Just a few more minutes of your time."

Jace sat down, albeit with a touch of impatience.

"My niece tells me the last time she saw you was the night Mr. Edwards—your cousin," she added pointedly, "—attempted to abduct her."

"That is true. I have spent these two days hunting him down. But he appears to have fled the country. A wise move," added Jace with murder in his eyes.

"My niece tells me you were not aware it was an abduction."

"I don't understand."

"Madeline said you arrived to find her in the arms of Mr. Edwards, and that you now despise her for it."

"*What?* That is a lie." As if remembering himself, he said, "I don't mean you, Lady Chesterton. I meant your niece, of course."

"Of course, that makes an insult more acceptable when not to one's person, but to one's niece." She let the dry remark hang between them for a moment. "She believes you entered the room and thought the worst of her, Mr. Remington. She was quite distraught."

"But I came to save her. I knew Madeline was not foolish enough to elope with my cousin. I know her to be more responsible than that. And," he continued, "how the devil would she have time to know what I was thinking, when her personal bodyguard once again decided to use me as his boxing bag? I had only just entered the room, when I was once again knocked unconscious by the brute."

Well, thought Glynnis, *this becomes more and more interesting.* "Yet you did not come directly here to tell her this yourself? She could have used a 'friend's' support when facing the lawyers this morning."

"Was it this morning? As I said, I left immediately for the hunt. Did it go well for her?" His concern touched Glynnis.

"Yes. It appears all went well, and she was able to reconcile with her sister as well."

Jace sagged with apparent relief. "You don't know how that pleases me. Madeli—Miss Pickett wanted nothing so badly as to establish a relationship with her sister Eleanor." He looked embarrassed of a sudden. "As I'm sure you must have already known."

"Yes, as all her 'close friends' know, Mr. Remington." Glynnis smiled, her first offering of friendship visible.

"I'd like to get on the road again, Lady Chesterton. You say she is returning to her grandfather's? Has he had a turn for the worse?" He leaned forward to await her answer.

"No, no, he is fine. Evidently he is recuperating well, and as expected, from the letters she receives." Glynnis hesitated, and then came to a decision. "Mr. Remington, may I be direct with you?"

"I would appreciate it very much, madam."

"I believe my niece left because she was suffering from a broken heart. She truly believed you blamed her for the fiasco with Mr. Edwards, and the loss of your good feelings toward her appeared to devastate her."

Jace closed his eyes and gave a quick shake of his head. "I am so sorry to hear that. The little twit. Oh, I beg your pardon." He at least had the grace to color.

"So I ask again, Mr. Remington. What are your intentions toward my niece?"

"Lady Chesterton, my intention is to marry your niece. If I may take my leave of your gracious hospitality, I shall be off to see her grandfather and to ask for her hand."

CHAPTER TWENTY-FIVE

By the time they reached the inn the rain had ceased, but they'd been forced to crawl due to the fog that crowded in upon the valley.

The two exhausted ladies were happy to be escorted upstairs to their rooms. Duncan had promised to bespeak dinner as well, and Madeline was looking forward to a hot meal in a warm, fire-lit parlor.

"Do you think Mr. Duncan will be joining us for dinner?" Mrs. Cork spoke casually as she moved garments between the traveling trunk and the wardrobe.

Madeline looked at her maid, who happened to have her back turned. "I don't know, Mrs. Cork." She watched for the reaction, which was quick to come.

Mrs. Cork turned, a neat stack of lace handkerchiefs sandwiched between her hands. "I was thinking he shouldn't have to eat in the common room, just because he's manning the coach. And you did say he's a friend of the family."

"Well, I suppose it wouldn't hurt to invite him to join us." Madeline wasn't about to tell Mrs. Cork it had already been arranged.

The three were in the midst of dinner when the serving lad knocked and was bidden to enter. "There's a gentleman asking to see you, sir." He addressed himself to Duncan.

"That's odd," said Duncan as he looked to the ladies. "Who would know we are here?" He demanded of the lad, "Did he give ye a name?"

The young lad turned red. "He said I'm to tell you it's your personal boxing bag, sir. He wants to know if you'll be needing to knock anyone unconscious tonight."

It was obvious the serving lad was hesitant to deliver this ridiculous message. However, the man had paid him well to deliver it, so deliver it he did.

Madeline felt a bubble rising right about where her heart was. "Mr. Remington? Here?" She looked to her two companions.

Duncan stood, but Madeline also jumped up and put a hand on his limb-sized arm. "Mr. Duncan, I did explain to you that Mr. Remington was not my kidnapper—this last time, anyway."

"Aye, ye did."

"So, you'll allow him to speak? I mean, before you hit him?"

Duncan nodded slowly, as he strolled to the door. "Aye, lass, I'll think about it . . . first." He followed the lad out.

"Why do you think he's here, miss?" Mrs. Cork buttered another roll.

Madeline walked to the window, but it was too dark to see anything or anyone in the courtyard. "I don't know. Perhaps he remembered another lecture he forgot to deliver while I was in London."

"You should finish your stew before it cools."

"No, but you go ahead, Mrs. Cork. I've . . . I've suddenly lost my appetite."

Madeline discovered she could now make out figures in the courtyard, just faintly, as the fog swirled in front of the lamps from the various carriages. She squinted hard, and then she was able to make out Duncan as he moved out from under the overhang of the entrance. It had to be Duncan, as there'd been no monolithic rocks in the courtyard that she'd recalled as they pulled in. Also, this one was mobile.

That was when she spied Jace. It would be hard not to. He stood with legs apart, facing Duncan. She'd recognize that stance and his height among other men. It was the stance of a man expecting to defend himself in a fight.

Furiously, she scrabbled for the latch on the window. She pushed upon the window frame that did not want to budge. It had perhaps never been opened since it's last whitewashing. Finally, it gave, and she shoved open the mullioned panes.

"Stop! Stop! Mr. Duncan, don't hurt him! Stop, I say!"

The few gentlemen and stable hands standing in the courtyard stopped talking, and turned to look up at the bright window, and the woman who stood in silhouette.

"For God's sake, Miss Pickett, could you please stop screaming like a fishmonger's wife? Mr. Duncan and I have business to discuss." It was definitely Jace's deep voice that carried through the thick air.

Well! How dare he yell at her in front of half the inn's guests? Madeline slammed the window closed, and spun toward Mrs. Cork with reddened cheeks.

"It appears they are working things out," Madeline said as she took a seat and picked up her soupspoon.

The door opened, and Duncan blocked the doorway.

"Mr. Duncan! How is Mr. Remington? Is he still alive?" Madeline's voice sounded hysterical to her own ears.

"Aye."

Mr. Duncan moved into the parlor, and Jace stood in the entry. Madeline had the maddest urge to run into his arms, but sat very still instead.

"Miss Pickett." Jace remained in the doorway.

"Mr. Remington."

"Come in, Remington," thundered Duncan. "Ye didn't ride all the way from London in this sorry weather to stare at one another, now did ye?"

Still Jace waited. "May I enter, Miss Pickett?"

"Yes." Madeline let out the breath she hadn't realized she'd been holding. "Yes, please do."

She'd never seen a shy side of Jace Remington, and neither would she now. The illusion was gone as he entered the room with a power that held her transfixed. She noticed he looked even more intimidating in his greatcoat, though its many layers dripped. As she watched, he shrugged out of the wet wool. She stared at the muscles of his back as he hung his coat on the pegs near the door.

He removed his hat, and she noticed water yet glistened on his long dark locks. He reminded her of a black panther that had lazily climbed from a pool. Then he turned to her, and it did seem he prowled as he approached gracefully, all strength and determination.

"I would talk to you, madam."

Madeline gulped. Why was she so nervous? "Yes?" she repeated, this time forcing air out of her lungs so she could be heard.

Jace looked at Mrs. Cork. "Evening, Mrs. Cork." A short bow accompanied this.

"Evening, sir." Mrs. Cork looked from Jace to Madeline, to Mr. Duncan.

"I'd like a word with your mistress." He addressed this to Mrs. Cork, but held Madeline's gaze in his hot steely look.

"Of course," murmured Mrs. Cork.

When Jace turned to Mrs. Cork, with one saturnine eyebrow raised, she took the hint.

"Oh . . . Oh." The maid turned to Duncan, who stood by the fire.

"Mrs. Cork," Duncan said, "I see yer stew is no longer steamin'. Might I invite ye to accompany me to the dinin' room downstairs for a hot supper and a bit of ale to wash it down?"

Mrs. Cork could not disguise the flame of her cheeks, nor could she disguise her pleased smile. "That would be delightful, Mr. Duncan." She turned to Madeline, and her shoulders slumped. "Oh, my. I'm sorry, but I couldn't leave Miss Madeline here alone with Mr. Remington."

"Yes, Mrs. Cork, you can." Jace's voice was more of a command than a confirmation.

"But . . ." Mrs. Cork looked at Madeline and then at Duncan in consternation.

"I think the lass will be fine for a bit, Mrs. Cork. We'll be right downstairs should she need us. But I don't think we'll have to worry about her. Isn't that right, Mr. Remington?"

Jace met the Scotsman's gaze, and nodded once. "Mrs. Cork, I give you my word that your mistress will be safe and unharmed while I am with her."

"All right," agreed Mrs. Cork quickly, ready to join Mr. Duncan's company.

"I beg your pardon! Do I have anything to say about this?" Madeline was clearly put out that everyone was having a conversation about her, and making decisions for her, without even consulting her.

"No, Miss Pickett, I'm afraid you do not." Jace took Mrs. Cork by the elbow, walked her to the door, and gave her a wink. Mr. Duncan followed, and Jace closed the door behind the two.

He turned to face Madeline.

She stood and folded her arms beneath her bodice. "This is most unseemly, Mr. Remington."

"Why is that, Miss Pickett?"

Now he truly did remind her of a panther as he stalked powerfully and slowly toward her.

Madeline retreated back a step from the table. "You know as well as I do that a lady should not be left alone with a gentleman who is not her husband."

"Ah, there is the rub. What if the gentleman is about to become her husband?"

Madeline's insides froze. She stood still, yet he continued to advance. She could smell the dampness rising from his clothes.

"I don't know what you are saying."

"If you were any other lady, I'd accuse you of coyness. However, I've learned that with you, Miss Pickett, it's simple stubbornness. You know very well what I'm saying. You just want to make me repeat it, don't you?"

He was so close, she felt the steam of his powerful body beneath the damp shirt. She had to swallow, her senses were so overcome.

She could not help herself. She had to put out a hand to feel the warmth of his chest. "Could you repeat that?" she whispered.

"Considering I intend to become your husband, Miss Pickett, I hardly think it improper we should be alone in this room. In fact, I intend to kiss you. Will that shock you further?"

She looked up into his eyes, and shook her head, but said nothing. He leaned forward and took her mouth in a long kiss. She knew his lips would be as warm as the body beneath her hand.

When Madeline opened her eyes he had already straightened. Yet he still stood close, his hands firmly on her waist.

Madeline moved her hands onto his forearms. "I . . . I thought you hated me. After you found me with Mr. Edwards."

"Why? I knew the scoundrel well enough to know you had nothing to do with it. I am only sorry you thought otherwise. I chased after him, all the way to the coast, but he'd made his escape to the continent. He won't bother you again. I won't let him." Jace put a hand behind her neck, and she leaned her head to his chest.

"I was so frightened. And I thought I'd lost your friendship as well."

"I'm so sorry. I came immediately to inquire after you, but your aunt informed me you'd already left. You should have waited for me."

"How was I to know? We'd never discussed anything this private, Mr. Remington."

"Well, that will change. We'll have many very private . . . conversations, I promise."

She felt a delicious warmth emanating from his large hands, as he slid them along her shoulders.

"Will you become my wife, Miss Pickett?"

"Madeline," she said.

"What?"

"I wish to hear you say my name, Mr. Remington."

"Madeline." He spoke it low and sensually, in three syllables of deep honey that surrounded her. In a deep voice that reverberated within her, he repeated, "Will you become my wife, Madeline?"

"Yes, Jace." She saw the smile in his eyes, and knew this was right.

Chapter Twenty-Six

"Stop! Please, stop the coach," she shrieked at Mr. Duncan, who was perched atop the rushing carriage. The ladies bounced forward as the coach came to a sudden stop.

Jace brought his stallion up alongside the window. "What's wrong?" He spat out a mouthful of the settling dust.

Madeline stuck her head out the window. "We've got to talk, Mr. Remington."

He looked at her in disbelief, then turned on his horse and surveyed the empty road, and the encroaching forest on either side.

"Now?" he asked. "Right here? Right this minute?"

"Yes!" She was most emphatic. "I've been worrying about something, and I decided it would be best if we discussed it sooner rather than later."

He considered this, raising his eyebrows, but acquiesced with a grim nod. "All right. Speak."

"I can't tell you right here, Mr. Remington. We're in the middle of the road, and there are people about." She couldn't believe he could be so dense.

Jace looked his confusion. "Then, where did you propose we talk? I'm not sure I follow."

The carriage door swung open, and Madeline stepped down, her reticule swinging from her wrist. "I'll be back shortly, Mrs. Cork. I promise."

Mr. Duncan leaned over from his perch, observing the

goings-on below.

Madeline looked up primly. "A little privacy, Mr. Duncan?"

He looked away. "Of course," he muttered, straightening. "Why not? Take yer time."

Madeline walked to the other side of the road, then turned and looked at the tableau of folks staring at her: Mr. Duncan, Mrs. Cork and Jace.

"Mr. Remington? A moment over here, please?"

Jace looked at the other two, and bowed from his horse. "You will excuse me?" He dismounted, tied the reins to the carriage, then stalked across the street to where Madeline stood.

"What the blazes is this about?"

"We have a problem, Mr. Remington," Madeline whispered.

"And we're going to discuss it in the middle of the highway?"

"I couldn't wait any longer. I believed it important you should know something as soon as possible."

He looked over at the carriage, as if debating whether to argue, but instead looked back, and said, "All right. What is it, Madeline?"

She still thrilled to hear him say her name. But she was saddened to think that after she told him what must be said, she might never hear it from him again. Surely he would end the short engagement. "I've realized we cannot marry."

"*What?* Wha—"

"No. No, don't interrupt me, please. Hear me out. I've made up my mind on this." She took a breath and blurted, "I'm disclaiming the money."

Jace stared blankly at her, but she rushed on. "I don't need it. Eleanor will take care of our stepmother. It's only fair she should keep the money our mother left. I plan on living my life in the country, Jace. I have no need of a London townhouse. I don't need a full staff of servants. I don't need an expensive wardrobe. I am happy with what I have."

"Living in a cabin?"

"It's not a cabin!"

"It's a country manor," they said in one voice.

Madeline frowned.

Jace was quick to add, "Truce! Truce; I was only teasing you. *This* is what you had to stop the coach to tell me?"

"Don't try to dissuade me." Madeline fiddled with the ribbons on her reticule. "I've made up my mind, you must know. At least, Grandfather already knows how stubborn I can be when I've decided something."

"Stubborn? I don't think I've ever noticed that in you."

Madeline gave him her "Don't start that" look.

"All right. What else?"

"What else?" Madeline repeated.

"You said you wanted to talk," Jace said. "What else did you have on your mind?"

"That's all," she said in a quiet voice. "So I don't blame you if this is the end of our relationship."

"What on earth is that supposed to mean, Madeline?"

"It means I am releasing you from our understanding. You are free. I am not inheriting any money, and . . . that's all, I guess."

She noticed that nerve on his right temple, the one that stood out when he was angry. Very angry.

"You little twit. How dare you think the only reason I'm interested in you is because of your damned inheritance? Do you equate me with my cousin?"

"Please, sir. Keep your voice down. I just—"

"I will not keep my voice down," he said loudly. "Hell, Madeline." He shook his head in disgust, and turned and stalked halfway across the road. He spun around, pacing back toward her. He looked about to speak, but instead pressed his lips together, and shook his head again. "I don't need your damned money. I've enough of my own to support a wife in comfort. And, I demand an apology."

"What?" Madeline was confused.

"I demand an apology from you, for believing my proposal was so shallow. For believing all I cared about was your money."

She looked down at the dust upon her slippers. "I'm sorry," she said quietly.

"What was that? Louder, if you please."

"I said I'm sorry."

"Sorry for what?"

"I'm sorry . . ." Madeline narrowed her eyelids. "Are you making me do this because I did it to you?"

He nodded his head in the affirmative. "You've got the right of it, Madeline. You were saying?"

She looked up at the canopy of the trees, as if reciting. "I'm sorry I was so shallow, Jace. I'm very sorry I was thinking like a male."

"That's a devious apology, and you know it, Madeline." But his laugh softened his response.

Madeline reached out and grabbed his sleeve. "I truly am sorry, Jace. Tell me again you want me, and not my money."

"Well, the money would have been nice . . ."

Madeline removed her hand, and slapped his arm instead.

"Ow! Yes, you are all I need. Now, get back in that carriage before I change my mind."

The countryside looked more and more familiar as they approached Grandfather's. Madeline didn't think her heart could be any happier. Even the skies had cleared up in a welcoming gesture.

"Well, Mrs. Cork, you've made a believer of me."

"A believer of what, miss?"

"Your arthritic weather predictor. Look at this glorious sunlight! I have to tell you I was not convinced there could be a square inch of land that was not being flooded in rain or shrouded in fog. What a beautiful day!"

"Do you suppose young love has something to do with the day?"

Madeline turned with a smile. "What's that?"

"I don't believe I've ever seen you this happy. Dear me, I just hope your grandfather approves of Mr. Remington."

"How could he not?" Madeline was scanning the countryside for familiar sights.

"Well, considering the man kidnapped you . . ."

"Oh. Oh, no." Madeline slumped back into her seat. "Mrs. Cork, I completely forgot about that. But . . . but Jace himself admits he was simply going along with the mistaken identity."

"Yes. I'm sure your grandfather will see it that way. He's always enjoyed a humorous mix-up as well as the next man."

"Ohhh, of a sudden I feel sick. Grandfather cannot possibly refuse Jace's offer for my hand. He can't! What am I to do, Mrs. Cork?"

"I'm sorry I brought it up, miss. It's nothing that worrying will solve. Besides, once your grandfather sees how much in love you are, he won't deny you. You've always been able to wrap him around your finger."

Madeline put her chin in her hand and was the picture of gloom. "I took a strange man camping. Grandfather is going to kill me, Mrs. Cork."

"Well, there you have it solved, nice and tidy. If there's no bride, then he won't need to refuse Mr. Remington, will he?"

"I must tell Jace! We must stop the coach."

Mrs. Cork reached over and quickly pulled down the shade. "Whatever you do, don't do that, miss! Or Mr. Remington will kill you before your grandfather has a chance."

CHAPTER TWENTY-SEVEN

The carriage clattered noisily across the cobblestoned manor entrance. Seeing Doctor Crombley walking down the porch steps dropped a stone into Madeline's stomach.

Duncan froze atop the driver's box, and Madeline opened the squeaky carriage door.

"Welcome! Welcome," the doctor greeted.

"Doctor Crombley, is everything all right?"

"Absolutely. Your grandfather is up and about and back to his old cantankerous self when he loses a game of chess." He assisted Madeline to alight. "I was having a bit of tea before going upstairs. He's not awakened from his nap yet."

Madeline closed her eyes and sighed loudly. "I'm so relieved to hear that, Doctor. Not that I'm not always happy to see you, but it startled me. I feared Grandfather might have taken a turn for the worse."

"No, he's been doing very well. And he'll be even better when he sees you've returned. Was he expecting you today?"

"No." Madeline bit back an explanation. "I should have sent word, but I was just . . . homesick. And missing him."

Duncan was at the coach door to assist Mrs. Cork. She descended slowly, as the rainy journey had been a bit much for her joints.

"Good morning, Doctor," she smiled at his familiar face.

"Mrs. Cork. A pleasure, as always."

"And this is Mr. Duncan, Doctor," said Madeline, "a friend

of Grandfather's."

"We've met." Doctor Crombley tipped his hat to Duncan. "Good day, Mr. Duncan. I trust you had a pleasant journey?"

"Other than bein' bathed by rain all day yesterday, it was uneventful enough." Duncan began methodically unstrapping the baggage.

Madeline took the doctor's arm, and pulled him along. "Doctor, I have another friend to introduce to you."

Jace had dismounted and tied his horse to the hitch. He strode over to join Madeline.

"Doctor Crombley, this is Mr. Jace Remington. Mr. Remington, Doctor Crombley is our family doctor and a very close friend of ours."

Jace eyed the man, who was young for a country doctor, and standing too close to Madeline. Just how close a friend was he? Jace gripped the doctor's hand and squeezed a little more firmly than necessary.

"Remington?" asked the doctor, cocking his head. "The name sounds familiar." He looked at Madeline. "Is Mr. Remington related to the man who kidnapped you?"

"It wasn't really a kidnapping," insisted Madeline, looking askance at Jace.

By this time, Mr. Duncan had ambled over, arms loaded with luggage, and overheard the conversation. "We decided it was Madeline who ordered poor Mr. Remington to accompany her to London. So it seems Madeline was the kidnapper, eh?" The Scotsman laughed at his own joke, and added, "and aye, this is the very same Mr. Remington, Doctor."

The doctor's eyes widened, mirroring his round spectacles.

Madeline nervously fiddled with her reticule. "Oh, dear, this is not going to be easy. Mr. Remington, perhaps you should come back and meet my grandfather tomorrow, after we've sorted all of this out."

"There should be nothing to sort out, Miss Pickett." Doctor Crombley looked at her, then at Duncan. "As I advised Mr. Duncan, there was no need to tell your grandfather about the kidnapping episode."

"Grandfather still doesn't know?" Madeline was incredulous. Could she possibly be so lucky?

"Duncan and I agreed that as long as he could track you down quickly and get word back to me, there would be no reason to say anything. I was concerned for your grandfather's health. Such news might have devastated him, and he was in a precariously ill position at the time."

"Doctor, I could kiss you!" Madeline clapped her hands together.

"I don't think so." Jace's voice was cold.

"Mr. Remington, it's a figure of speech." Madeline was too excited to allow Jace's prudery to dampen her enthusiasm.

"That's not what I meant." Jace looked at each of them, including Duncan. "I meant I do not think there is any need to cover this up. I will not be party to deceiving your grandfather. I intend to tell him the truth."

"You cannot be serious." Madeline looked from the doctor to Mr. Duncan, hoping they would back her up. "There was no harm done. It was all a misunderstanding. Grandfather need never know."

"Miss Pickett." Jace's tone would brook no argument. "Your grandfather and I will not start our relationship with an unspoken lie. If he should learn of this in the future, it would reflect poorly on all of us." He touched Madeline's arm to soften his words. "I believe it is a matter of honor and trust that I tell him exactly what transpired. I am confident he will understand."

Madeline's shoulders slumped. "You don't know Grandfather, Mr. Remington. He will most likely throw you out."

"Of his cabin?" Jace smiled.

"This is not a time for jokes, sir." Madeline frowned. "I am very serious. You are making a mistake. I insist you take my lead on this, as I know my grandfather."

"And I insist I won't begin our relationship any other way. So I believe you will take my lead on this, madam." Jace no longer smiled.

The others shifted uncomfortably, and moved toward the door, leaving Madeline and Jace, two stones glaring at one another.

Madeline tiptoed into her grandfather's room, prepared to find him in bed.

"Madeline!" To her delight, he stood by the cheval glass, his tilted reflection mirroring surprise. He spun around, halfway through tying his cravat.

"Grandfather! You look wonderful." She hurried across to the hug awaiting her.

"You're barely returning my hug, my dear. Did you become so weak in the little time you were gone?"

"No. I'm . . . I'm just afraid to hug you too hard. How are you?"

"I won't answer until I get a decent hug from you."

Madeline pulled her arms tighter around his thin body, smiling against his shoulder.

"That's much better. Now, help me with this damned cravat."

Madeline took the tie in hand, and it seemed like yesterday. Except . . . Grandfather had become thinner. If it were possible, he looked older in this short time.

"This is a wonderful surprise, Madeline." He hugged her again.

"I expected to find you in bed, and here you are up and about. Doctor Crombley said you were doing well."

"And I am feeling quite fit. Even dropped a few of those

pounds that have been following me down the hall of late." His eyes twinkled. "But you are the best medicine for me, Grand-daughter." He pulled back to study her. "There is a healthy flush to your complexion. I feared after spending time in the city, you'd be sallow and listless."

She laughed. "Actually, there was so much to do in the city! I had a wonderful time."

"As I gathered from your letters, unless they were full of happy made-up stories to put an old man at his ease. I worried about you, you know."

Madeline sat on the stool next to his mirror. "To be honest, at first I did make up happy news. Grandfather . . . my recep-tion was so awful. They didn't want me there."

"The devil take them!"

"But by the end, everything turned out well. My sister Eleanor and I became close." Madeline smiled mischievously. "You will enjoy her when you meet her. She is a bit shorter, with hair a bit darker than mine, though I'm told we look quite alike. And, she's ever so honest with her opinions. She amazes me. At first, she did not want anything to do with me, but we straightened all of that out."

"And her mother? Your stepmother, I mean?"

Madeline made a face. "Dreadful, Grandfather! You *don't* want to meet her. She's a dragon."

"Any brothers? Other kin?"

"No. Other than Aunt Glynnis and Uncle Rupert, that is. I already wrote about them. Oh! But there is someone I especially want you to meet."

"I see that dimple. A gentleman, I take it? Though, I warn you, if he thinks to become a suitor, I shall grill him ruthlessly."

"Grandfather, you're teasing, aren't you? Tell me you are, for this man is very special to me."

Her grandfather eyed her with speculation. "Mmm. How special, miss?"

Madeline smiled down at her hands. "Very."

"Well, well. We shall see if he passes muster. Is he in London, then?"

Madeline looked up quickly. "He's here. He escorted me home."

"Ah. I see," he said, frowning.

"Grandfather, it's important to me that you approve of him. Please?"

"Is there a reason I would not?"

Madeline flushed.

"Madeline, is there something you are not telling me? I warn you, Doctor Crombley will not want me to get overly excited, and you are making my stomach acid rise. What is wrong?"

Madeline jumped up and took his hand. "Nothing is wrong. Just . . . unusual. Oh, Grandfather, I promised not to discuss it with you until Mr. Remington is present."

"Mr. Remington, eh? Is there something physically wrong with this young man? Did he lose an arm or a leg in the militia?"

"Oh, no, nothing like that. Please, do come downstairs and meet him."

"All right. I think I'm finished here, and I am quite ravenous. I assume your friend will join us for tea?"

Madeline chuckled. "His stomach is a veritable quarry pit. I think I can convince him to take tea with us."

"All young men soon dent a larder, Madeline."

They left the room. On the stairs, Madeline paused. "And if he calls this manor a cabin, tell him you'll shoot him. Would you do that for me, Grandfather?"

"I'd be glad to." He kissed the top of her head. "Anything for you, miss."

Jace stood when Madeline and her grandfather entered the

parlor. Madeline made the introductions, and Jace bowed low to the gentleman.

"Sit, Mr. Remington," Sir Arthur said. "We were just about to have tea. Will you join us?"

Madeline watched Jace nod. She noticed he did not seem nervous or intimidated by her grandfather. She didn't know why she should feel pride in that, but she did. He was so handsome, and his shoulders were so powerfully broad. She caught her grandfather watching her from the corner of her eye.

"So. How did you and Mr. Remington meet, Madeline?" Her grandfather turned from her to Jace. "I'm sure you were properly introduced in London?"

"Yes," Madeline jumped in. "Mr. Remington is a cousin to Eleanor's fiancé. Well, Eleanor's former—"

"No," said Jace, "that's not quite true."

Madeline went speechless. She gave him a pointed scowl, afraid of what he was going to admit.

Her grandfather watched the interplay, then cleared his throat. "Please proceed, Mr. Remington."

"I met Madeline earlier, Sir Arthur. You see, I was sent here to spy on your granddaughter, before she ever left for London."

Madeline groaned. This was not going to go well.

"I see," said her grandfather, but his frown showed he did not.

"My cousin—who, as Madeline pointed out, was engaged to her sister Eleanor—believed Madeline was not whom she claimed to be. I was asked to investigate. I acted upon a sense of family loyalty in ferreting out the truth, as I'm sure you would have done."

Madeline looked at Jace, wondering how he could be so unbearably blunt. Grandfather would eat him alive with the currant muffins that were on their way.

"I came here, to your home," continued Jace, "and Madeline

mistook me for your man, Albus Duncan. I didn't correct her, though I should have. Instead I took on the role and escorted her to London."

"You, a stranger, escorted my daughter and Mrs. Cork?" Sir Arthur was incredulous.

"Yes, sir, I did. Though I assure you your granddaughter was well guarded. Well . . ."

Madeline caught Jace's eye. Her eyes were like saucers already, but she tried to make them larger.

He didn't seem to get the signal, and continued, ". . . the only misadventure occurred while we were camping—"

"Camping! You did say 'camping?' " Her grandfather sat forward on the seat of his chair. A vein began throbbing on his left temple.

"Yes, sir. It was Madeline's idea, and I did my best to dissuade her. Well, as you can imagine, knowing your granddaughter, *that* didn't amount to anything. So I decided to humor her. But, then there was the near-drowning incident—"

"Stop!" Madeline stood. "Just stop!" She turned to Jace with her hands on her hips. "Mr. Remington, do you have any idea what is happening here?"

Jace remained seated, waiting to continue with eyebrows patiently raised. "I told you, Miss Pickett, that honor demands I be totally honest with your grandfather. As should you be," he added pointedly and primly.

Madeline ignored that last remark, and waved a hand toward her grandfather. "Put yourself in my grandfather's position. Please. I can't believe you are confiding all of this. He will lock me up in the future, and never allow me out. Not—even—to—marry. Do I make myself clear, Mr. Remington?"

"Marry? What is this about marriage?" her grandfather asked in an agitated voice.

Jace turned to her grandfather. "I wish to marry your granddaughter, sir," he said as if requesting another scone with his tea.

Madeline held her breath, but the only sound was the turning of the doorknob. Mrs. Cork knocked as she entered with the tea tray. She noticed the frozen, silent tableau before her, set the tray down next to Madeline, and closed the door quietly behind her as she left.

Madeline watched her grandfather, waiting for the eruption.

"Would you serve us, Madeline? Mr. Remington, a little sherry?"

Madeline was dumbfounded. "Grandfather, this man has just told you he kidnapped me, he almost drowned me, and—oh, yes, Mr. Remington, I'm surprised we didn't mention the near-compromise in the conservatory!"

"Or," Jace reminded her, "your running off to elope with my cousin Emerson."

Grandfather lifted a finger. "Excuse me. Was this the same cousin who was already engaged to her sister?"

"Yes, sir. Very astute." Jace gave him an approving nod.

"And," continued Madeline on a hysterical note, as if there'd been no interruption, "he is now asking for my hand in marriage!" Her hands still on her hips, she turned to her grandfather. "And you are asking me to pour tea?"

Grandfather's eyes twinkled. "Madeline, I have a confession to make. Mr. Remington came to see me while he was looking for his cousin."

"*What?*"

"I must admit I was a bit taken aback, but," he nodded to Jace, "Mr. Remington was diligent in being truthful, and I like his honesty and forthrightness. I have agreed to his suit. I think the two of you very well-matched." He chuckled at her expression. "Assuming you still wish to marry him, of course."

Madeline stared at her grandfather, a sternness about her

mouth. She turned to pin Jace, her eyes narrowing. If she'd been Gorgon, they'd both be stone by now.

"I've half a mind to dump this cream upon your head, Mr. Remington," she said very, very quietly.

"Well, as you can see," Jace said as he winked at her grandfather, "he has not yet thrown me out of his cabin."

Madeline spun on her heel. "Men," she muttered loudly as she left the room. "Serve your own damned tea!"

Dinner was lively. Madeline watched her two favorite men in conversation. When the mushroom broth was removed, Jace eyed the rabbit casserole with appreciation. Small potatoes and a rich gravy accompanied the dish.

"Thank you for your gracious hospitality, Sir Arthur."

"Please, Remington—Halvering or Arthur will do. Speaking of a wedding, will you be married here, Madeline? Have you honeymoon plans?"

"I was thinking Italy—" began Jace.

"An outdoor adventure—" Madeline stated at the same moment.

Grandfather chuckled. "It sounds like you two have a few things to discuss."

Jace reached over to pick up Madeline's hand. "What do you think about an outdoor adventure, followed by a side trip to Venice?"

Madeline squeezed his hand. "I would very much enjoy that! Oh, and, Venice too, I suppose."

"Then, we are settled." Jace raised his fluted glass. "May I propose a toast?"

Madeline and her grandfather also lifted their glasses, looking expectantly to Jace.

"A toast to a happy marriage. And to the outdoor adventure we shall take every year to mark our anniversary. Hopefully, with no collapsing tents."

Madeline looked her love. "Thank you, my darling. But . . . you *will* learn to fish?"

"After I teach you to swim," he promised.

CHAPTER TWENTY-EIGHT

Madeline strolled out to her grandfather's garden, a tiny parcel in one hand and an open letter in the other. She stopped at the masonry bench and sat. She became so engrossed, she was startled when a shadow crossed the page.

"Jace! Good morning." She moved over, and he took up most of the bench, wrapping an arm about her.

She leaned into him as she continued to read. "It is from Aunt Glynnis. She is sorry I won't be coming to town for the Season, but she's most pleased to confirm she and my uncle will be making a trip to the country for the wedding."

Madeline smiled up at him, squinting in the sun. "She says she knew all along that you and I would be together, you know."

"A very astute woman. Any news of Bennett or Emerson?"

"No. Though she does say Eleanor has visited with her once, which quite surprised our aunt. She believes there may be hope for my sister after all. Oh, and you should hear this part." Madeline scanned the second page. "She writes, 'By the way, as your sister Eleanor was leaving, she said to tell you she has discovered the culprit behind your midnight rendezvous, and to tell you also that she no longer wears the same perfume as your stepmother. She promises to go home and pen a letter of explanation to you. I must confess I was intrigued, for as you know, I love a bit of good gossip. So I made her promise as well to pay me a return visit so I might hear the entire story.'"

Madeline folded the pastel sheets and looked thoughtful.

"Well. What do you make of that? Do you think Mary Pickett wrote those notes to meet in the conservatory the night of Aunt Glynnis's party?"

"If she did, she botched it. If only we'd been caught out and forced to wed at that time, she'd have saved me a lot of trouble."

Madeline harrumphed. "Trouble? I don't recall you going to the trouble of courting me, sir. And I would have refused to marry a man I was caught in a compromising situation with. I would only marry a man whose love I was assured of. Love cannot be circumstantial."

"Ah, but think of the circumstances of our meeting, Madeline. Sir Arthur, unfortunately, fell ill. Duncan was late receiving your grandfather's bidding. I owed my despicable cousin a favor. I arrived here when you were impatient to leave. Could all of that not be called circumstantial?"

Madeline's eyes went wide, then sad. "I suppose, when you tally it like that. Then our fate was nothing more than a series of circumstances, Jace?"

He laughed and pulled her closer. "No. I am teasing you. That was not circumstance, Madeline. That was destiny."

She smiled, then turned her attention to the wrapped parcel in her lap.

"And who is the packet from?"

"I don't know." Madeline balanced it in her hand. "It was enclosed in the letter." She gently pulled the wrapping away. "Oh, Jace, look! It's beautiful."

A cameo lay nestled in her hand, the ivory silhouette in miniature.

Jace took her hand in his, and studied it with her. "It certainly bears a likeness to you. Did you have this done while in London?"

Madeline shook her head. She unfolded the single note page that was wrapped around the cameo. "It's from Eleanor. She says our mother Jeannette wore it." Madeline choked on the last word, but forced herself to continue in a wavering voice. "She says our mother wore it on her wedding day. Eleanor wishes that I should wear it on mine." A frown clouded her soft features. "You don't suppose she'll not come? Because of our stepmother's refusal to do so?"

"I think if you write a letter to your aunt, she and your uncle will be more than happy to bring Eleanor along, if Mrs. Pickett is 'indisposed.' "

"Yes, that's what I'll do. Oh, Jace, I hope she will come."

"Would you like me to go to London and fetch her?"

"I shall threaten her with that, if she does not agree to come with Aunt Glynnis." She laughed at his indignant expression, and kissed the tip of his nose. "Thank you."

Madeline looked around the ring of those most familiar and beloved to her. The group stood on the manicured lawn, before white rose trellises that granted access to the gardens of Redfern Manor.

Eleanor stood at her side, radiant in peach silk, a nosegay of white and apricot roses clasped at her waist. Crystal beads separated the pearls roped around her neck; a matching strand wove through upswept hair.

"You look beautiful, Eleanor." Madeline touched her sister's hand, and Eleanor returned the affection with a squeeze and a shy smile. Thankfully, Eleanor had succeeded in coming to Redfern Manor, even though Mrs. Pickett still had a mysterious ailment, and had sent her regrets.

Madeline's gaze moved past her sister. Duncan, his whiskers trimmed, and his hair pulled back like a warrior's, looked more intimidating than ever in the belted plaid that draped his body and made it look even larger. The tassels on his stockings did nothing to soften the image.

Mrs. Cork, in muslin gown and a shawl of sky blue to match her eyes, stood dwarfed at Duncan's side. She beamed at Madeline, her cheeks rosy and her eyes wet, a lacy handkerchief clenched in her fist. As she raised the handkerchief to her eyes, the sun glinted from the slim wedding band with its delicate ruby chips that encircled her third finger.

Madeline's eyes moved on to the next handkerchief in line, hidden in the folds of a periwinkle satin skirt, and she raised her eyes to meet those of Aunt Glynnis. Her aunt lifted her brows in acknowledgement, pressing her smiling lips together firmly to belie their slight tremble. At her side, Uncle Rupert winked his support to his niece, while his hand gave an affectionate squeeze of support to his wife's.

Madeline looked to her grandfather next, and that was her undoing. Tears made stars on her lashes when she noted his proud fierce look. Only a scowl was keeping his emotions in check. She knew this man so well. She nodded her love to Grandfather, then turned back toward the vicar.

Her brother-in-law-to-be, Bennett, stood straight, his broad shoulders almost touching Jace's. When Bennett's eyes met hers and the corners of his lips twitched up, Jace caught his brother's smile and turned his head toward his bride.

Madeline's eyes moved to Jace, to the man who closed and completed this circle of love.

As the vicar pronounced them man and wife, Jace pulled her into a scandalous kiss in front of their guests. Madeline glowed, and the two laughed as they were pelted with white rose petals.

"I was afraid of forgetting my vows," confessed Jace in her ear.

"What fustian! All you had to do was repeat what the minister said. And I was much more nervous than you. What is that?" She noticed the worn paper he pulled from his pocket.

"I don't know. I thought it was my copy of vows."

She took it from him, and unfolded it, then burst out laughing. "You rogue."

"What are you two looking at? Come and join the celebration." Her grandfather came up and planted a kiss on his granddaughter. Putting his arm around her, he shook Jace's hand.

"It is a list," Madeline answered.

"A list?" Her grandfather read it over her shoulder. "A list of what?"

Madeline smiled at the long sheet of paper.

Her grandfather read the list aloud: "Going fishing, grilling the fish we catch over a fire, brewing tea in an iron kettle, doing our laundry in the river—"

"It's my outdoor adventure list," explained Madeline. "My husband kept it."

Jace was so happy to hear the word "husband" on her lips, he had to kiss them before it escaped.

ABOUT THE AUTHOR

Sharol Louise and her husband live in the Pacific Northwest, where her psyche was born. However, her body was born in downtown Los Angeles, so it took about twenty-five years for the two to catch up. As a youngster, she thought people were referring to the dictionary when they said, "the good book," as she grew up in the library reading Edgar Rice Burroughs, Mary Stewart, and Sir Arthur Conan Doyle. She's been known to miss her bus stop when engrossed in a good book, and wishes that her books may do the same for you.